HANGTOWN HEARTS

Love in Gold Country

HANGTOWN HEARTS

Love in Gold Country

c. 2025 VIRGINIA HULL WELCH

Dedicated to all lovers of clean and exciting western romance.

Virginia Hull Welch, October 2025

ISBN Paperback – 978-0-9888739-8-8
ISBN E-Book – 978-0-9888739-9-5
Hangtown Hearts

Published by Virginia Hull Welch, 2025
Www.virginiahullwelch.com

Cover Design by Salar Seif

i

Other Books by Virginia Hull Welch

Crazy Woman Creek
Western Romance

The Lesson
Romantic Comedy Based on a True
Story

What to Do When the Blessings Stop
When God Sends Famine

The Hiss from Hell Only Women Hear
Is It Truth or Is It Tradition?

Hangtown Hearts is a work of fiction.

Hangtown, California (renamed Placerville years ago) and surrounding mining camps described in the story are or were real places. Some of the crimes and criminals mentioned to establish setting, such as Pretty Juanita—the first woman to be hanged for a crime in California—were also real. But names, characters, and incidents germane to the story are products of the writer's imagination or have been used fictitiously and are not to be construed as real. Any resemblance to persons, living or dead, actual events, or organizations is entirely coincidental.

CHAPTER ONE

Hangtown, California
Late Summer, Early 1850s

Madeline Whittaker pulled the reins to halt the oxen. She should have been jubilant. They had finally arrived in Hangtown after months of difficult travel and agonizing loss. But the weight of her awful secret made her jumpy.

"Look at all the reprobates. This is the wickedest place I ever saw." She shook her head in disbelief.

"Look at all the *men!*" cried Caroline, clasping her hands with excitement.

Madeline looked askance at her younger sister. "Don't go casting your eyes on any of them. God willing, we'll be out of here in a week and enjoying dinner at Auntie Hannah's back in

Independence soon enough." But it would be a very long time until they were settled in at Auntie Hannah's, even if travel plans were ideal, and they were anything but. Until then, how would she rein in the pretty coquette on the wagon seat beside her? Four hungry oxen were more docile.

The two young women spent a few minutes wordlessly taking in the sights of Hangtown, formerly called Dry Diggins, the scrappy mining camp comprised of three-sided, plank-and-canvas saloons, gambling houses, and hotels. The town was surrounded by wide, deep, abandoned mining pits, large enough to swallow the girls, the oxen, and their wagon. Empty liquor bottles littered the ground, polluting the beauty of this clear and crisp fall morning in the mountains. Pa had been so excited when he described the booming mining town to his children on the long journey from Independence. Had he been lied to?

"They drink," said Madeline.

"Surely not all of them," said Caroline. "You exaggerate."

"Unwashed, unshaven, uncouth. Probably smell like tar."

"A girl who hasn't had a real bath in more than a month should not disdain of another's fragrance." Caroline wrinkled her nose to drive home her point.

Madeline looked up. Some luckless soul, lifeless and pasty, hung by his neck from a tall tree on one side of the bustling street. Yet at street level townsmen went about their business obliviously, as if a gray-faced cadaver swaying above their heads was no more remarkable than a flickering gaslight. Her chest tightened. Hangtown was more hedonist than she had imagined.

"Caroline," she said, holding forth the reins, "take these. I'm getting the rifle."

"Whatever for, Maddy?" Caroline wrapped the reins around her dainty hands. "I'm sure they're all gentlemen." She was still admiring them as she said this.

"Yes, I'm sure they are," said Madeline, turning around on the wagon seat. "But the rifle has a magical way of charming ordinary gentlemen into downright princes."

By the time Madeline had settled herself with the rifle across her lap, all of Hangtown had ceased its business to stare at the rare sight of not one but two unescorted young women. It seemed even the sun had halted its western trudge to observe the petticoat spectacle.

"Go," said Madeline.

In a rare display of obedience, Caroline did as she was told and urged the oxen. The wagon began to creep forward. Madeline sat rigid, striving for dignity while avoiding any provocative eye contact.

"Heaven help us," she said out of the side of her mouth. "We will never be able to go about our business here without causing a scene. We're being ogled like chanteuses in silk stockings. And there are no women."

"I know," said Caroline, smiling at a nice-looking young miner on her side of the wagon. "Isn't it glorious?"

The young man tipped his hat and smiled in return. Madeline jabbed her elbow into her sister's side. Caroline turned and made a face but then capitulated, looking straight ahead like her sister— most of the time. They had rolled a few yards when two dirty, bearded miners approached their wagon, hailing them. Caroline jerked the reins.

"Yes?" said Madeline.

"Miss," said the taller of the two, tipping his hat. "My friend and I were wondering how much?"

How much? Madeline thought of their few remaining foodstuffs and costly mining supplies piled high in barrels and crates and hanging in sacks swinging from the sides of their wagon.

"What is it on our wagon you wish to purchase, sir?" she said. The two men exchanged a startled look and then at once began to guffaw like stupid braying mules. Other men standing around the wagon chuckled. What on earth was so hilarious?

Caroline whispered into Madeline's ear. Her eyebrows shot up. "Let's go," she said, "Go!"

But before Caroline could snap the reins, another man, calm and well groomed, broke through the crowd and stepped up to the wagon.

"Wait, miss," he said. He turned to the two miners, who were still laughing and slapping their thighs with their grubby black felt hats. "Go on. Leave these ladies alone," he said, dismissing the two miners with an angry wave of his hand.

The miners' amusement at Madeline's response had evidently inured them to offense. Without argument they rakishly tipped their hats to the girls in a pretentious display of chivalry then shuffled toward the dusty street, still chuckling.

Quite a crowd had formed by now, surging dangerously close to the wagon and preventing its movement. Madeline was keenly aware of a whole lot of eyes watching them. But she was so angry at the two miscreants she forgot to be embarrassed.

The man turned back to the wagon. His pale green neckerchief distinguished him in an ocean of blue flannel shirts, gray pantaloons shoved into boots, and broad-brimmed felt hats. Madeline was sizing him up, her heart beating wildly, when he made the mistake of stepping too close to the wagon box. She reflexively lifted the rifle, aimed it at his head, and cocked the trigger. At once the man took a step back.

"You want to purchase something too?" she said.

Caroline's eyes grew round as a mining pan. The hubhub about the wagon dropped to a hush.

"No, miss," said the man as he slowly removed his hat. He glanced at the business end of Madeline's rifle and then back at her face. "My name is Jesse Garry. I thought I might be of some assistance, that's all."

"Thank you, Mr. Garry. We do not need any assistance." Madeline, still pointing her rifle, said this loudly and distinctly so any man who thought otherwise would be thoroughly disabused of his foolishness.

Jesse nodded grimly, put his hat back on his head, dipped it, and then wordlessly turned and disappeared into the crowd.

Madeline scanned the stunned miners standing about and, seeing nothing to threaten, slowly brought the rifle back down to her lap but kept her finger on the trigger. "Go," she said. Without further ado Caroline snapped the reins and the two girls continued rolling down Main Street, all eyes fastened on them like burdock on wool.

"You've lost your mind," said Caroline after a few terse seconds. "If you're going to go poking that rifle in people's faces, why not that grizzled old sapper and his friend instead of the handsome one who's trying to help us? He was quite gallant, I think. We're never going to meet some eligible fellows if you go threatening to blow their heads off with so little provocation."

"Exactly," said Madeline.

"But we need friends here, Maddy."

"Not that type."

Caroline sighed dramatically and turned back to the street. In minutes they were approaching the end of the few buildings that comprised town. Other than the two-story wooden hotels and a few prosperous retail establishments, most of the buildings had canvas fronts, and there were even many low tents, some no more elaborate than pine boughs with cotton shirts thrown over them. And more abandoned mining pits.

"Now what?" said Caroline.

***

Earlier that morning, Jesse Garry had hung back a few feet from the blackened corpse, the smoky stench of burned flesh filling his nose, incongruous with the brilliance of a mountain morning in early fall. Like a word he has always known but could not bring up, he couldn't shake the feeling he should know the identity of this grotesque thing. But shaken by the macabre scene, he averted his eyes and studied instead the shadowy depths of nearby woods. For the first time they seemed menacing, even evil.

"Any idea who it is?" His even tone masked his horror.

"Miner, no doubt, though killers don't usually go to so much trouble with the body."

6

Harlan Turpin kicked a few stones off the pyre. Blackened fingers emerged. "Pile of rocks over the body. It's like the killer didn't want a grizzly to get it. Strange."

Jesse stared. It didn't seem human, this desiccated piece of flesh. As if someone had dropped a large slab of meat into the fire, decided it was too risky to retrieve, and abandoned it to the ashes. The analogy unsettled him. This was no hunk of meat. It was a man, his body all in one piece, limbs splayed crudely. A few hours ago he had stood upright, felt icy creek water splash his face, gave thanks for steaming cornbread, slipped aching legs under a rough blanket after rocking a placer for hours in a hot September sun. Now he was dead, some lonely miner, likely one who had camped an easy walk from this ghostly site. The creek bank where they'd found him was down the way from multiple diggings, but very near Diamond Spring.

"Claim dispute, probably. See it all the time," said Harlan. "Here, help me get these off him."

In a few minutes the two men had cleared all the stones from the body. When they uncovered the face, mouth open in terror, eyes melted away, Jesse grimaced and turned away, searching the tree line again for anything to explain this horror.

"Stones are warmer than they should be for this hour," said Jesse. "He was killed sometime after midnight. Someone didn't want to be seen out here with the body. Waited till the saloons cleared out."

"But they always leave clues." Harlan bent down to examine the body, knitting his bushy white eyebrows in thought. "Cuts on the bones. Bullet hole in the head. Rope around the neck. Don't think he was killed here, though." He scrutinized the area.

"Nothing disturbed. No drag marks. Like he was carried to this spot."

"Wasn't a big fella," said Jesse. "Californio? Maidu?"

"Maybe. But the killer wouldn't bother to hide a Mexican or an Indian. They dump those anywhere."

Jesse nodded but stayed standing. He couldn't bring himself to squat close to the body. It seemed unholy to poke a corpse with a stick like his friend was doing. "See anything?"

"No. Pretty much everything is burned up. Clothes too, if he was wearing any. Hard to tell. Someone tried mighty hard to burn away the evidence."

"Wedding ring? Timepiece?" Jesse peered closer.

"Either he wasn't wearing any or it got filched." Harlan scraped some ash on one side of the body. Something small and round dislodged on the opposite side and fell to the dirt.

"What's that?" said Jesse, pointing.

Harlan looked to see what Jesse was referring to and then reached over the corpse to pick it up. "Suspender button, I think. Metal. LeFevre. L-E-F-E-V-R-E. That's French. European or French Canadian."

"That describes half the men for a hundred miles."

"Not much of a clue," said Harlan. He slipped the button into his pocket, lowered himself again, and poked the corpse with his stick. "Here's another one," he said, dislodging a second ashen button.

Jesse took one last look at the corpse, removed his pale green neckerchief and hat, wiped his forehead, then replaced the items. "Sun's high. I gotta get back to the hotel before Clint burns it down, and you gotta get this body into town. I'll send Clint with a wagon. Anything else I can do, let me know."

"Thanks. I'll look around for whatever I can find. Killer must have left some evidence, at least tracks. I'll stay here till the wagon comes. Afterward I'll go on up to the camps, see who's missing. Gotta check my traps too. I'll be a while."

***

"Pull in over there." Madeline pointed to some patchy greensward. "The oxen can graze what they can while I go find us a room and someplace to store the wagon for the night and someone to help us with—"

"Can't I come too?"

"No, I need you to stay with the wagon." She turned in her seat toward the dim interior of their cramped conveyance. She began to shuffle things about, digging for something.

"Why, Maddy? We've left the wagon unattended many times since Independence. No one's ever pilfered our belongings."

"Really, Caroline, I would think I shouldn't have to explain things to you." Madeline's voice was muffled as she fished through a canvas sack, her back to her sister. "Things are different now. Dry Diggins—Hangtown—is wilder than any stretch of the trail we've traveled thus far. We've arrived in Sin City, dear sister." She shook her head, remembering. "And to think how we pined for civilization." She turned back to the wagon seat and sat down. "Here," she said, extending a pistol. "Take

this and keep it on your lap where you can get to it
quickly. And be careful. It's loaded."

Caroline stared soberly at the handgun while
Madeline retied the ribbon under her straw bonnet
and reached for her drawstring poke. She alighted
from the wagon, and once both feet were on the
ground, reached up for the rifle.

"You aren't going to carry that thing down
the street, Maddy? What would Pa say?"

She knew exactly what Pa would say. *Make
every bullet count.* She'd heard him say it to her
brothers many times. "Do not leave this wagon for
any reason. If nature calls, draw the curtains and use
the pot. Everything we own in the world is in this
wagon, Caroline. Promise me."

"I promise." Then, "Maddy, go into one of
the stores and buy me a fizzy bomb, *please.* All I've
thought of since San Francisco is a hot fizzy bath
with scented soap. I'm dreaming and dreaming of
it."

"I'll try, sugar bun. Now do as I say and stay
in the wagon."

Once in the center of town, Madeline pushed
aside the heavy door of the Garry Hotel. The faint
scent of cigar smoke, acrid and manly, met her
nose, but it was eclipsed by the feel of plush
flowered carpet, green and thick and lavishly
spongy under her boot. Gaudy crystal oil lamps
suspended from brass chains attached to a crude
shingled ceiling cast a heavenly glow.

Suddenly a hot bath was all she could think
about too. She could hear the delicious whoosh of
boiling kettle water, feel the steam, smell the
flowery fizzy bomb. She glanced down at her soiled
dress and scuffed boots. She looked hideous and
smelled worse. They had run out of soap days ago,

and she had no fat to make a fresh batch. It was laughable how men would gobble up any rumpled excuse for womanhood; every man at the bar stopped drinking at stared. She sighed. There was nothing to be done but make the best of an embarrassing situation.

She searched for the service desk, averting eyes away from the men at the bar. She saw the clerk to the right, behind the front desk, his back to her. She walked to the desk and pressed the service bell.

At the sharp *ding* the clerk turned around, and when he did, Madeline locked eyes with Mr. Green Neckerchief.

CHAPTER TWO

Jesse Garry had seen few women during his eighteen months in gold country. He'd heard there were two of them for every ninety-eight men—his experience confirmed it was no rumor. But he'd seen enough of these curious beings to know only two types of unmarried women made their way to the mining camps. The first was a man pleaser, the type who danced and sang and warmed a miner's bed while she shook his pockets to glean his last bit of gold dust. The second type would steal your britches then scold you because the fit wasn't right. You knew this second group by their guns, their itch to do men's work, and their cussin', boozin', and fondness for tobacco. These were the women-turned-men, the worst wild beasts he'd come across on the western frontier.

He already knew by the public dressing down he'd suffered on Main Street that the filthy

12

trail tramp who had dragged through the door of the Garry Hotel was a founding member of the second group. As if to underscore the point, she had the *cojones* to show up in the lobby of his uncle's fine establishment accompanied by her ridiculously oversized rifle.

Shame. She could be pretty if someone took a stiff brush and some lye to her grime, not to mention her attitude. Her snug fitting basque outlined nicely rounded breasts.

"Yes?" Jesse did not favor her with a smile, and with wicked pleasure he noted how startled she looked. Her eyes got wide and her mouth dropped open slightly. He didn't wait for her to stop gaping. "You rang the bell."

"Uh, yes. I need a room for the night. My sister and I."

"One night?"

"Yes."

"That will be one-half ounce. More if you want a bath."

"Pardon?" Her face flushed as she set her bag on the desk. The dainty accessory seemed out of place on a woman who carried enough firepower to take out an elephant herd.

"Gold dust. One-half ounce." His mouth drew a grim line.

"Oh," she said. "I don't have any gold dust. Will dollars do?"

"In that case it will be ten fifty, plus another two dollars for the second occupant. Another dollar for a bath. We have Russian steam, galvanic, or iron and sulfur. Fifty cents for hot, cold, or shower baths. No animals in the room. Damage anything with your pipe or cigar and you pay. Intoxication or any ruckus that disturbs other guests and you're out."

Madeline gasped.

"What? Is it the rate or the rules you can't abide?"

"Your rates are robbery."

"Our rates are market rates, same as the Golden Casbah across the street. Now do you want the room or not?"

Jesse crossed his arms and waited. She looked to be about twenty. Where were her parents? No doubt she'd blown them to kingdom come with her stupid gun. Who would let two young women travel to this rough gold camp unescorted? He shuddered at the thought of all the perils from wild animals, the elements, the fevers, and the men of every color and stripe who crawled these woods looking for gold or worse, looking to steal it. He thought of the three corpses left swinging on Main Street when he arrived in '49, strung up for murder and theft.

Miss Big Gun had no idea what she was up against.

"Only a fool would pay such a sum for a room. Hangtown isn't some big city like Boston or New Orleans. It's a tiny mining camp." She drew herself up with indignation.

He gave her a cool, even gaze. "Respectable people pay these rates every day."

Madeline pursed her lips, blew through her nose, and returned the gaze. "Then perhaps you should keep it ready for state visitors. You never know when Queen Victoria might drop in."

There were a few seconds of tense standoff. He refused to take her bait. No gun-toting snippet was going to get the best of him—at least not twice.

"Do you have another room not quite so royal?" she finally asked.

"We have one vacancy."

Her shoulders drooped. "Do you know of another hotel besides the Golden Casbah that can accommodate my sister and I, the oxen and wagon? I must secure our goods for the night."

"Hangtown has two inns, though I suppose any one of the saloons would make room for you somewhere." He smirked. "Affordably too."

She seemed upset. Good.

"There's the fandango hall a few doors down," he continued, fueled by her annoyance. "They're always looking for dancers. But I can't recommend you to the owner without first seeing your legs."

The men standing about the lobby broke into laughter. Madeline grabbed her bag and turned from the desk in a huff.

"Anything else I can do for you, miss?" he called as she turned toward the door.

She did not look back. Hurriedly she swiped at the door latch. In a moment she was gone.

***

Dozens of men surrounded the wagon by the time Madeline returned. Caroline sat on the wagon box smiling and chatting and looking ever so innocent. It was the same everywhere they traveled. Men were smitten at once by that fair face and sun-soaked curls. Caroline was shorter than Madeline, but what she lacked in stature was compensated for handsomely by hair like flax and a chest like two ripe melons. Nectar to the bees.

15

Madeline stopped, wide eyed. The little vixen had exchanged her work bonnet for the one trimmed with handmade lace, her Sunday topper. She tightened her grip on the rifle.

"I stayed on the wagon, Maddy," Caroline called out merrily as Madeline approached.

"Excuse me, gentlemen," said Madeline as she made her way through the crowd. The chatter stopped and the men parted to allow the little lady with the big rifle to approach. She walked to the front of the wagon, handed the long arm to Caroline, and started to climb up. Suddenly one of the men nearest her extended a hand. His clothes were unusually refined for a mining camp, and his tone was calm, not desperate like the others. He seemed at once a gentleman. Madeline smiled faintly at him, placed her hand in his, and let him help her onto the wagon box.

"Alonzo Moore at your service, miss. If there is anything I can do to help you get settled, I do hope you will call on me."

"Thank you, Mr. Moore. But my sister and I must depart Hangtown at once."

"Leaving? We just got here, and you promised me a bath," said Caroline.

All the men chuckled.

"Hush," said Madeline. "Grab the reins." Caroline did as she was told but drew up her mouth in a well-practiced pout.

"But ladies, you just arrived. You aren't going to leave us already?" said one of the men. A murmur went through the crowd.

"Miss," said Mr. Moore, removing his hat, "should you discover you have any creature needs before you leave, I invite you to visit my store along Main Street here." He gestured to a stylish storefront across the street. "I have every comfort a body could desire, and a few select items for ladies such as yourselves."

Items for ladies. Ah. A fizzy gardenia bath bomb burbling deliciously in a big tin tub of hot water. But that was impossible without a room for the night. Besides, he may look like a decent sort, but what did he want for his precious bath bomb? Every item on her wagon and her firstborn child, no doubt.

"We have an urgent matter to attend to, Mr. Moore, but nothing in your store can help us in that regard." Madeline's thoughts were never far from their secret in the wagon.

"If you are possibly seeking a position here in Hangtown, I have the ideal situation for a young lady," added Mr. Moore. A few in the crowd guffawed, but most watched with intense interest. He ignored them. "I refer to my establishment, miss. I have more customers than I can serve, and most recently my sister left my employ."

"I will remember your kind offer. But my sister and I have situations waiting for us in San Francisco," said Madeline. "However, before we depart we have urgent business that requires the services of a minister. Perhaps you would be so kind as to direct us?"

"Hangtown has no preacher, miss."

Madeline's face went slack. A town with no minister?

"There is a man with a rancho not far from here. I've heard he used to be a man of the cloth. But he's a monte dealer now."

It took a second for Madeline to absorb that. "I see. Thank you, Mr. Moore. You have been very

kind." "If you will excuse us," she said to the
crowd. "Caroline, let's go."

The men stepped back from the wagon and
the girls started up. After making their way through
a maze of pits, they managed to turn the wagon
around and retrace their trek down Main Street. All
eyes followed them as before. In short order they
reached the entrance to town. Caroline's glum
silence accompanied them like a threatening black
rain cloud the entire parade route.

"Why do we have to go back, Maddy?
Hangtown has everything we need."

"If it's a swarm of panting swains you lack."

"But Maddy—"

"Enough. We're leaving."

"But Maddy, I want to stay in Hangtown.
The air is nice."

Madeline regarded her brazen little sister.
"Air? I have to get us out of here before you make a
fool of yourself. You don't know what these men
are like."

"You don't know, either." Caroline shoved
the reins at her sister, crossed her arms, and stuck
her chin in the air.

"Oh, sweetie," said Madeline after a while.
Caroline was such a child. "Can't you see why we
can't stay? There's nothing but frustrated men here.
Did you see any women on the street? All this
flattering male attention is meaningless under the
circumstances. These men would throw themselves
at any scarecrow in a corset. And besides, we can't
afford a room."

"That's not true!" Caroline turned in her seat,
eyes flashing. "I got three proposals while you were
not getting us a room and a bath. And they were all

from nice men, too. One gentleman said he even had a cabin."

Madeline gaped. "Three? They're desperate. I rest my case."

"Would've been four if you hadn't interrupted."

Madeline shook her head in disbelief. "I never promised you we'd settle in Hangtown. I told you we would stay long enough to take care of our obligation to Pa before we returned to San Francisco to make our way home. How was I to know it would be so rough and crude, with strumpets to set an example? I never could have envisioned a wild place like this. Surely you realize that. No wonder the miners misconstrued us as a couple of harlots. There is no possible way we can spend the night in this Babylon without a room with a lock and key."

Caroline stared at the ground, her face set like stone.

"Besides," she added, "they want the moon and the stars for a room and a bath. High living will eat up our little bit of money like locusts on barley. It's out of the question."

"But it's such a long way to San Francisco, Maddy. That's dangerous too."

"I am well aware of what the trail is like between here and San Francisco. But we made it safely on the way here. We'll do fine on the return, especially if this nice weather holds."

"But we were with others most of the way here. We're alone now. You know this isn't wise. You're panicking. I saw you shaking when you pointed your gun at that young fellow. Oo, he was handsome! You're worried we'll get stuck in

Hangtown and you'll never inherit Uncle's medical clinic back home."

Madeline pursed her lips, stung by the truth. But it was more than panic. She had a bad feeling about Hangtown. An inexplicable evil was out there. She could feel it, and it was not something fit to be shared with a flighty sixteen-year-old. Caroline was already worked up, and nothing Madeline said would change her mind.

The trail from San Francisco had been long and difficult, but unlike Hangtown, Madeline knew its dangers, and the girls had survived and still had each other. Returning to San Francisco to work and wait out the winter for the next wagon train back to Independence seemed the wisest path. Hangtown, with its hordes of women-hungry, intoxicated miners would not be easily tamed. She glanced at her sister, so young, so ignorant of the perils of the early loss of innocence. Surely they would be safer in the woods, at least for one night, while she reassessed their next step.

"You think it's your job to carry the world on your shoulders," said Caroline. "You're not God. You should ask for help."

"Don't be ridiculous. You have no idea what the world is like."

"And what did you mean about us having positions in San Francisco? We have nothing waiting for us there."

"We *will* have positions in San Francisco," said Madeline. "We *will* get home too. Be patient. We'll find something. Work through the winter, save all our money, book passage East in the spring. I'll sell all these supplies, too. They will fetch a goodly sum. You'll see."

"I don't want to go home. We don't have a home."

A wave of exquisite sadness washed over Madeline. Caroline was right. They had no home.

"But we still have family in Independence. Auntie Hannah and Uncle Finney will be glad to see us." She hoped. She hated the thought of returning to Missouri unmarried and penniless. That wasn't the rosy picture of their future she'd carried in her heart the last six months. Would Aunt and Uncle be willing to feed them until they found a better situation? Until they married? How long would that take? Nearly all the eligible men in Missouri had hightailed it for the gold fields.

"So where will we be tonight, then? Slapping mosquitoes in a hot wagon while losing sleep to grunting bears, doubtless," said Caroline. "I want a bath!"

Whine, whine." You needn't work yourself into a pet," said Madeline. "We'll go till sunset. Get ourselves far enough from the mining areas to safely set up camp. We've been doing this for months. We'll be fine. We have food, arms, plenty of bullets, and there's the creek."

"You're trying to convince yourself, not me."

There was a long, sad silence.

"You're right, sugar bun," said Madeline. "I'm not sure what's best right now, and I am a little afraid. It's not safe for us to spend the night in the wagon in this wicked town, and we can't afford a room. We'll get a good rest tonight and discuss plans again in the morning. Everything will be fine."

Caroline chewed on that a minute. "But Maddy," she said, "what will we do with the body?"

CHAPTER THREE

"Aren't you the charmer? Explains why we never have any handsome women putting up here for the night."

Clinton Garry, long and muscular like his older brother, leaned lazily on the long oak service desk. Jesse's back was to him as he sorted mail. He didn't respond.

"Charm. Like a rattlesnake," added Clint.

Jesse silently sorted away.

"Pretty little lady blasted a hole in your pride without even pulling the trigger."

"Word gets around this town awfully fast," said Jesse, still fixed on the mail. *Clint! Irksome assistant manager-bucketful-of-irritation-baby-faced-kid-brother. Mouth always running.*

"Pride goeth before—"

"Shut up." Jesse stopped sorting and whirled around to face his brother.

"What are you trying to do? Drive all our business to the Casbah?" said Clint, shaking his head. "A darling thing behind this desk would draw 'em in faster than clean towels twice a day and monte on Sunday."

"I'm not worried about the Casbah. Not my lookout," said Jesse. "Gull keeps the Casbah full no matter what happens this side of the street, and the Garry's doing fine."

"You want her to end up serving suppers over there? Or her shapely little sister? She's as fetching as the older one. Whole town's talking about 'em. Biggest story since Pretty Juanita got strung up in Downieville." Clint closed his eyes and sighed noisily. "I'm going to marry that pretty little blonde butterfly."

"I hope Gull does get saddled with them. He deserves all the persecution Providence can hurl at him."

"You don't know for certain Gull was involved in the fire. Besides, how will you explain your lack of management skills when Uncle Justus shows up and those girls are working at the Casbah instead of the Garry? It's not like pretty ladies show up every day in Hangtown. You're missing the chance of a lifetime."

"Uncle nearly threw me out on my ass because of that maggot. He'll get his due."

"Don't be an angry fool. You have no hard evidence he started the fire in the buttery. Why blame Gull? Maybe it was an accident. If there's frost on the ground tomorrow morning, you'll blame that on Gull too."

Jesse scowled. "Those girls are nothing but trouble, and I don't have time to go over it again. I need you to get a wagon halfway to Diamond Spring. Harlan found a body up there this morning. Burned to cinder and covered with rocks. I told him I'd fetch it to town."

"Who is it?"

"Don't know. Miner, probably. Harlan's up there now waiting for you so he can ask around. He needs the body brought to town for examination and burying."

"There's no road. A mule train can't get through."

"Then bring a spare horse and plenty of old blankets. The body is mighty charred."

"Why am I elected for the job?"

"Harlan's my friend and you're available. But if you prefer, I can send Tien," said Jesse.

"Why don't you?"

"Because if I send Tien, that leaves you to dump jerries and clean vacant rooms."

Clint made a face. "Why isn't Harlan draggin' it back to town?"

"Get moving or I'll send Tien." Jesse reached for a pencil, scribbled a few directions on a scrap of paper, and shoved it toward his brother. "If you get to Diamond Spring and haven't met up with Harlan, you've gone too far. Ask around. By the time you get there it will be all the miners are talking about."

No, that wasn't exactly right. The two unattached damsels on the wagon and the elder one's proclivity to blow the brains out of anything more threatening than a hunk of coffee-soaked rusk were bigger news in the camps than another dead miner. His humiliation was now complete.

"Body won't be hard to find," said Jesse. "Now hurry. Harlan's waiting."

Clint scoffed. "Alright, I'm leaving. But you'll regret letting those pretty things get away."

"I can't hire any more help around here unless I fire someone first."

It was Clint's turn to glare. "Fire someone? I have a suggestion for who to fire. We're the only business in town with a coolie for a chambermaid. What if Uncle finds out?"

"Don't call Tien that. He does a good job, I trust him, and he'll never run off and marry a miner who's struck it rich. As long as I make money, Uncle doesn't complain. Right now, Tien's all we've got. If you're unhappy with a Chinaman working in the hotel, you're free to fill his shoes and I'll start looking for someone to replace you. Might be nice for a change to have an assistant manager who doesn't bellyache so much."

"Women's work." Clint shook his head, muttering something indiscernible. "Those girls are what we need to resurrect this place. Colorful dresses, sweet-smelling cologne. Especially the curvy blonde." He closed his eyes.

Jesse yanked hard on the bell pull behind the desk. "Keep your mind on your work."

Clint left. After a while a shrunken older man with a long plait of salt-and-pepper hair hanging down his back appeared in the lobby. Tien was a sad little bag of bones: wrinkled, ashen, and perpetually bent over. His puffy tunic and baggy trousers were threadbare and stained. Most of his teeth had retired and moved away years ago. But his most notable physical characteristic was a swelling as big as an apple along his jawline.

No sin to be ugly, but no blessing, either.

Regardless, Jesse's conscience would never let him throw Tien out on the street, no matter what Uncle or Clint thought about him. Tien was old and alone. He'd starve.

"Tien, find out where those two girls on the wagon are going. Don't get near them, and don't let anyone see you. Come back and tell me where they settle for the night. Understand?"

Tien nodded, unsmiling, and said something unintelligible, which Jesse took as Chinese for yes. He watched with interest as Tien left on his errand.

The Garry Hotel was a fine hospitality establishment, every bit as modern as the Casbah and certainly managed better. And that pretty younger sister was free to work wherever she chose whether Gull liked it or not.

CHAPTER FOUR

"We'll bury him ourselves," said Madeline.

"Alone? We can't."

"Yes, we can. Maybe not as well as those helpful soldiers back in Kansas Territory, but we have a shovel, and there are two of us."

"But he's so heavy. Don't you remember how hard it was to get him into the wagon?"

"We are not pantywaists, Caroline. We do what we must do."

Perhaps it was the unrelenting sameness of weeks of traveling in a bumpy wagon. Or perhaps it was the surprising disappointment with Hangtown after so much anticipation. Perhaps it was the gathering gloom of dusk, which seemed a little eerie on their first night alone in the woods. Whatever it was, it had taken a toll on Madeline. She suddenly felt overwhelmed with tiredness, drained to the marrow. Tired of having to do what one must do, which for the last six months had involved too much meaningless suffering. Then again, maybe she was asleep. Maybe this was a bizarre, terrible dream. She glanced over her shoulder at the lumpy bundle in the dark wagon interior.

No, not a dream.

"Besides, getting him out will be easier than getting him in. Gravity is with us," she said.

"But there are all those strong, willing miners in town. Why are you so contrary?" Caroline started to cry.

Madeline sighed. She wanted to finish their unthinkable business and then lay her head down on a soft pillow and sleep—long, deep, and oblivious. It had been a grueling day, but she must be patient with Caroline. After all, she was older of the two, all of twenty-one. Her behavior should exemplify maturity, even if all she wanted to do was crawl into the wagon, pull one of Mama's quilts over her head, and sob.

By nightfall they had settled into a small clearing near a creek. Neither one had any appetite, so they agreed to forego an evening meal. They watered and tethered the animals, built a fire, and checked over the wagon for any damage. A full moon began its silent ascent into an iridescent, blue-black late summer sky. Soon the thick woods encircling their lonely campsite were alive with eerie shadows from the fire.

"This place would be pretty if it weren't a graveyard," said Caroline, looking up at the twinkling stars.

Graveyard. Madeline stirred from her grim reverie. "We've put off this awful task long enough," she said, rising from her resting place by the fire. She inhaled deeply and scanned the edges of the camp site. "We'll bury him over there," she said, pointing, "underneath that tree. You take his feet. I'll grab him under the shoulders. The torso's the heaviest."

Grunting and huffing, the girls dragged the corpse from the wagon to the ground with an irreverent thud. They stared at the body.

"You used all your medical knowledge to heal him," said Caroline. "Uncle Finney would have been proud to see how you doctored Pa. You did every bit as good as when you assisted Uncle in his clinic. Too bad you can't follow in his footsteps."

"Maybe if we'd had quinine..." Madeline rubbed her eyebrows. "I don't know. I never saw a patient in Uncle Finney's clinic with a fever accompanied by a bloody rash like Pa had. Must be something indigenous to these mountains."

"Do you suppose we'll burn in Hell for this?" asked Caroline, her voice cracking.

"What?" Madeline reached for the shovel hanging at the rear of the wagon. "Hell?"

"I mean, for not burying him in a town with a preacher to conduct a proper service. This doesn't seem holy."

"You heard Mr. Moore. Hangtown has no preacher," said Madeline. "Likely none of the other camps do, either. And you're right. It's *not* holy. Death is an outrage. But it's no time to worry about righteousness. It's been nearly a whole day, and it's hot. I'm surprised he's lasted as long as he has."

Caroline nodded morosely and said no more as they worked, digging, resting, taking turns, digging some more. They worked doggedly to break up the unyielding earth. Suddenly Caroline stopped digging and pushed the shovel toward her sister. "I'm tired. Can't we finish in the morning?"

"No. For shame, thinking we'd leave his body out here all night."

Caroline whimpered, wiped her face with a filthy sleeve, and dropped onto a fallen log. "I can't dig anymore. We'll never be able to make a hole deep enough to properly cover his body."

"We will if we don't stop," said Madeline, beginning her turn with the shovel. She was itchy with dirt and sweat. Her back ached. She slammed the shovel into the ground repeatedly, but the hole never seemed any deeper. Digging a grave was more work than she had realized, but they couldn't quit. He'd been dead since early morning. He would start to stink soon. They had no choice but to keep digging. After a while she paused and leaned on the shovel, panting. The hole was long enough but only about a foot deep, not deep enough to properly cover a full-grown man.

"Your turn." Madeline thrust the shovel toward her sister.

Caroline didn't move. "I can't."

In the dim orange glow of the fire, Madeline saw the tear streaks on her little sister's face and was moved with pity. She was too drained to be angry. "It's alright, sugar bun. Go to bed. I'll finish. I think I can drag him in there by myself." She stepped close enough to stroke Caroline's hair. "We'll have a little service for him in the morning. We'll read the Bible and sing a hymn. It will make us both feel better. You'll see."

Caroline nodded, stood up, hugged her sister tightly, and then climbed into the wagon. Madeline glanced over to a nearby tree where she had set her rifle. *Still there.*

It was nearly midnight when Madeline acknowledged the futility of it. She couldn't dig a grave as well as a man. She didn't have the strength to drive the shovel deep enough to protect a corpse from four-legged predators, though she had given it her best try. Defeated, she began to drag her father's body into the shallow hole when she heard the crunch of a boot behind her. At the same moment a hand flew over her mouth and a muscular arm, unmistakably male, reached around her middle and slammed her against his body.

"Don't scream," he said.

Madeline's heart pounded wildly. She was wide awake now, all fatigue flown away. Heat from the man's body radiated against her back.

"I'll remove my hand," he said, "after you nod your head to tell me you won't scream."

Madeline nodded. The stranger removed his hand from her mouth but placed it on her upper arm, gripping it painfully. His other arm remained tight around her waist.

"Who's the dead guy?" he said.

His breath was warm on her ear. "My father."

"You better have a good explanation for burying him here, outside town in the middle of the night."

"My sister and I don't feel safe in town."

The stranger tightened his grip. Madeline yelped in pain. "You have reason to worry," he said. "Less than an hour with us and you threaten to kill one of our citizens. Your reputation precedes you."

Madeline's breathing was so shallow she feared she would faint from lack of oxygen. The man's arm crushed her diaphragm.

"When and how did he die?" demanded the stranger.

"Very early this morning, before sunup. About three hours from town. He'd had a fever for days, and a rash."

"Why drag his body all the way to Hangtown? You cover plenty of burial ground in a three-hour ride."

"We did it for him. We'd come so far, all the way from Independence. Pa's dream was to mine gold here. He told us we would reach town today by midday. After all he suffered to get here, we thought the respectful thing was to keep going, get his remains to town so he could have a Christian burial in the place he tried so hard to reach."

The man's thighs pressed against Madeline's, and one of his knees smashed against the back of one of hers, making balance difficult. She smelled his sweat and the familiar scent of tobacco—like Pa. She shook herself for making the comparison. This man was nothing like Pa.

She had never been so physically close to a man. The feel of him, raw and powerful, increased her terror. *Why is he here? What does he want? Will I die out here? What will happen to Caroline?*

"There's no minister for miles around," said the man.

"We didn't know that until we arrived."

"Where's your sister?"

"In the wagon, asleep."

"Anyone else come from Missouri with you?"

"Three brothers."

"Where are they?" said the man.

"They died of cholera at Fort Atkinson."

"Why weren't you with other travelers? Or with the pack train?"

"We were, but Pa didn't agree with the wagon master on a few things, so we broke away from the group when we reached San Francisco."

The man glanced at the grave where Pa's head and torso were exposed. "You should have stayed in town. Any man would have stepped forward to help you bury him ... if he's really your father."

Madeline could not respond. A moment of silent terror followed in which she was aware of his hot, hard body pushing against hers and the wild pounding of her heart. *Is his mouth on my neck?* She shivered with panic while a weird, tingling excitement ran through her entire body, which horrified her.

She saw her rifle a few feet away. She tried to think of a way to break from his grip and grab it, but his hold on her was like steel.

"I told you already. We feared to spend the night in town."

The man kicked at the loose dirt around the shallow grave. "Your hole's not deep enough. Animals will tear into it within hours after you leave this spot."

"Better to look out for the living," said Madeline. The thought of Caroline, asleep in the wagon, suddenly helped her focus. "I had to get my sister out of town. She is sixteen. Hangtown's no place for her. And I know the grave is shallow. I planned to cover it with rocks from the creek in the morning."

"Rocks?"

"Yes, to deter animals. And if I couldn't dig it deep enough, I planned to set the body on fire so there'd be nothing to attract them. It's not what we wanted as a final resting place for our pa, but we had no choice. Will you help us get his body to town for a proper burial?"

The man regarded the body in the ground a disturbingly long time. Madeline's heart pounded in her ears in the silence. She willed herself to stay calm to stem the wooziness.

"Please let me go. If my sister wakes up and sees you, she'll be frightened. And if she starts screaming there's nothing either of us can do to stop her."

"I'll let you go. But you and your sister are going back to town. With me."

"Why? We've done nothing wrong. Please let us go."

The man gripped her harder. "A dead body turned up this morning not far from Diamond Spring, a mining camp south of here. Your habit of shooting quick and burying bodies in the dark makes you both suspects."

Suspects?" Please leave us in peace. Our pa died of fever. I've told you the truth. We know nothing of a body at Diamond Spring."

"Go stand by the wagon," he said, releasing his grip and shoving her away.

Madeline, tasting freedom, ignored his instruction and with nary a thought of the risk, lunged for her rifle. But the stranger was quicker. In less than a second, he grabbed the longarm and slammed its butt into her back. Madeline went sprawling, hands and face in the dirt. She screamed in pain. He aimed the rifle at her head.

"Please don't shoot my sister!" Caroline thrust her head out from the rear of the wagon. Her long blonde hair hung loosely around her shoulders, taking on an unearthly pale sheen in the moonlight. She wore a thin cotton nightgown and a look of terror.

"On the ground," barked the man, using the rifle as a pointer. "Next to your sister."

Caroline glanced at the rifle and then clambered barefoot out of the wagon. She threw herself onto the ground next to Madeline. The man kept the rifle pointed at both girls.

"I'll shoot if I have to," he said. "You pull a stupid trick like that again and it will be your last."

"Are you going to lynch us?" Caroline asked in a high-pitched voice, latching hard onto her sister's arm.

"Shh," said Madeline.

"We heard how those miners lynched that woman in Downieville," Caroline said, ignoring her.

"California does have the distinction of being the first state to lynch a lady." He cocked the trigger. "Pretty Juanita might not be the last."

Caroline started to sob.

"Who are you, and why did you follow us out here?" Madeline asked.

"Gull Dupont."

"Gull Dupont?"

"I followed you because I figured someone else would, to make sure you got out of town unmolested. Untold number of scoundrels around here."

"We appreciate your concern, Mr. Dupont," said Madeline. "But having our own rifle pointed at us invokes the opposite effect. We do not feel safe."

"How you feel is not my business. A man's been murdered. The miners are riled and searching for the killer, and you two are out here hiding a body. You're going back to town with me."

"What will happen there?"

"There's a man, Harlan Turpin. He acts as a justice of the peace among the miners. He presides over most criminal matters. Hangtown has no sheriff. The miners respect him, and he's a friend of mine. I'll speak to him."

"Why is all this necessary? He is our father," Madeline said, gesturing toward the body. "All we wanted to do was get his remains to the gold fields, to bury him properly and honor his desire to arrive in Hangtown. I told you that."

"These mountains are teeming with miners, and more arrive every day. It's a matter of time before someone stumbles across this grave, especially one so shallow. If someone finds out I discovered you in the act of burying a body but didn't speak up, they'll string me up for collusion. Even if I believed your cockamamie story—and I'm not sure I do—I have no choice."

"It's a simple matter of speaking to a U.S. Marshal," said Madeline. "It's not uncommon for someone to succumb to fever on the trail. A marshal will understand."

"Marshal?" Gull scoffed. "California swore in the marshal service last year, or so we've heard. But I'll give you twenty dollars in gold if you see a marshal this far east of San Francisco. Miners are their own marshals here. Judge, jury, and executioner, too."

Madeline froze. "Executioners? Surely you won't turn us over to them. Surely you believe what I've told you."

Gull regarded the girls coolly. Caroline was wailing now. Madeline put her arms around her.

"You're upsetting my sister," she said. "I beg you to leave us be, Mr. Dupont."

"You both get in the wagon. I'll finish with the dead fellow. Don't even think about fleeing in the night. I'll still be here when the sun comes up."

CHAPTER FIVE

"They're back!"

Clint Garry blew through the door of the hotel kitchen with his news. The cold air of a mountain morning blew in with him, carrying mingled scents of a hundred campfires and frying salt pork.

"I heard it," said Jesse. "Whole town's heard it."

"What about the mule train? We're out of nearly everything," said the Garry's cook, Bartholomew "Biscuit" Pyle. He jerked his head toward the haphazard heap of limp burlap sacks and empty wooden crates pushed into the corner.

The cluttered kitchen at the rear of the Garry Hotel was dominated by a large worktable covered with red oil cloth and piled with wet porcelain dishes and cups. Oversized cast-iron cookware hung on the walls. Biscuit sat on a wooden chair to one side of the table, near the greasy black cook stove, peeling potatoes and dropping the creamy spuds into a bucket of cold water. Peeling was a sit-down job, a position granted to him on account of his age and girth. Standing tired him. His abundant belly rested on his lap, his bushy white beard softly undulating with each noisy exhale.

"Haven't seen it," said Clint with a dismissive toss of his head. He turned to his brother. "Now are you going to try and get one of them over here? I put my money on the blonde. She'll look real sweet behind the lobby desk."

"That blonde would look sweet anywhere," said Biscuit.

"Even sweeter at the Casbah where Gull put them up," said Clint.

"Gull?" Jesse paused from his dish drying. "What's he got to do with those two girls?"

"He's the one who brought them back to town."

"Brought them back? What do you mean?" asked Jesse. "Did he follow them out of town? Did he go searching for them this morning?"

Clint shrugged. "Does it matter? Gull offered the younger one a job at the Casbah. You should have hired her when you had the chance."

Jesse mulled this news. Tien had reported the girls had camped about twenty minutes from town. But he had said nothing about Gull following them. Could Gull have slipped past the little man? What was Gull up to? Nothing good. He shoved his dish towel toward Clint, who dutifully took it, reached for a cup, and started drying.

"What happened to Sadie Shaw?" asked Jesse. "From what I heard, she did a good job running the lobby for Gull."

"She's marrying some miner who struck a big one on Rich Bar. They're on their way to San Francisco right now. She talked him into settling in the city. She has family there."

" Sadie was a wanton little Christmas plum," said Biscuit.

" Younger sister take her job?" asked Jesse.

"Don't know," said Clint.

"Something's not right." Jesse shook his head.

"Yeah, you should have offered the younger one a job first," said Clint.

Jesse bit his lip. Clint knew nothing about business. If that lowlife Gull Dupont was involved, a scandal was brewing. Jesse would put money on it.

"Aren't you going to ask about Madeline?" said Clint.

Jesse gave his brother a blank look.

"The older one." Clint smiled, his eyes glinting with secret knowledge. "Caroline is the younger one."

Madeline. Such a silken name for such a scabrous fishwife. "You spend too much time listening to scuttlebutt at Moore's," said Jesse. "We could use more of your help around here."

"Hear, hear!" said Biscuit without looking up from his paring knife.

"It's all I can do to keep this place filled up and help Biscuit in the kitchen without you lollygagging around town half the day. There are no women to help with domestic duties in this hotel and every man within a hundred miles is panning."

Clint's smile disappeared. "I do my part," he said. He gave his towel a smart snap. They eyed each other.

"Well? What about her?" said Jesse.

"Twenty-one. Never married."

"What's she going to do if her little sister starts at the Casbah?"

"I thought you didn't care," said Clint.

"I don't. You brought her name up." Jesse reached for another dish.

Clint and Biscuit guffawed.

"Moore offered her a job in his store," said Clint.

"Good businessman, Moore," said Biscuit. "Supply and demand. Women are scarce as hen's teeth in this camp, and he's managed to take half the supply and lock it up good and tight."

"Good businessman? Moore's looking for a wife for himself and a nurse for his loony mother," said Jesse.

"Then he's the smartest businessman of all," said Biscuit. "Employee and nurse for one price. And if he marries her, he gets all three for free."

Jesse regarded his cook. Startling amount of wisdom inside that old bald head.

"With comforts," added Biscuit.

The three men chuckled.

"What'd you do with the body?" said Jesse, turning back to his brother.

"I locked him in the buttery."

"My larder?" Biscuit stopped paring and slapped a beefy hand on the table.

"Where else was I supposed to store a hunk of charcoal that big? The lobby?" Clint crossed his arms.

" There's vittles in there," barked Biscuit, his face growing red.

"Not much," said Clint. "Like you said, few supplies left. Plenty of space for a stiff."

Biscuit began to wheeze.

"Keep your boots on," said Clint. "A handful of miners from Diamond Spring are riding to town this afternoon to bury him. He'll be gone before supper."

"He'd better be." Biscuit turned back to his bucket of potatoes, mumbling under his breath.

"It's alright," said Jesse, trying to defuse the situation. "Body's wrapped well in several old blankets. Clint will make sure it's gone today." He turned to his troublesome sibling. "Anyone missing? You asked around town?"

Clint shook his head. "Didn't get much. One or two locals sold their claims and left in the last couple of days. Makes 'em hard to account for. Then there's Rich Bar, Indian Bar, Diamond Spring, Sutter's Creek, and all the others. All kinds of comings and goings in those camps. New faces every day. No one can keep track."

Jesse nodded. "What about Harlan? Run into him down there?"

"No. By the time I arrived he was gone."

"He's probably asking around at the camps," said Jesse.

"That's what I heard."

"Jesse," said Biscuit, lifting the flaccid burlap bag at his feet as high as the table, "not enough potatoes for tomorrow's breakfast."

"I'll run down to Moore's and see if he has any left to hold us till the mules get in," offered Clint.

"You stay here and help Biscuit and Tien," said Jesse. "I'll go myself this afternoon after I get this place squared away."

"You're going to offer Madeline Whittaker a job. I knew it," said Clint.

"When frogs grow hair."

"Then why can't I go for potatoes?"

"Because I don't want to trade every piece of furniture in this building and half a month's receipts for a couple sack of tubers," said Jesse.

***

"Who could that be?" said Madeline, sitting up in bed. Someone was knocking on the door of their room at the Casbah. Both girls looked toward the sound as an unseen hand slid a cream-colored envelope under the door, then the sound of steps retreating down the hall.

"I'll get it," said Caroline, throwing off the bed covers.

"If it's Mr. Number Four, tell him no," said Madeline, falling back onto her pillow. She'd believe anything to be possible at this point, no matter how bizarre, even another marriage proposal.

"It's addressed to you," said Caroline, frowning.

"Me?" Madeline sat up again.

Caroline handed over the envelope. "I wonder why he didn't leave it at the front desk."

Madeline stared at her name in disbelief, then tore open the envelope to find a single sheet of paper.

Caroline plopped herself nearby on the edge of the bed. "Who's it from?"

Madeline ignored her little sister, her eyes growing wide as they moved down the page.

"Madeline? Who's it from? What does it say?"

"Lord have mercy." Madeline dropped the letter onto her lap, leaned back on the bed frame, and covered her eyes with her hand.

"What, Madeline, what?"

"Mr. Dupont has sold our oxen and wagon and everything in it."

Caroline gasped. "Why would he do that?"

"I have no idea. It's not from Mr. Dupont. It's from Mr. Moore, the man who owns the mercantile. Here," she said, pushing the paper toward Caroline.

Madeline slumped down in the bed as Caroline read in silence. That blackguard! How could he do this? *Why* would he do this? He had no right. What kind of infernal underworld had they tumbled into? A godless place in which barbarous men thought they could trample with impunity upon the rights of two unescorted young ladies.

And what would they do now? What happened to the money Mr. Dupont had obtained for the sale of their gear and supplies? Would they ever see that money? How would they ever get out of this lawless town without their wagon and team and no money? How would they ever get back to Independence? With no inheritance and no education, Uncle Finney's offer to leave his clinic to her was her only hope of ever ministering to the sick and wounded.

"Mr. Moore seems quite pleased with the trade," said Caroline as she reread the handsome script. "He seems to think you ordered the sale."

"I know." Madeline's words came out in a groan.

"*Your obedient servant.* Ooh. Now who's got swooning swains? You have an *obedient servant* to wait on your every whim, m 'lady. Order a coach and four, won't you, so we can be about town this afternoon in style."

"Don't be silly. That's the polite prose of an educated gentleman. It means nothing," said Madeline.

"At least he repeated his offer to set you up with a position in his store. That could be providential. You know how Ma used to say, silver lining and all that."

"Silver lining?" Madeline shook her head. "How can you see things so simply? We are in dire straits."

"Maybe not. I could accept one of those marriage offers and then you wouldn't have to look out for me. I know I am a burden to you. You could return to Independence more easily if I were married off."

Madeline scowled. "Don't be ridiculous. You'd be going from the pot right back to the fire. Besides, you've got what you wanted. We have returned to Hangtown. In fact, we are stuck in Hangtown. I hope you're content." She paused. "And you're not a burden, sugar bun."

Caroline shook her head madly. "I don't know how you can use that word, *content*. We're in Hangtown, but Pa is not. Neither are the boys. I wanted to arrive in Hangtown, of course I did. We all did. But not like this."

Madeline sighed. "Forgive me, I am uncharitable."

Caroline reached for Madeline's hand and gave it a squeeze.

"You seem to rise above all these tragedies, and so quickly too," said Madeline. "I don't know how you do it. I miss Pa and the boys so much."

"I miss them too," said Caroline. "You think I don't?"

Madeline didn't answer. She reached for a feather pillow and hugged it tightly.

"Pa wouldn't want us laying around bawling over what we can't change. He wouldn't put up with it," said Caroline.

Madeline nodded. Caroline was right, though the truth didn't make her feel any better.

"I cry at night when you're asleep, Maddy." Caroline managed a weak smile and began stroking her sister's hand. "At least we can be thankful Mr. Dupont is letting us stay in this room in his hotel without charging us." She glanced around at the simply appointed but clean and private room. "And that tub and scented soap he sent up. He had our trunks delivered to the room too. He can't be entirely evil."

Oh, he can t? Madeline bolted upright in the bed. "Scented soap or no, I'm going to find that weasel and get our possessions back. And then I'm going to call on Mr. Alonzo Moore."

"And if he doesn't give them back?"

"I'll demand he pay me their full value."

"And if he refuses, what then?"

Madeline looked across the room where, under ordinary circumstances, her rifle would have been leaning against the wall. But the weasel had purloined that, and the handgun too.

"I don't know," she said. "May God help me to get them back without violence. But get them back I will."

CHAPTER SIX

Caroline wasn't scheduled to work at the front desk until noon on their third day at the Casbah, so she helped Madeline ready herself for her urgent errand. Being clean in body after enduring weeks of grime was a celebration not to be wasted. Madeline adorned herself in her one good costume, a morning dress, pale pink with a domed skirt ringed with multiple rows of pale pink flounces and printed with dainty pink-and-green flowers that matched flowers bordering the bell sleeves. The tightly fitted bodice fell to a blunt point at the waist. Underneath the yards of delicate pink cotton she wore her well-worn but serviceable pantalettes.

She heated the sadiron in the fireplace and used it to press her wrinkled white chemisette. And over all this indulgence she draped her one true luxury: Ma's crocheted shawl to guard against the chill morning mountain air. She plaited her thick brown hair and pinned it up. Her old straw bonnet would turn no heads but it's all she had. She tied it under her chin, kissed her sister good-bye, and left the room.

Gull Dupont was not in the lobby. Annoyed, Madeline consumed a quick breakfast of coffee and toast in the hotel dining room and then returned to the lobby where she found Hank, the dim-witted front desk boy, pulling mindlessly on his one chin hair. She figured he was the same person who had pushed Mr. Moore's letter under their door. She inquired as to Mr. Dupont's whereabouts, but Hank knew nothing. She thanked him and left the hotel.

Once outside the cold mountain air hit like a slap. Fall was here. She shook herself and pulled Ma's shawl more tightly around her shoulders, wishing she had chosen her gray wool dress. Despite the cold, she stood a moment to take in the scenery and people of Hangtown. Despite its many drunkards, crude gambling houses, brothels, and weird honeycomb of abandoned mining pits on every side, Hangtown was a pretty settlement surrounded by tall, ancient pines that climbed the side of soaring mountains, backed by ever-present, brilliantly blue sky. The air was fresh and invigorating, far more refreshing than the heat and humidity of Independence. Pa and the boys would have loved the energy, the promise of this dynamic gold town.

Pa. He was still out there. Her chin trembled momentarily at the memory of his lifeless body in the ground. She had watched from the wagon as Mr. Dupont shoveled dirt over her father's face as irreverently as if he had been covering an old latrine pit. The memory of the thudding shovel sickened her still. She was still contemplating her father's unholy burial when someone addressed her by name.

"Miss Whittaker," said Gull, tipping his hat. "It's a chilly morning to be out. I will escort you."

"Thank you, Mr. Dupont, but I don't need an escort. What I need is the money Mr. Moore gave you for our oxen and wagon and mining supplies."

Madeline stood at least eight inches shorter than Gull Dupont. In the bright morning sun and clear mountain air, he seemed exceedingly handsome, chiseled even, with a strong jaw, piercing dark eyes, and that unusually thick black hair. She was embarrassed to notice the weasel's charms.

His mouth turned upward ever so slightly on one side. "You look very pretty in that pink dress."

She consciously glanced downward. "Thank you," she said. His gaze made her squirm, as if he knew all too intimately what she was wearing under those yards and yards of pink cotton.

"Did you find your room comfortable?"

"Yes, thank you, I forget myself. The room is comfortable in every detail." She thought of her long hot soak in that delicious tub, but it didn't seem appropriate to bring up such a picture to a gentleman. "My sister and I are grateful for your generosity, but you have not answered my question. Why did you sell our belongings without consulting me first?"

"Let us walk." Gull extended his arm. "We have important things to discuss."

Madeline glanced at his arm. Well, why not? The weasel on the end of that arm had all their money—their singular hope of returning to Independence. Reluctantly she linked her arm in his.

"Where to?" he said.

"I need to speak with Mr. Harlan Turpin."

Madeline was flustered even more when Gull reached over with his free arm and began patting her hand. The gesture was confusing. Was he genuinely concerned or merely inclined to patronize her? He made her feel like a child.

"My friend Harlan Turpin has not yet returned from his investigation," said Gull. "And as I told you, I will deal with Mr. Turpin. You're not to speak to him."

Something steely in his tone made Madeline reticent to argue. He had made up his mind, they were in a public venue, she and Caroline were eating and sleeping on his largesse, and he had all their money. And perhaps Mr. Dupont did know the ideal way to handle the matter. At home Pa would have taken care of everything.

She felt very disoriented.

"Mr. Dupont, why did you sell our gear and supplies? Where is the money?"

"For your welfare and that of your sister, it is preferable for the duration that a neutral representative look out for your affairs."

"Neutral representative? You?"

"Don't make a scene."

Madeline buttoned her lip in frustration. They started down the "street," which had no boardwalks and was dusty from months of dry summer heat. Men stared at them on every side, though she noticed her escort's commanding presence seemed to part the crowds like Moses and the Red Sea, giving them a strange sense of privacy. She felt, once again, as if she was being paraded down Main Street. But at least with an escort she needn't fear molestation. A frightening percentage

51

of Hangtown's all-male citizens took to drinking as soon as the saloons opened in the morning.

They walked a while in silence, but Madeline could not keep quiet. "You said we'd talk. I have to know—why did you sell our gear and supplies, and where is our money?"

"Your things had to be sold. It is in your best interest to make people think you and your sister returned to Hangtown of your own accord."

"But that's a lie."

"You *did* decide it was in your best interests to return to Hangtown, did you not?"

The wretched man forced them to return at the end of her own rifle. And where was her long arm, anyway?

"You have a skewed sense of truth."

"It suffices for our mutual purposes."

"What are you talking about?" She stopped and looked him in the face.

"Considering the unsavory and illegal activity in which I recently found you and your sister involved, I deem it much safer for you both that your return to Hangtown appear to outsiders as entirely innocent, even planned."

"I beg your pardon?"

"For the time being, your story is you changed your mind about returning to San Francisco and have decided, at least for a season, to build your fortune in our bustling gold town. Therefore, you have decided to accept the position Mr. Moore has offered, and your sister Caroline has decided that working at the Casbah suits her equally well."

Madeline gaped.

"Consequently," Gull continued, "you have no need of oxen or a wagon full of mining supplies.

You cannot deny this is a perfect plan. It provides you protection against the disquieting violence of an angry mob of vigilantes."

Vigilantes. Madeline's chest tightened. "I told you, the body we were burying is our father's."

He leaned into her face. "It is your only plan."

He stood too close for comfort. She looked away. "How long must we keep up this ruse?"

"Long enough for me to speak to Harlan Turpin about your father."

"And when will that be?"

"He's away from town right now, searching for the killer … or killers."

Killers. She and Caroline might be mistaken for killers. The dark thoughts this idea evoked were incongruous with the sunny morning. She took a deep breath to slow her racing heart. How she wished she had someone to lean on. Now that Pa's body was buried, unmarked, in the dark forest, she and Caroline were alone in this unfriendly place. Their plan to return to Independence seemed all but hopeless, and all these distressing circumstances had happened in a single day. This couldn't be real.

Was she dreaming? No. Her wagon, oxen, and supplies hadn't vanished into thin air.

"What about our money? And my rifle and handgun?"

"I sold everything to Mr. Moore."

Madeline snorted. "My rifle is one of my personal effects, like my clothing."

"Consider the wisdom of selling all your things," he said as he began to lead her down the street again. "Total divestiture of your mining and traveling supplies is in keeping with the actions of two sisters who mean to settle themselves permanently here in Hangtown, is it not? You're safe from suspicion this way."

How dare he.

"You mean all we have left in this world is the contents of our trunks and bags in our room? What about our money?"

"Bail."

"Pardon me?"

"Bail money. Security. I'm keeping your money in a safe place to make sure you and your sister don't abscond to San Francisco before the matter of a certain dead body is resolved."

Madeline was incredulous. To whom could she turn?

Gull stopped in front of a narrow but prosperous-looking store. Two large windows flanked a central door. Moore's Mercantile was elaborately inscribed in large gold letters over dark green paint.

Gull turned the knob and pushed open the door. "After you," he said.

CHAPTER SEVEN

Jesse looked up from where he leaned on the counter, chatting with Alonzo, when he heard the tinkle of the bell over the door. An airy puff of pink, like a silky cluster of mimosa blossoms released by a sudden spring gust, floated across the threshold. He stood upright and stared. In all her frothy glory this vision of femininity was the most beautiful, most captivating thing he had ever set eyes on. Her striking loveliness made the store and its contents appear colorless and drab.

The trail tramp?

Gull stepped in behind Madeline, shut the door, and ostentatiously reached for her arm. An alarm went off inside Jesse. Something about this visit was crooked.

"Good morning, Miss Whittaker, Gull," said Alonzo, smiling broadly.

Yes, she had transformed overnight into angel's breath. But wait until Alonzo tried to sell her something. Jesse well remembered the tussle over the hotel bill—she might be all pink froth on the outside, but she was all green pinch fist on the inside.

Jesse nodded to the couple, noted her discomfort as their eyes met, and watched intently to see what Gull was up to. Though her metamorphosis rendered him nearly speechless, he did manage a barely civil "good morning" to Gull.

"Miss Whittaker asked me to assist with her business affairs this morning," said Gull, ignoring Jesse and directing his comment to Alonzo.

"Splendid," said Mr. Moore. "Splendid, splendid. So, I trust you have reconsidered my offer?"

Madeline opened her mouth to speak but Gull interjected. "She has," he said, patting her hand in a fatherly way. "She's decided to settle down here in our friendly town. And I've offered the younger Miss Whittaker a position at the Casbah."

Gull glanced at Jesse, who couldn't hide his disgust. In Gull's eyes he saw the same disgust reflected in equal measure.

"Can you begin at once?" asked Alonzo.

Madeline blinked. "I thought perhaps—"

"Of course, of course, I understand," Alonzo interrupted. "The accommodations. You needn't concern yourself. Mother has the big bed across the hall, upstairs." He pointed to the stairwell in the rear corner of the store. "Plenty of space since my sister left us. You will be most comfortable, and Mother is used to sharing."

Jesse watched as Madeline's eyes darted around like a cornered cat searching for an escape.

What had gotten hold of that briery tongue? The girl was clearly cowed by her dark escort, but this milquetoast response was odd coming from a fishwife such as Madeline Whittaker. He had crossed mountain bobcats with better manners.

"I didn't know that—"

"An ideal solution to difficult circumstances," said Gull, cutting her off. He looked down at Madeline. Her arm was still wrapped around his, his free hand still clasping hers protectively. "You'll be near Caroline and will be spared the expense of a room at the Casbah," he said. "Meanwhile, you and Caroline can get some much needed rest in my establishment." He turned back to Alonzo. "I'll arrange for her things to be transferred here in a few days, maybe a week."

"But I…"

"Yes?" said Gull.

Jesse watched as a strange and slimy something passed between Gull and Miss Whittaker. There was more to the story, and whatever it was, it wasn't good. Yesterday she was a brawling termagant. Today she was a dispirited waif. He didn't know her from Eve, so the sudden change in her bearing since the scene at the Garry befuddled him.

On the other hand, he had no confusion about the likes of Gull Dupont.

After a few awkward exchanges, Gull and Madeline left. Jesse watched them with keen interest until they were out of sight.

"Good business sense, that one," said Alonzo. He reached to the floor and pulled up two lumpy burlap sacks and set them on the counter.

"You think this is about business?"

"Sure. He wants a pretty face greeting guests in his hotel lobby. Don't you?"

"The Garry is profitable without all the trouble skirts bring in," said Jesse. "Likely he's looking for cheap labor to replace Sadie. She ran off with a miner who struck pay dirt on Rich Bar."

"I heard about Sadie," said Alonzo. "Regardless, I think you wish you'd made an offer to one of those pretty sisters before Gull did."

Jesse drew his mouth into a grim line as he reached into his jacket for his pouch of gold dust. Best to keep mum about his plans. "How much for the potatoes?"

Alonzo chuckled knowingly. Jesse paid his bill and was about to hoist the two bags when Alonzo asked, "Seen Harlan lately?"

"Not since we found the body. He's still making the rounds at all the camps, looking to find who roasted that miner and left him under rocks by Diamond Spring. Why do you ask? Heard anything?"

"Not about the murder. Brown's back in town," said Alonzo. "Back from Marysville."

"William Brown? I never thought that Swede would deliberately poke his stupid head into a rope necklace. You sure it's Brown?"

"Saw him this morning. I hear he's settled in at a rooming house in Rich Bar, but he was in town this morning looking to buy a shovel, supposedly for mining. He was so hooched up, the only thing he'll be digging up is trouble. He's done nothing but lounge around one saloon after another since he arrived, interrupted by a little bit of mining."

"Why come back?"

"He was acquitted of stealing the gold from his partners, Jesse. He's a free man."

"He's a free fool." Jesse hoisted the potatoes over his shoulder. "His partners are bent on getting their gold back, and the whole town believes he's guilty. His freedom to walk about town increases his chance of taking a bullet to the head or a swing from a noose. Why risk his neck by coming back?"

Alonzo mindlessly fingered his emerald cufflink. "Probably too potted all the time to think it through. He needed a shovel, so I sold him one."

Jesse shook his head again in wonderment. "Coming back to Hangtown confirms in a lot of miners 'heads he's got a stash of stolen gold dust shoved in a coyote hole up the mountain somewhere."

Alonzo shrugged. "Then I hope he comes back and buys more mining supplies."

Jesse left the store with his potatoes. As he walked back to the Garry, he scanned Main Street for the younger Miss Whittaker. She should have received his note by now. Gull Dupont was going to be sorry when his newest conquest rejected the Casbah for a better position at the Garry. And if there was anything Jesse wanted in this life, it was to make Gull Dupont sorry.

Very, very sorry.

CHAPTER EIGHT

Madeline pushed open the door to the Casbah. As she approached the front desk, she was surprised to see Hank behind it and not Caroline. Alarm bells went off in her head.

"Miss Whittaker," said Hank, before she could speak, "I'm glad you've returned. Miss Caroline still ain't come down for her shift."

"Have you rung our room?"

"Yes, ma'am, several times. Knocked loud on the door, too. She don't answer."

"I can't imagine what is delaying her. I'll get her for you," she said.

A sickening sense of dread accompanied her to their second-floor room above the lobby. She shouldn't have brought her sister here. Caroline had never been reliable, but she had been excited to have her first situation, a means to make money and

… Madeline stopped short. *A respectable way—a fast way—to meet eligible men.*

She opened the door to their room. Caroline was not there, which was odd, but by itself not necessarily alarming. Her muscles relaxed when she found the room orderly and everything in place. The bed was made neatly. The vanity had been tidied up after both sisters 'morning toilettes. The wash towels were folded and hung straight on their wooden stand. Nothing about the room seemed askew. Its perfect ordinariness would have made her feel silly for worrying, if it weren't for Caroline missing her first day of work.

Caroline had evidently rummaged through her trunk, because Madeline found it unlocked and the contents disturbed. She sorted through Caroline's things, figuring she would choose, inappropriately, her best summer dress, a frilly white lacey thing, for her first day of employment at the Casbah. Aha. The dress was not in the trunk. Madeline had been right.

But where was Caroline? Madeline swept the room again and noticed a folded piece of paper on the vanity, tucked slightly under the porcelain bowl on the dry sink.

Dear Miss Whittaker,

I would like to offer you a position at the Garry. I am in need of an agreeable young woman to greet customers and efficiently run the front desk. Whatever Mr. Dupont has offered you in the way of compensation, I am prepared to double. Please meet me at the side

*entrance to the Garry at 11:00 a.m.
today. Considering the sensitive
nature of this request, I ask that you
use great discretion and share this
business with no one.*

*Cordially,
Jesse Garry, Manager
Garry Hotel*

So that was it. Caroline had run off to the
Garry for better wages. She folded the note and
placed it where Caroline had left it. She would
return shortly, doubtless all bubbly and excited over
her new position and fat pay packet.

Meanwhile, Madeline needed to placate
Hank. She descended the stairs to the lobby and
made an excuse about Caroline being a little
delayed, then returned to her room for a nap. The
angst of the last few days had sapped her strength.
She was exhausted. She would leave Caroline to
deal with the mess she'd made by failing to show
up. There wasn't anything she could do about it
now, anyway. She disrobed down to her chemise
and stockings and climbed into the soft feather bed.
She was asleep in a moment.

She awoke to the sound of someone
knocking on the door. It seemed late—the room was
shadowy. For a moment she was discombobulated.
Where was she? What time was it? Then she
remembered the morning's events. She threw off the
covers and called through the door.

"Who is it, please?"

"It's Hank, ma'am."

"Yes?"

"Miss Whittaker never showed up at the desk. Is she in there with you?"

"I'll find her, Hank. I'll be downstairs shortly." With that, she threw on her clothes. She would begin at the obvious beginning, the Garry Hotel and that onerous desk clerk, Jesse Garry. Inwardly she groaned at the thought. She was about to leave the room when she remembered Mr. Garry's handwritten note. She slipped it into her bag.

She was unnerved to see it was five o'clock when she stepped into the lobby. Caroline should have returned to the Casbah hours ago. Hank eyed her strangely. Not knowing what to say, and embarrassed at her sister's misbehavior, she merely smiled then exited the hotel. In seconds she was across the street, standing at the front desk of the Garry Hotel.

***

To say Jesse Garry was shocked to see Madeline Whittaker across the front desk was putting it mildly. Her face was drawn looking, but unlike before, her distress was not a source of entertainment. She had been duped by the maggot. He had the grace to pity her.

But pity wasn't enough. As fetching as this young woman was since she'd cleaned herself up, her visage still resurrected the memory of an oversized rifle poking in his face and the sting of public humiliation. Acting cordial required extraordinary grace, and he didn't have it.

"We're full," said Jesse.

"I'm not here for a room. I'm looking for my sister."

"Haven't seen her."

"She had an appointment with you this morning. *You* invited her here."

The younger Miss Whitaker must have spilled the contents of his note to mama bear. " I invited your sister here to discuss a business matter, but she never showed."

Jesse saw the spirit drain from her. For the second time, he felt sorry for her. Despite all the bluster, the lady needed a big, strong man at her side.

"She didn't arrive?" She pulled his note from her bag, unfolded it, and pushed it across the desk.

He pushed it back across the desk. "I had a messenger deliver it to the Casbah. I was surprised your sister didn't show or send a note. But I assure you, she has not been here today."

Madeline blew through her nose. "Why, sir, did you insist my sister not tell anyone about your meeting?"

"I didn't want her employer to find out."

She glared at him. "And why would you entice her with *double* wages? How could she turn that down?"

"Business. That's the way business is. You wouldn't understand."

She eyed him for an overlong minute. "I understand, Mr. Garry," she said slowly and loudly, "you requested a private meeting with an impressionable young girl and offered her the moon and stars to make sure she responded the way you desired."

Jesse surveyed the room. All eyes were upon on them. "We will talk outside," he said. Before she could object, he was around the desk and taking her arm, firmly, guiding her to the door.

Once outside, he turned her toward him and released his grip on her arm. "You have to understand about business in this town," he said. "It's competitive. Customers want to see a pretty face behind the hotel desk, but Hangtown doesn't have enough women to fill these jobs. I thought it best to meet with your sister privately considering her recent agreement with Mr. Dupont. That is why I asked her for discretion. But she did not show up. I would not lie to you."

The sun was sinking, bathing the buildings and tents along Main Street in soft shadow, but Jesse was aware only of the shadow passing slowly across Miss Whittaker's eyes. He watched as her bravado melted away.

"I see."

"Shall I escort you to the Casbah? It's getting dark."

She opened her mouth to speak but nothing came out.

"I can see you're worried about your sister. I can get a search party together if you're convinced she's in danger."

"No, no," she said, shaking her head. "That won't be necessary. I'm sure my sister will show up soon enough. I'm probably worried over a trifle. Likely she's finishing up errands. Thank you for your offer. It is very kind of you."

With that she turned and walked across the street to the Casbah.

***

At the front desk Hank reported Caroline had not returned to the hotel, so Madeline asked him to alert her at once if he heard any news, then she returned to the sanctuary of her room. She sank onto the bed and stared at the ceiling.

What should she do? Whom could she trust?

Mr. Dupont? Not for one second would she unburden herself to that weasel.

Mr. Turpin? Mr. Dupont warned her about communicating with him, and in this small town— hardly a town, just an upstart mining camp—Mr. Dupont would undoubtedly find out she had spoken to him. She feared the consequences.

Mr. Garry again? He seemed more gentlemanly than she had assessed on their first day in Hangtown, and it was gallant of him to offer to help search for Caroline, but he could be lying about Caroline's not appearing at the Garry. He was, after all, the self-confessed author of the note designed to draw the girl out of her room. He seemed sincere, but it could be mere smokescreen.

Mr. Alonzo Moore? He was well spoken, courteous, and thoughtful of women, at least as it concerned the goods he stocked in his mercantile.

She got up and looked out the hotel room window. The street wasn't fully dark yet. Perhaps the doors of his mercantile were still open.

CHAPTER NINE

Madeline was surprised to see a strange older woman standing behind the counter when she entered the mercantile. Emphasis on *strange*. The woman, about fifty, wore a thin, tattered nightgown paired with a garishly broad hat trimmed in a profusion of lime green and purple ostrich feathers. Underneath the hat her tangled gray hair hung loosely about bony shoulders.

At the sound of the bell tinkling above the door, the woman looked up from whatever she was doing and stared at Madeline, rudely looking her up and down. "We're sold out," the woman said. Then she glared.

"I'm here to see Mr. Moore," she stammered. She clutched her bag more tightly than usual, aware of some vague need for self-defense.

"My agent is not accepting new clients."

"Clients?"

"You're here to audition, are you not?"

"Audition for what?"

The woman walked from behind the counter and stepped toward Madeline, who was shocked to see bare feet sticking out from a torn hem. A nasty smell of urine clung to the ragged nightgown. Madeline recoiled.

"The show is *full*," said the woman. "And I told you, my agent isn't accepting new clients. Now get out."

"I'm sorry, ma'am, there seems to be a mistake. I've not come here to audition. I—"

"Hah! I know your type. You think you can bamboozle your way into show business with your flouncy flock and pretty face. But those aren't enough, not nearly enough. You need talent, and plenty of it. Talent is what matters. I was born with talent oozing from my fingertips—buckets of talent, barrels of talent. You young lassies think your looks will carry you to stardom. I had to claw my way into the best theaters in New York."

The woman suddenly stepped a little closer, uncomfortably close, thrusting her face practically into Madeline's. The smell of urine mingled with sour breath. Madeline shrunk back.

"Are you a virgin?"

"I beg your pardon," said Madeline

"Hah! I knew it. Damn town is full of tarts. Last one wasn't a virgin, either, though they all claim to be as pure as snow. Everyone wants to be on stage no matter the cost."

"I think I should go now." Madeline started for the door.

"Amorous congress won't make you a star, missy," the old woman hollered after her. "You can frolic every night with your agent, but no matter

what he promises, he can't make up for no talent.
You'll end up like that other trollop! I'm warning
you!"

Madeline raced through the door and shut it
with a bang. She shook herself in the brisk evening
air to calm down. *Who was that awful woman?*

She had wasted precious time sparring with
the crazy lady in the feathered hat. But perhaps in
that short interlude Caroline had returned to the
Casbah. She decided to return to check their room
before inquiring at the few shops in town, though by
now most had locked up for the night.

At the Casbah Madeline questioned the
night clerk, but he hadn't seen Caroline come or go.
But, he said, a gentleman had left an envelope. The
clerk reached into a cubby behind him, retrieved it,
and handed it to her. Her name was on the front.
She recognized Caroline's pretty script at once. She
thanked the clerk and rushed to her room.

The room was undisturbed since Madeline
had left it an hour earlier. She lit a candle, slit the
envelope, and began to read.

Dear Maddy,

*Please do not be angry, and
do not worry about me. I have fallen
in love with the nicest man. He is a
true gentleman, and he is rich too,
with a big house and horses. We are
leaving right away for our
honeymoon home. When I get settled,
I will send you a letter.*

*Please do not search for me.
I know you think I am flighty and
silly, but I know what I am doing,*

and now that I am no longer your burden, you are free to return to Independence as soon as you can arrange passage. And soon I will be Mrs. Number Four! Please be happy for me.

> *Your Sugar Bun,*
> *Caroline*

CHAPTER TEN

Caroline eloped? Madeline stared at the words. It couldn't be true. She scrutinized the handwriting. It surely was her little sister's penmanship, flowery but neat and uniform. Then the awful truth sunk in: Caroline had abandoned her for a man, a stranger at that. Now she was truly alone in this filthy, forbidding mining camp.

She dropped her head into her hands. She had felt alone when they first rolled into this wretched town, but it was nothing like the aloneness she felt now. Perhaps she was walking through the valley of the shadow of death she'd heard so much preaching about. Was she being punished? Or was this all a terrible, purgatorial nightmare sent to scare her into living right?

Would she ever wake again to the morning songbirds in Independence? Home, Pa, Ma, and her brothers, and now Caroline—gone. Was her dream of inheriting Uncle Finney's medical clinic dead too?

She sat a long time trying to make sense of all that had happened to her in the last few days. Finally, after a lengthy spell of reflection and self-pity, she shook herself. She wasn't one to wring her hands and stew in hopelessness. Pa would be disappointed in her.

She grabbed a wrap and hat, tucked the note in her satchel, and made for the door. She had only one choice left, nauseating though it was.

***

Jesse was alerted at once to the sexiest sound in all Hangtown—the rare silken rustle of a woman's long, flowing skirts—that followed the more familiar clunk of the door to the Garry Hotel as it opened and closed. He stopped thumbing receipts when he saw the elder Miss Whittaker walking through the empty lobby.

He noted, with relief, she wasn't carrying her elephant gun.

"Isn't it late for you to be in the street without your rifle?" he asked as she approached the front desk.

"I have urgent business."

That meant one thing. "Your sister returned?"

"No. I received a note." She pushed the envelope across the scarred wooden counter.

Jesse slipped the note out of its envelope and read it. His eyebrows knit into a question. "Mr. Four?"

"She's had four marriage proposals since we arrived in town."

72

"Any idea who Mr. Four is?" he asked, passing the note back to her.

"No, I know nothing. Neither his name nor occupation."

Jesse saw her upper lip quiver and felt a pang of compassion. But his ego still smarted as he remembered his public dressing down at the hands of this confounding woman. And his ego was vastly bigger than his compassion. He put on a poker face.

"You sure this is her handwriting?" he asked.

"Yes, very sure."

"How old is she?"

"Sixteen."

"She is of age." Jesse turned back to his work.

Madeline's shoulders drooped. "She is. But how old is the man she's with? She's a child at heart."

"Did she take her things with her?" he said without looking up from his papers.

"The room hasn't been disturbed all day. Other than a favorite white dress she wore for your meeting this morning, I saw no evidence she took anything from the room. For that matter, I didn't see evidence she returned to the room—after her appointment with you."

Jesse flinched. "I told you, your sister never showed up for our appointment. When she didn't show, I assumed her answer was no."

"Yes, you told me. But where is my sister? Why didn't she show up at the Garry? Why didn't she return to the Casbah? All she had to do was cross the street."

He pushed aside his paperwork and looked at her directly. "If I had meant harm to your sister by drawing her to the Garry on a pretense, wouldn't I deny being the author of this incriminating invitation? Wouldn't I? Didn't I freely admit it's my handwriting?"

Madeline's mouth drew into a straight line. She was silent for several seconds. "Your point is well taken." She slipped the note into her bag.

"I have nothing to hide," added Jesse. "Can you think of any reason why your sister would want to leave so badly and in such a hurry? It's odd she took nothing with her and didn't say goodbye. Could she be running from something?"

Madeline breathed deeply. "We've suffered a lot of losses. Caroline was grieving. Perhaps she thought marrying would bring her happiness."

"Losses?"

"Our mother died a few years ago. But since we left Independence in the spring our three brothers all died of cholera. At Fort Atkinson."

"And your pa?" said Jesse.

"Our pa—our pa is not here. He died on the way also."

Jesse studied her face. Why be cagey about her pa's whereabouts? He tucked away that question for later.

"Well," he said, "sounds to me like she started for the Garry this morning to talk to me about the position but changed her mind before she got here. Or, she never had any intention of keeping our appointment. Maybe she used my note as cover to meet her beau without the Big Gun's interference."

Madeline's mouth fell open.

"Or," he said more deliberately, "maybe someone or something interfered with her attempt to keep our meeting. Perhaps Mr. Number Four.

Perhaps someone else." Jesse saw panic in her eyes. "Which scenario do you think is the right one?"

"I don't know. I'm so confused. Caroline was flattered at all the gentlemanly attention she's received, and like most young girls she's smitten with the notion of marriage. But I can't believe she'd intentionally run off and leave me alone. And she didn't take her things. I'm worried something awful has happened to her. She is very gullible."

Madeline wasn't the only one confused. That sister of hers had run off with a gold-digging yokel, like Sadie Shaw before her. What a team these two sisters were, a complicated, messy, troublesome duo. Nevertheless, the older sister seemed awfully distressed. It didn't seem right not to help.

"As soon as I can find someone to cover this desk, I'm going to make inquiries around town about your sister. But right now I'm going to walk you back to the Casbah so some drunk doesn't proposition you on the way. You wait there. I'll send word. Alright?"

Madeline nodded. "Thank you."

Clint flung open the front door as Jesse was reaching for the bell pull. He closed the door a little too loudly and strode toward the front desk. He greeted his brother and Madeline.

"Everything alright?" said Clint.

"Miss Whittaker's sister left the Casbah early this morning and hasn't returned," said Jesse. "I need you to watch the lobby. I'm going to escort her back to the Casbah then search town for the younger Miss Whittaker."

"I'll search with you," said Clint, practically salivating. He turned to Madeline. "We'll find your pretty little sister. We'll have her back within the hour."

"You're staying here," said Jesse.

Clint made a face.

Jesse reached for his hat and sidearm, then took Madeline's arm to lead her to the door.

"Jesse," said Clint, "Can I talk to you a minute? Outside?"

Jesse excused himself to Madeline, and he and Clint stepped outside. The night sky was inky blue, blanketed with stars and rich with wood smoke from dozens of campfires.

Jesse crossed his arms. "I said no."

"It's not about the girl," said Clint. "But maybe it is. Another body has turned up at Diamond Spring. Just like the first one, burned to a crisp and buried under a pile of rocks."

CHAPTER ELEVEN

Madeline could hardly sleep, and what sleep she got was shallow and fitful. There was no escaping the truth: Caroline had eloped or had fallen into serious trouble. The weight of this thought pressed hard on her chest every waking minute.

An envelope was waiting for her in the hotel lobby next morning. True to his word, Jesse Garry related he had visited as many businesses, mostly saloons, as he could during the night, but no one had seen Caroline. Starting at daybreak he would ask others to search the area outside Hangtown, particularly the camps, with him. He closed with a promise to do all he could to find Caroline.

She folded the note and slipped it into her bag. Caroline had spent a night away from the hotel.

This was bad, very bad. She felt faint again. She stepped to the nearest chair and sat down.

"Miss Whittaker," said a familiar male voice. Every muscle in her body went rigid in defense at the sound.

"Good morning, Mr. Dupont."

"I heard the disturbing news of your sister's disappearance. I want you to know that all my resources are at your disposal. And I've sent two Casbah employees with Mr. Turpin to help find your sister."

She noted his impeccable clothes: crisp, dark slacks and a pristine waistcoat with starched collar. He wore no hat, as they were indoors. His abundant black hair shone under plenty of pomade. Such dandy clothing made him stand out from all the other men she'd met in Hangtown. Somehow she sensed he was trying to set himself apart from the rabble. But that was a wicked thought, wasn't it?

"Thank you. That was very kind of you." It *was* kind of him. Maybe she had misjudged him? The scintillating memory of his lips on her neck popped up suddenly. The man unmoored her.

"Do you have news?"

"At least three dozen men are searching for her," said Gull. "It's nearly nine o'clock, so they should have reached the farthest camps by now. We'll know more by this afternoon."

She nodded.

"Have you been outside the hotel yet this morning?"

"I was about to leave for Moore's Mercantile."

"Then you are unaware of the news," he said.

"What news?" She stood to leave.

"Another dead body has been found at Diamond Spring."

"No!" Her hand flew to her heart.

"Nothing is known yet of the identity. It would be premature to presume."

At this he took her hand in his. Madeline stiffened, taking care not to let even a baby finger respond in kind.

He looked directly into her frightened eyes. "The killer set the body on fire."

His words struck their target. Madeline's heart started pounding hard. Blood rushed past her ears in a roar. She let go of his hand and gripped the edge of the chair.

"And," said Gull, leaning in close and lowering his voice, "The perpetrator covered the body with rocks, like you planned to do for that unlucky fellow in the woods."

Their eyes locked. Madeline instinctively took a step back from him. "I will be moved out of my room here at the Casbah as soon as I can arrange it. Thank you for your hospitality and for your concern for my sister's welfare."

"As you wish. Let me know if I can be of any assistance."

Madeline started for the door.

"Miss Whittaker."

She stopped and slowly turned.

"I will make sure to speak to Mr. Turpin about your situation as soon as he returns to town. I would have spoken to him sooner, but I've been taken up with affairs here at the Casbah, and he's been away searching for the killer or killers. After this latest upsetting news, I don't think I should wait any longer."

***

Jesse dismounted his sweaty horse, handed the reins to the stable keeper, and headed for the Garry Hotel kitchen. "Biscuit!" he called before he was through the door. "Biscuit!" He glanced around the oversized kitchen. Only Tien was there, wide eyed at his employer's unusual irritation.

"Tien, where's Biscuit?"

"Store." Tien stopped his work at the enormous stove. Two huge pots of simmering coffee sent plumes of steam into the air.

"And Clint?"

"Not here."

At that moment Clint walked into the kitchen. "Heard my name. What's all the ruckus?"

"Did you see the younger Whittaker sister, Caroline, yesterday morning?" said Jesse.

"Wish I had," said Clint. "Whole town is looking for her. I'd love to be the one to find her."

"I mean, was she here? Did you see her anywhere around the hotel?"

"No."

"And Biscuit? Did he see her around here?"

"Don't know. I suppose if he had he would have mentioned it. Caroline Whittaker is news. Why?"

"Gull's been running around telling the whole town Caroline disappeared from the Garry," said Jesse.

Clint swore. "Jackass couldn't tell the truth if a knife was at his throat."

"It's worse. She had an appointment here, with me, right before she went missing."

"An appointment with you?" said Clint. He leaned against the doorway. "This sounds good. Keep talking."

"Don't let your imagination out of the barn. I was planning to offer her a position at the desk, that's all. Told her I'd pay her twice what Gull was paying."

"What took you so long to figure it out?"

"It's not about the Garry. I told you, we're doing fine. But she never showed up for our meeting."

They heard the breathy huffing of Biscuit carrying a load. He pushed open the kitchen side door with his foot, his arms full of packages. "Help me with these," he said with a wheeze as he noisily dropped the items onto the central worktable. "There's more outside."

"They can wait," said Jesse. "Did you see Caroline Whittaker anywhere around the hotel yesterday morning?"

"This hotel?" said Biscuit.

"Yes, of course this hotel."

Tien wordlessly slipped out the side door and began bringing the remaining packages and bags into the kitchen.

"Never saw her," said Biscuit. "But I bet I know what this is about. Got an earful at Moore's. Figured it wouldn't take long to get back to you."

Jesse repeated his accusation against Gull.

"Gull Dupont, origin of every dark scheme," said Biscuit, shaking his head. "He's going to keep at it till he pushes you so far down you can't get up again."

"How did he know?" said Jesse.

"Know what?" said Clint and Biscuit in unison.

"Miners I talked to this morning knew all about the note I had Tien deliver to the Casbah asking Caroline to meet me."

81

Tien heard his name and stopped loading packages.

"Maybe she wanted to keep her job at the Casbah. In that case she would have never come to the Garry," said Biscuit.

"I've no idea if she wanted the job, but she got my note. Her sister found it in their room at the Casbah. She said Caroline's favorite white dress was missing from the room. She figures Caroline wore it to make a good impression."

"She'd make a better impression without it," said Clint.

Jesse gave Clint a dirty look. "I suppose the note isn't proof of anything, is it?"

"Not hardly," said Clint.

Biscuit shook his head. "She took a white dress because she ran off to marry some rich miner."

"You suppose that second dead body at Diamond Spring has anything to do with Caroline's disappearance?" asked Clint.

The men fell silent. Should he tell his brother and trusted employee about the note Madeline had received from Caroline, claiming to have voluntarily left town? Knowing Clint's inability to keep his mouth shut, it occurred to Jesse it might be a good idea for a second rumor to make its way around town, one that invalidated the first, because soon all eyes in town would be on Jesse Garry, Girl Kidnapper. He'd far prefer to have them talk about Caroline Whittaker, Girl Eloper.

"I don't know what to think right now," said Jesse. He ran a hand through his hair. "There's another note—from Caroline herself. Yesterday afternoon someone delivered it to the Casbah."

Tien, who had finished unloading the foodstuffs from the wagon and was standing at the stove preparing breakfast for the second wave, stopped what he was doing. Clint and Biscuit looked expectantly at Jesse.

"It said Caroline had met a man with some money and they've left Hangtown to get married."

"Told you." Biscuit cut the string on the largest package and began to unwrap hunks of salted pork.

"Madeline doesn't know who this fellow is. No name, nothing. We don't know if he's a miner or something else. We don't know where they're going, either."

"So which is it?" said Clint. "Which note is the right note?"

Jesse shook his head. "I don't know."

"Who delivered it?" said Clint.

"I didn't think to ask."

"Is she sure her sister wrote it?" said Biscuit. "Perhaps someone has the girl and is trying to throw everyone off by delivering a counterfeit."

"Madeline insists her sister wrote the note," said Jesse. "She's certain the handwriting is Caroline's."

"Well," said Biscuit, "could be both notes are right. Maybe she met her new husband on the way to the Garry and decided against meeting with you. And then they took off to get married."

"That would be the fastest wedding I've ever heard of," said Clint.

"You said yourself she wore white that morning," said Biscuit. "Likely the dress was for her wedding, not a meeting with a hotel manager. This isn't hard to figure out."

Biscuit made sense, to a point. But something was off, seriously off. "Madeline told me her sister didn't return to the Casbah all day once she had left in the morning to keep her appointment with me."

"Then she was wearing the dress when she left for your meeting," said Biscuit. "She knew she was leaving town to get married when she left the Casbah in the morning. That was her intent all along. She never had any plans to meet you here." Biscuit started toward the buttery, his arms loaded down with hunks of pork.

"Or something bad happened to her on the way over here," said Clint.

Biscuit poked his head out from the door to the buttery off the kitchen. "You need to start thinking like a lawyer. You may need one."

Jesse and Clint exchanged a knowing look.

Biscuit emerged from the buttery and eased his heavy body into his chair by the work table. He went back to opening packages. "Anybody know anything about that new dead body?"

"Nothing for sure," said Jesse. "Miners will speculate about anything. I'm waiting to talk to Harlin."

"Any idea who he is?" said Biscuit.

"None," said Jesse. "Probably another miner." He hoped this was true. But the fact was, he wasn't so sure.

"You think it might be Caroline Whittaker?" said Biscuit.

"I hope not," said Jesse.

Each man was alone in his own thoughts for several seconds. Finally, Clint got up to go. "Now that you're back, I'm going to go search for Miss Caroline."

"Not quite yet." Jesse pulled his sidearm from his holster and checked to see if it was loaded. "I need you to watch the desk a little longer. I'm going to go talk to Harlin." He reholstered his gun. "I'm going to find the elder Miss Whittaker and offer her a job and room and board at the Garry."

"Really?" said Clint.

"Gull will lose this war," said Jesse.

CHAPTER TWELVE

Madeline was touched by the expressions of concern she received from miners and storekeepers alike who stopped her as she headed toward Moore's Mercantile. They seemed sincere. But each time another man stopped to say he was praying for her sister to be found, it heightened Madeline's fear. Perhaps something truly awful had befallen Caroline.

She was certain of two things: She must find Caroline, and she must move out of the Casbah immediately and get as far from Gull Dupont as she could. She would focus on these two tasks. It would give her purpose and keep her sane. And when Caroline returned, Madeline would forbid her to work for the awful Mr. Dupont.

She was a minute away from Moore's when she saw Jesse Garry walking toward her. When their eyes met, she knew he intended to speak with her.

"We are doing all we can to find your sister," he said.

"I'm sure you are. I received your note late last night. Thank you. Any news to share with me since then?"

"I've heard nothing. Several dozen men are still out, visiting all the camps and asking about her."

She nodded morosely.

"I'm on my way to speak to Harlin."

She gave him a weak smile.

Jesse removed his hat. "I know we met under poor circumstances, but I need a desk person and you need a way to keep body and soul together. Would you consider working for me at the Garry? The work is easy. I'd provide a small but private room, and all your meals would come from the dining room."

"As you know, Mr. Garry, I already have a position."

"You haven't started yet," he said with a smile. "And you won't have to cook your meals at the Garry like you would at Moore's."

"I—"

"I'll pay you double what Moore is paying you."

She crossed her arms. "What is going on here? Why are the two hotels in this town risking financial ruin to get me and my sister behind their front desks? I'm no businesswoman, but it occurs to me that neither of us have ever held a job, and certainly not a job waiting on the public. Except for my time helping my uncle with his medical clinic, our skills are entirely domestic. You can't last in business long if you foolishly overpay your employees."

Jesse looked away briefly. "Alonzo Moore," he finally responded, "will work you long hours. And he'll expect you to care for his mother."

That odd woman is Mr. Moore's mother?

"Is Mr. Moore's mother quite elderly, thin, with long gray hair?"

"Yes, that's her."

But for the crazy lady with the ostrich feathers, working in a clean, well-stocked mercantile was more appealing than laboring in the hotel where Caroline may have disappeared. Could she trust Jesse Garry's word that he was not involved?

"Well," said Madeline, "I think ... I think Moore's Mercantile is a more genteel place for a lady to work. I'm sure I can be of greater service to Mr. Moore and his mother than I would be at the Garry. I'm sure you understand. Thank you for your offer, but I must decline."

***

After about half an hour Jesse tracked down his friend at the public stable where he was dismounting after his long ride to the camps. Harlin's shoulders sagged.

"Learn anything?" asked Jesse after they had exchanged greetings.

"Walk with me," said Harlin as he removed his saddle bag from his horse. "We'll talk over a drink."

They found an empty table at the rear of the nearly vacant saloon and sat down. Most of the town's residents were out in the gold fields, madly digging and sluicing as fast as they could, knowing the warm weather would soon be a memory. The saloon was poorly lit and reeked of smoke and unwashed bodies. The two men ordered their drinks.

"News?" asked Jesse. Waiting for Harlin to speak strained his patience.

"Not what you want to hear," said Harlin. "Whoever killed that first miner at Diamond Spring surely killed the second fellow I saw this morning. Same everything—charred body, clothes burned off, same rock pile. Second body wasn't far from the first. Maybe quarter mile."

"Another miner?"

"I collected part of a suspender. No buttons this time, though. Just a leather piece that didn't burn. But I don't think it's a miner."

"Why?"

"Someone is trying awful hard to hide the identity of the dead. If it were a miner, it would be another claim dispute, and those are public."

"We have tribunals for those."

"Exactly," said Harlin. "There'd be no need for secrecy. Most miners who are defrauded of their claim or their gold or any other property want other miners to side with them. They prefer a public hearing over these sneaky, middle-of-the-night doings."

"Anything on the body to tell you how he died?"

Harlin shook his head. "And it wasn't burned where it was found. Burned elsewhere and carried to the grave site."

"Like the first one," said Jesse. "Anybody missing? Besides the young woman, Caroline Whittaker, I mean."

"I asked around. Everyone seems to be accounted for, at least within a mile of where the body was left. I haven't heard back from the boys I sent to Shingle Spring or Coloma. I'll let you know when I do. The searchers are doing double duty, scouring the countryside and the camps for anyone or anything that doesn't seem right."

"What about William Brown?" said Jesse. "He has reason to kill his former partners. They sent him to jail."

"His name came to mind when the first body turned up. But I checked on his former partners. They're panning in Coloma. Saw them myself. Brown should be worried about taking a bullet from either of them, not the other way around."

Their drinks arrived. They each took a sip and sat a minute, thinking. Finally, Jesse couldn't keep quiet any longer. "Harlin, what about Caroline Whittaker? Has anyone outside of town seen her?"

"No. She's evaporated like smoke."

Jesse debated. It was inevitable that Harlin would find out about the two conflicting notes. It was only a matter of time, and a short space at that. Still, he was reluctant to disclose them to Harlin because he didn't want the focus of the search for the girl to lose steam. After Sadie Shaw had run off suddenly to marry a rich miner, everyone would logically assume Caroline had done the same and stop looking for her.

On the one hand, he had no stake in seeing that Gull's newest desk clerk got installed back at the Casbah. Gull could rot in Hell and his hotel could go down with him for all he cared. On the other hand: *Madeline.*

In a moment of clarity, it struck him that he cared about what happened to Madeline. The thought unnerved him.

And he needed to clear his name. Best to feed the information to Harlin himself before he heard the story from some inebriated miner.

Jesse told Harlin about both notes, his and Caroline's, and how sure Madeline was that the latter one was written in Caroline's own hand.

"Do you think she ran off with a miner or got snatched against her will? Or got lost in the mountains?" asked Harlin.

Jesse let out a long, audible sigh. "Caroline never showed up for our appointment at the Garry. That leaves me to think she ran off with her man. I find it hard to believe something sinister happened to her between the Casbah and the Garry. They're across the street from each other."

"Any witnesses to her leaving the Casbah that morning?" asked Harlin. "Maybe she had no intention of keeping your appointment."

"No."

"Anyone see her arrive at the Garry?"

"No."

"Hmm," was all Harlin had to say.

"But then, she ran off without her belongings and without saying goodbye to Madeline. The sisters seem close," said Jesse.

Harlin's pointed questions and intense gaze made Jesse uncomfortable. He reached for his drink.

"You seem to take an inordinate interest in those two girls," said Harlin.

"Doesn't every man in town?"

"Particularly the older one." Harlin smiled a small, knowing smile. "It's hard to believe a pretty

little thing like that, one of a handful of young
women in this town of hundreds of men, would not
be noticed crossing the street from the Casbah to the
Garry."

"I think about that constantly."

Harlin put down his drink and leaned in
close. "You realize that if the girl doesn't turn up,
some will think you had something to do with her
disappearance?"

"I know it."

They chewed on that a while and sipped
their drinks. "Miners weren't all that disturbed when
the first body showed up," Harlin finally said. "One
dead miner isn't news. Miners are too busy digging
for the next big vein to be worried about one cold
miner—if it is a miner. But it's different in the
camps now. I got a lot more cooperation this
morning than with the first body. Miners are jittery.
I had no trouble getting dozens of volunteers to ride
out to all the camps within a few miles of town. A
second stiff and a missing young woman make this
a different story indeed."

Jesse nodded.

"The good news is that the miners 'readiness
to volunteer can help. We'll find her quicker. And
we will find her. People don't disappear into thin
air. She's somewhere, probably not far from here.
We'll find out who killed those two fellows along
the creek bank too. Meanwhile, keep your eyes
open and your sidearm with you. At times I may
need you to take over my duties for me. I'll let the
miners know. Hopefully they'll cooperate with you
despite the note you wrote."

Harlin's last comment made Jesse's chest
feel heavy.

"Jesse, if Caroline never showed up at the Garry, is there any evidence proving she ever left the Casbah? Maybe something happened to her there."

"I've thought of that, and the thought makes me sick. And if anything *did* happen to her, you can be sure Gull Dupont is involved." Jesse's voice rose a bit. "It's that bastard Gull who's been blasting the news all over town that Caroline Whittaker disappeared from the Garry."

"Take it easy. We have nothing to go on," said Harlin.

"You're right. We've got nothing. Not yet. But if I find out Dupont is involved, I will kill him," he said. Then he remembered something. "Madeline believes Caroline did leave the hotel the morning of the day she went missing. She told me Caroline has a favorite white dress she likes to wear for special occasions. She noted the dress was not in their hotel room, so she believes Caroline wore it for the interview for the position with the Garry, to make a good impression."

Harlin's eyes grew wide at the mention of the dress. "That brings me to this," he said. He put down his drink and wordlessly reached for his saddle bag. He untied the leather straps, reached into the bag, and pulled out a muddy, damp, torn piece of fabric about the size of a man's hand. Underneath all the filth, it had once been white. "Did it look like this?"

"Where'd you get that?"

"Along the creek bed about a half a mile from the body we found this morning."

CHAPTER THIRTEEN

The bell over the door at Moore's Mercantile tinkled as Madeline entered the store. Alonzo Moore flashed a too-big smile when he saw her.

Madeline's hair stood up on the back of her neck.

"Miss Whittaker, how nice, how nice to see you this morning. We weren't expecting you for a few days. Perhaps you are here this morning to peruse my fine goods for ladies?"

"Good morning. I've come to talk to you about that."

"You need more time?" asked Alonzo.

"No, quite the opposite."

"It's about your sister, isn't it?" asked Alonzo. "I heard the news. I'd be out searching for her with the others, but the shop," he said while making an arc with his hand toward the inventory.

94

"I wouldn't expect you to abandon your responsibilities."

"Harlan and the other men will find her," said Alonzo, "like he brought in William Brown."

"I'm sure he will," she said, though she was sure of nothing except she needed to get far away from the malignant Gull Dupont as soon as possible. "Mr. Moore, would it be acceptable for me to move into your spare room within the next few days and start working for the Mercantile immediately?"

"So soon? '

"Yes."

"I can arrange for your things to be removed from the Casbah the day after tomorrow," he said. "Is there a reason why you feel an urgent need to start right away?"

She felt foolish. She should have anticipated this question. But she was utterly dumbstruck at the next one.

"Is there something or someone making you uncomfortable at the Casbah?"

She madly cast about in her mind for a noncommittal answer. "The Casbah is comfortable," she said. "But I need to be earning, and I think keeping my hands occupied while I wait for Caroline to return would be healthful too."

"Of course. You make eminent sense."

Just then she heard the scuffle of feet above her head. She glanced up. Alonzo didn't seem to hear it.

"Mr. Moore, at our first meeting you mentioned your mother lives with you."

"Yes?" The plastered smile disappeared.

"As part of my position with the Mercantile, do you expect me to care for your mother?"

Alonzo's chin went up. "What makes you ask such a question?"

She spoke slowly. "I came to the shop yesterday morning, but you weren't here. There was an older woman behind the counter. She was dressed in a nightgown and a big plumed hat, like the type women wear in the theater, and she was barefoot. She seemed to believe I had come to audition with her agent."

Alonzo abruptly shut his accounting ledger. "You do realize how ridiculous you sound?"

Madeline opened her mouth and shut it again.

"Do you mean to say this phantasm you think you have encountered could possibly be my mother?"

Madeline was so shocked she could not speak.

"Any young lady I take into my employ must be committed to speaking the truth. Tall tales will not be tolerated. No woman, particularly my mother, would enter this shop garbed as disgracefully as you describe. You have greatly insulted Mrs. Moore."

"I'm sorry, but—"

"Do you even know with certainty this, this poltergeist was my mother?"

"No, I don't, but—"

Madeline was ashamed. She had presumed the bizarre old woman to be Mrs. Moore. She had lost this argument.

"No, you don't. Therefore, as my employee, I forbid you to repeat such slanderous fiction to anyone at any time for any reason. Gossip hurts business. Do you understand?"

"I wouldn't dream of repeating such a report."

"As for caring for my mother, Mrs. Tamsan Moore does not need a nurse. She's of a sound mind and directs an orderly and peaceable home."

"Of course."

"And she is in charge of that home," he added with an air of finality.

Madeline nodded meekly.

"Now," said Alonzo, and the smile was back, "I will have a man come by the Casbah by five o'clock for your things. Is this sufficient time?"

"Yes," said Madeline. "But, sir, we haven't discussed—"

"We will discuss your hours and wages in the morning once you are moved into the shop. Do we have an agreement?"

Deep down, Madeline believed she had nothing to fear from Mr. Moore. Best of all, he would get her away from Mr. Dupont by tomorrow—only one more night at the Casbah. But why was he so touchy—even secretive—about his mother?

"We have an agreement."

***

Madeline approached the front desk at the Casbah. Hank had no news of Caroline. She thanked him and climbed the stairs to the second floor. The door of her room was locked as she had left it, yet her whole being went on alert as she touched the knob. She saw and heard nothing, but she had an inexplicable bad feeling about entering.

Don t be silly. She turned the knob and opened the door slightly, gazing into what little she could see in the dimness. Unsatisfied, she opened the door fully then gasped. Her room was in disarray. Someone—not Caroline—had been here. Clothing, toiletries, and other personal effects were scattered on the floor. Both girls 'trunks were overturned, and the fabric lining had been ripped away. The bedcovers had been pulled from the bed. The feather tick had been yanked from the bed too, though not torn apart. Furniture had been dragged away from the walls.

Surely someone had been searching for something. The room was small. There was nowhere for an intruder to hide, nevertheless, Madeline bent down to make sure no one was concealed under the bed. She was relieved to see darkness.

She ran out of the room and flew down the staircase to the lobby.

"Hank, someone was in my room." Several guests in the lobby stopped what they were doing to listen.

"Miss Caroline?"

"Not my sister. The room is completely torn apart. Someone was clearly searching for something."

"Is anything missing?" said Hank.

"I ... I don't know."

"I'll call Mr. Dupont."

Madeline groaned within. Anyone but that man.

Hank pulled the bell cord and shortly a paunchy, older man walked into the lobby. Hank dispatched him to fetch Mr. Dupont. Madeline waited, twirling her handkerchief into a wrinkled rope. How would she survive another tense conversation with the awful man?

In a few minutes Gull was standing in front of Madeline.

"You look lovely this morning," he said, his eyes traveling down her body.

Why did this man's gaze feel like a disrobing? She could never shake the feeling that Gull Dupont saw her naked underneath her clothes and read her thoughts to boot. Every encounter with him unnerved her. She clutched her bag to her body and glanced at her bosoms, relieved to see nothing carnal peeping through her bodice.

"How can I be of service?" he asked.

"Someone has been in my room this morning and left it in awful disarray."

Gull blanched, then glanced around the lobby. "We will continue this conversation in my office," he said, taking her arm. "Come with me."

He led Madeline to a small room behind the front desk before she could object. He pulled a key from his breast pocket and unlocked the door. "Please have a seat," he said, gesturing to a hard-back chair across from his desk.

A neat but modest oak desk filled most of the windowless room. Madeline noted Gull's agitation as he peppered her with questions.

"Did the perpetrator break in?" he asked.

"No, it appears he had a key. There's no sign of damage to the door. And when I returned to the hotel this morning, the door to my room was locked like I left it."

"Anything missing?"

"I haven't had a chance to determine that," she said. "But then—everything my sister and I owned of any value was sold. We were left with nothing worth stealing."

Gull gave her a cold stare.

"I left the room as soon as I realized an intruder had been there," she added.

"I see," said Gull.

This news seemed to sober him in a way she had not seen before. She sensed genuine distress in those dark eyes.

"Have you given anyone your key?"

"No, of course not. There's one key, and I've always had possession of it."

"May I see it?"

Madeline fished in her bag for the key and handed it to him.

"This is the key issued by the Casbah" said Gull, rubbing his chin and pacing the room. He handed it back to her. "Are you positive the thief used a key to enter your room?"

"Go see for yourself." She held out the key again.

Gull took it from her. "Please wait here."

She nodded. While she waited for him to return, it dawned her that her lace knickers were strewn about the room. She moaned.

Oh well.

She stood and walked around Gull's office. Spartan, neat, functional. An ink pot on the desk at the corner of his blotting pad, an ornate wall clock ticking away, a handsomely carved filing cabinet with many shallow drawers. All the customary accoutrements one would expect to see in an important man's place of business.

"Miss Whittaker." Gull stopped in the doorway.

"Oh," she said, flustered at being caught nosing around, "you have an attractive office, Mr. Dupont."

Gull regarded Madeline with his steely gaze, making her heart pound.

"Did you learn anything?" she said as she reseated herself as calmly as she could muster while scooting around to the public side of his desk. "Did you see any sign of a break-in?"

"No," said Gull. "They used a key." His mouth moved but his eyes didn't. They bored into her.

She was certain he was reading her mind. She shouldn't have been snooping around his office. She squirmed. The room was small and claustrophobic, and he was blocking her exit. "I'd like to gather our personal items now," she said. "Mr. Moore is sending a wagon this afternoon."

"Fine. Be sure to report to me if any of your items are missing. The Casbah will reimburse you."

"I will." The room seemed terribly small, the atmosphere thick with tension, as she stood across from the weasel. She was anxious to end this conversation and distance herself from the dreadful man.

"If I learn anything pertinent, I'll send word to you at Mr. Moore's. But," he said, leaning in closely and lowering his voice, "speak to no one of this matter. I will question my employees myself and see if anyone has seen anything or observed anyone near your room this morning."

"Yes," she said. Oh, how she hated being under the thumb of this nasty man.

"If anyone around town becomes privy to this matter, I'll know who has been discussing it," he added.

Madeline shrunk back. "I understand. But what about Hank?"

"I'll deal with Hank."

CHAPTER FOURTEEN

"Can I see it?" said Jesse as he reached for the piece of fabric.

Harlin handed the muddy thing to Jesse, who examined it, looking for clues while fingering the delicate rows of once-white lace, some of which had been torn from the fabric and hung half on, half off. He turned it over. Immediately he noticed the stains.

Jesse raised his eyes to his friend. "Blood?"

"I think so."

Jesse sucked in a noisy breath. "It looks fairly fresh."

"Probably because of the damp."

Jesse stared at the stains, his mind running wild with every possible mishap, intentional and unintentional, that could befall a young woman in the rugged country surrounding Hangtown. After a few seconds he pushed the piece of fabric aside.

"This looks bad," he said, shaking his head. "Madeline needs to see it."

"If it's her sister's, she'll know."

"If it's Miss Caroline's, we need to know exactly where it was found and search the area as soon as possible."

"They found it a half mile from here. Along the bank of the north fork. As you know, there's a lot more miners working the south fork. Mostly isolated cabins near where they found the dress. I want you to show it to her."

***

Clint was working the desk when Jesse walked in carrying the cloth sack Harlin had given him. "You look like you swallowed a Cane toad," said Clint.

"A poisonous peeper in my gullet seems like a small problem right now."

"What's wrong? You got news about Miss Caroline? Or the dead guy?"

"Maybe."

Despite his proclivity to chase skirts and neglect his hotel duties for more exciting shindigs about town, Jesse had not found his brother to be a man of guile. But the kid couldn't keep a secret, especially one as explosive as a bloody piece of fabric—most likely torn from a woman's dress. And besides, deep down Jesse felt Madeline should be the first person to see the fabric.

"Where's Tien?"

"Around somewhere," said Clint. "What's going on?"

"Get Tien out here."

"What for?"

"Can't you ever take an order without guff?" snapped Jesse.

"Whoa. Something is bothering you for sure," said Clint. "I'll bet it's that missing girl." He threw the day's mail onto the front desk. "You sort it." He grabbed his hat from a hook and stepped out from behind the desk.

"Where you going?" said Jesse.

"Going to join Harlin's men and search for Caroline Whittaker."

"Get back here. You can't abandon your shift."

Clint didn't respond or even look back. He walked out the front door of the Garry.

Jesse yanked angrily on the call bell. While he waited for Tien, he pulled out a sheet of paper and hastily wrote a note to Madeline, asking her to meet him at the Garry. He debated how frank he should be in a note. At last, he decided it was best to say the meeting was about her sister. That would surely bring her across the street.

In a few minutes Tien's drab form stood across the front desk from Jesse. As before, he instructed Tien to deliver the note to the Casbah. Tien nodded. Jesse watched him exit the lobby onto the street. He was filled with dread.

In less than an hour Madeline walked into the lobby. At once Jesse saw the fear and strain on her face. He made a conscious effort to look calm, knowing the effect his news would have on her.

"Can we speak in my office? It's private," he said, pointing to the door.

Madeline followed him into the cramped office. He motioned for her to sit down then pulled the muddied, torn fabric out of the cloth sack and laid it on the desk. He stood next to her, watching for her response.

"Do you recognize this fabric?"

Madeline turned it over, examining it in silence. Her eyes fell on the red stains, and as if to confirm what she was seeing to be real, she gingerly stroked the spots with a finger. Then she turned and lifted her eyes to Jesse and began to breathe noisily, as if she was struggling for air. Wordlessly she slumped over the side of the chair in a dead faint.

Jesse sprang into action. In a few seconds he had laid her across his desk. He yelled for Tien to bring water. After what seemed like minutes he arrived with a bucket. Jesse used his handkerchief to sponge Madeline's face. Slowly she began to gain consciousness.

"You fainted."

Madeline looked confused. After several minutes, Jesse helped her from the desk and guided her back to the chair.

"You recognize the fabric?"

"I helped Caroline make the dress it came from. And the lace was made by our grandmother."

"You're certain she was wearing this dress when she left the hotel?"

"I didn't see her leave the hotel. But this is from her dress. I know that lace."

"Of course," said Jesse. "I know these stains look like blood. But look here," he pointed, "the stain isn't heavy like blood pooling from a serious wound. The blood spots are scattered, like someone got scratched. The rips look like that too. See? If Caroline was wearing this dress, the evidence doesn't point to a fatal injury. It's more like a lot of scratches caused by walking through brambles."

"Everything she owns except this dress is in our room at the Casbah," she said.

Then she did not elope. Jesse kept this disturbing thought to himself. Madeline was traumatized enough for one day.

"Mr. Garry," said Madeline, "where did you find this?"

"I didn't. A couple of fellows searching with Harlin Turpin found it along the north fork about half a mile from town. Harlin brought it to me."

"Only half a mile. I see."

"Also, Mr. Turpin asked me to tell you he will be coming by the Casbah after nine tomorrow morning to talk to you about the search. Is this acceptable to you?"

"Please tell him I'll be waiting. And," she paused and looked down at her hands, "I apologize for causing a disturbance in your office."

Disturbance? Holding her seductive femininity against his own hot body was a first for Jesse—the best thing that had ever happened to him. With effort he hid his thrill.

"You are no disturbance, Miss Whittaker. Rest up now. I promise you, we will find your sister."

Jesse watched Madeline exit the Garry, her wide skirts swishing through the door. *Are you crazy? Making promises you might break?* He didn't care. If promises kept him connected to the alluring Miss Whittaker, he would keep making them.

CHAPTER FIFTEEN

Madeline smoothed the skirt of her brown poplin as she sat in the Casbah dining room waiting for her appointment with Mr. Turpin. The dress was old and worn, discreetly patched in places, but serviceable. However, in light of Caroline's disappearance, the state of her clothes seemed trivial now. Besides—she had noted after a few days in this woman-hungry town—men didn't notice what a woman wore. They were far more interested in the female items under the garment.

How inappropriate to be thinking about something as silly as my attire considering the seriousness of the conversation I am about to have with Mr. Turpin. She was ashamed. She pulled her shawl around her shoulders a little tighter. It was unusually cold for early fall, and she was seated far from the dining room fireplace.

"Ms. Whittaker," said Harlin. "I'm Harlin Turpin."

Madeline looked up to see a middle-age gentleman standing across the table. He was dressed in drab attire, held a worn hat at his side, and had thinning white hair. He was forgettable in his appearance, except he seemed calm, not desperate like all the panting miners in town, and he had kind eyes. She invited him to sit with her. A waiter approached and Harlin ordered coffee.

"I suppose Jesse told you why I wanted to speak with you," said Harlin.

"He said it was part of the investigation."

"True. But before we start, I want you to know how grieved I am about the situation with your sister. All the men in town feel the same. We are doing everything we can to find her."

"I am grateful."

"Likely you know by now that Hangtown has no sheriff, and the marshal service hasn't arrived here yet, so I serve as a volunteer de facto sheriff when I'm not trapping. The men cooperate with my orders. Dozens of them have been working with me to search for your sister. We will find her."

This man seems so sincere, so kind. Like Pa. Someone in this town truly cares. Madeline was relieved. She unwittingly slumped in her chair, her muscles releasing days of tension.

"I'm sorry. My questions will upset you," said Harlin.

"It's alright. I was upset before you arrived."

"I'm sure."

His coffee was delivered to the table. He poured some cream into his cup and sat quietly, sipping it. After a space, he said, "Do you think you're able to answer some questions for me? The more I know about your sister and her habits, the better able I'll be to determine what happened to her."

"Yes, of course." She braced herself and sat upright.

"Tell me about the people you and your sister have met since you arrived in town. Is there anyone you've had dealings with who made you uncomfortable? Did your sister meet anyone who was overly friendly or took interest in her? Did she have feelings for any man?"

"We've met a handful of men." She drew in a deep breath. "I don't believe she was fond of any of them. She never mentioned anyone by name. We met the mercantile owner, Mr. Moore. He offered me a job in his store, which I accepted. And Jesse Garry, of course. He also offered me a position, but I declined. However, several men made proposals to Caroline the day we arrived, but of course I put a stop to that immediately."

"Who were these men?"

"I don't know. It was while she was watching over our wagon as I tried to find us a room."

"And the wagon? Where is it now?"

Madeline paused. Should she tell this man about the involuntary sale of her oxen and wagon and its contents? If she did, it would inevitably lead to talk of Mr. Dupont, and she didn't want that awful man to make good on his threats. The thought sent a chill into her soul. He had forced her to promise to keep quiet about their transaction. How risky would it be to divulge the details to this caring older gentleman who wanted to help her find her sister?

"Miss Whittaker?"

"Yes, well …" she bit her lip, debating.

"Where are your wagon and oxen?"

"Mr. Moore has them."

"You sold them to Mr. Moore?"

"Not exactly."

"I don't understand," said Harlin.

Madeline gulped then plunged ahead. "Mr. Dupont sold them to Mr. Moore."

Harlin set down his coffee cup. "And what is Mr. Dupont's involvement in all this?"

Madeline felt lightheaded. She took a sip of coffee. Then it all tumbled out. She told Harlin about Mr. Dupont coming upon herself and Caroline their first night in Hangtown as they tried to bury Pa's remains in the woods. She explained she understood about the first body found charred and covered with rocks near Diamond Spring and how a second body had been found under similar circumstances—the news was all about town—and how someone might reasonably link herself and her sister to both crimes based on the way they tried to bury their father under rocks and because they were newcomers to the area.

"I see." Harlin pushed aside his nearly full cup. "And your money? You have it now?"

"No. Mr. Dupont told me he would hold it as bail."

"Bail?" Harlin's eyebrows shot up to the sky.

"Yes. He was waiting for you to return to town to discuss our situation. He said since my sister and I were under suspicion for murder, he would hold our money as bail to make sure we didn't flee."

Harlin looked somberly at Madeline. She began to squirm. Had she said too much? Mr. Dupont's threat loomed large in her mind.

"Can you show me where your father's body is buried?"

"I think so. But Mr. Dupont told me he'd arrange to have the body moved to town. He has been most kind. He didn't want us to be seen as murderers, so he told me to keep quiet about Pa's burial in the woods, so there wouldn't be an uproar in town. And he gave us a room here in the Casbah without charge until we could find positions. The night after tomorrow will be my last night in the hotel. I plan to move in with Mr. Moore and his mother."

Harlin nodded and began stroking his chin, thinking.

"And Jesse," said Harlin, "tell me about your conversations with him."

Madeline clammed up at the name of the man who tried to lure her sister to his establishment. She was loath to accuse a man without evidence, but other than the fatherly figure across the table, she trusted no one in this wicked town.

"I heard he had an appointment to interview your sister on the day she went missing. Is this true?" said Harlin.

Madeline stared into her cup. "It's true she was invited to meet with him. Whether or not she decided to accept is uncertain. No one claims to have seen her leave the Casbah or enter the Garry."

"Jesse sent a note. Did you see it?"

"Yes. He sent a note to Caroline asking her to meet him at his hotel. He was prepared to offer her double what Mr. Dupont was paying her to do similar work."

Harlin nodded. "So, what happened that morning?"

"I had left the hotel earlier to speak with Mr. Moore. When I left the room Caroline was still there. When I returned, she was gone. I found the note in the room. I haven't seen her since. I assumed when I saw the note she had gone to meet Mr. Garry."

"Do you still believe that?"

She took a deep breath. "I don't know what to believe. I don't know Mr. Garry, but I know my sister. She's sixteen. Why wouldn't she keep the appointment? He offered her *double* wages for the same work."

"Of course. And I hear there was another note, this one from Caroline," he said.

She struggled to keep back tears. "Yes, I received a note supposedly from Caroline saying she had eloped."

"*Supposedly* from Caroline? You don't believe your sister wrote the note?"

Madeline bit her lip, aware of all the big ears in the dining room. It seemed everyone was listening. "I'm confused. The note with Caroline's name on it was surely written by her hand. But she wouldn't run off without saying goodbye to me, and she surely wouldn't run off without her clothing." Madeline gulped in some air to keep from crying. "I want my sister back and I want to go home to Independence. If you can help me, I'd be so grateful."

Harlin waited patiently while Madeline calmed herself. "Jesse showed you the piece of fabric we found?"

Madeline sniffed. "Yes."

"And it's from your sister's dress?"

"Definitely."

"I know this doesn't look good, but the material evidence doesn't prove Caroline is dead. It suggests she left town."

"Mr. Garry explained the blood stains were superficial. He said they would have been larger if she had suffered a fatal wound."

"Jesse is correct. Concentrate on thinking hopeful thoughts about your sister. Caroline may have merely gone for a walk and lost her way in the woods. It happens even to miners sometimes."

"But they don't leave notes behind saying they're running away."

"You are very astute, young lady. Miners don't do that."

She gave him a weak smile.

"Now, as for Jesse, he's my partner—also a volunteer in keeping the peace. I trust him without reservation. If he says he didn't see your sister on the morning she went missing, you can rest assured he did not see her. I hope you'll continue to cooperate with him in the investigation."

"I will," said Madeline, softly.

"Is there anything else you think I should know?" asked Harlin.

The hotel room break-in popped into her mind. But Mr. Dupont had made her promise to share the news with no one. Suddenly Madeline felt very tired of all the secrecy. The weight of it crushed her spirit. She'd do anything, divulge anything, if it helped this man find Caroline. She leaned across the table.

"Someone broke into our room here in the Casbah," she whispered. "They were searching for something. They tore apart all our things, even pulled furniture from the walls. I don't think they found what they were looking for though. Nothing is missing."

"When did this happen?"

"After my sister went missing. About two days ago."

"Any idea who did this?" asked Harlin.

"No idea at all."

Harlin ruminated on this bit of information. "Who knows about this?"

"Just you … and Mr. Dupont. But he told me not to tell anyone."

Harlin barely hid a grimace. "Anything else to share?"

She thought a minute. "That's all."

"You and your sister will get your money back," said Harlin. "I'll speak to Mr. Dupont about it, and about moving your father's body to town. Don't worry." He stood up, thanked her for her time, and left. She watched as he walked out of the dining room toward the lobby.

For the first time since Caroline disappeared, she had hope.

***

"All the evidence leads to Gull," Harlin said into the darkness from the crude wood platform that served as his bed. Sleep eluded him.

Those poor girls, stranded and alone. They were guilty of nothing, that was a fact. They were too innocent for a place like Hangtown—they'd actually trusted a lowlife like Gull. When it came to their wagon and team, he'd surely swindled them. Alonzo Moore may have been in on it too. Bail? *Bail?* Hangtown had no sheriff, judge, or jail. Of course it had no bail. But the girls didn't know any better. They had believed Gull's story and lost everything they had.

Where was their money? Who broke into their hotel room? What was the intruder looking for? If Gull had taken their oxen, wagon, and its contents, what valuables could possibly be left behind to tempt a thief? The Whittaker sisters did not strike him as young ladies of means.

He would talk to Gull as soon as he could find him. He wasn't at the Casbah earlier when Harlin stopped in. He would seek him out first thing in the morning.

Harlin was finally getting drowsy when there was a knock at the door.

"Who's there?"

CHAPTER SIXTEEN

Madeline awoke to her last full day at the Casbah
with many empty hours to fill. Her things and
Caroline's were packed. Mr. Moore's men would
arrive in the afternoon to load their few possessions
onto a wagon. Reading was out of the question—
she couldn't concentrate, and currently she didn't
have a needlework project to occupy her. She had to
keep busy or thoughts of Caroline would make her
insane.

A peek out the hotel room window revealed
gray, lowering skies. When she touched the glass, it
was very cold. But lounging in the room all day
with thoughts of Caroline her only companions was
intolerable. She bundled up well in wrap, bonnet,
and muff, and headed downstairs to the lobby. She

figured walking briskly would keep her warm and clear her head of so many frightening thoughts.

"Excuse me, Miss Whittaker, this came for you," said Hank as she neared the door. He slid a small white envelope across the counter. Her name was written in neat cursive on the front. The handwriting looked familiar.

Madeline took the envelope and thanked him, then made herself comfortable on a nearby settee to open it. Inside was a note from Jesse Garry asking her to come to the hotel to speak with him. Her heart did a little flip. Surely he had news of Caroline. Anxious for any snippet, she hurriedly returned the note to its envelope, tucked it into her muff, and exited the Casbah.

She shivered, walking quickly to get inside the lobby of the Garry Hotel where she knew there would be a toasty fire in the wood stove. A portly older gentleman she did not recognize was working the desk. He glanced up and smiled. More than half his teeth were missing and nearly all of his hair had jumped ship long ago.

"Miss Whittaker," he said before she'd reached the desk, "welcome. I'm Bartholomew Pyle."

"Pleasure to meet you, Mr. Pyle."

"Around here they call me Biscuit," he added.

"Biscuit?"

He patted his substantial belly with both hands.

"I see," she said, smiling demurely. "I've not seen you before at the hotel, sir."

"I work the kitchen most of the time. I get drafted for lobby work when there's no one else

available," he said. "I'm sorry about your sister.
Have you heard anything? Has she contacted you?"

"We've heard nothing."

"Not even a good-bye note?"

She blinked.

"Your sister is a pretty little thing. Probably
had a dozen suitors from the day she arrived."

"There's some truth to that."

"She probably took a liking to one of them
and ran off."

She stared, baffled by how dense men could
be, not to mention the boldness of this oaf.

"I wouldn't worry too much. I'm sure your
sister is doing fine, setting up a home somewhere,
probably not too far away too. The boys will find
her."

"Thank you for the encouragement, Mr.
Pyle," she said, the smile all but drained from her
face. "Is Mr. Jesse Garry in? We have an
appointment."

Biscuit gestured toward Jesse's office. "He's
in. Knock."

***

Jesse stood when Madeline entered his office. At
once she noted the grim look on his face. Her
stomach fell and her knees locked.

"Please have a seat," he said, gesturing to the
chair opposite the desk.

She shook herself and sat down. Her heart
was beating so hard she could hear the blood rush
past her ears. Why his grim look? There could be
only one reason.

Jesse seated himself. "I have bad news.
Harlin Turpin was murdered in the night."

Madeline's hand flew to her mouth. "No."

"I just got back from his cabin. It appears he was attacked in his sleep. Someone slit his throat."

"But why? He was such a dear man."

"Harlin was investigating two murders and the disappearance of your sister. That makes him someone's enemy, and perhaps more than one."

"You must be mourning your friend greatly. I am very sorry, Mr. Garry."

Jesse nodded.

"Do you have any idea who did this?"

"I have a few clues to pursue."

They sat in silence a few seconds, contemplating their mutual loss. Then Madeline, now composed, said, "Will the search for Caroline continue?"

"Yes. I was his partner. His responsibilities fall to me."

"I see."

"Losing Harlin doesn't change anything. My brother Clint is out with others right now scouring the area where we found the bit of her dress. I am distraught over the loss of Harlin, but the search will go on."

Madeline nodded.

Jesse leaned forward and clasped his hands together, resting them on his desk. "I need to talk to you about something. It won't be easy to hear."

"Yes?"

"Unless Caroline is found soon, at some point it will not make sense to continue the search. It's been five days. The men have left their places and businesses to search. But—"

"Thank you, Mr. Garry," said Madeline. Abruptly she stood to leave. "If you need to get word to me, starting tomorrow I'll be boarding at Mr. Moore's Mercantile."

"Miss Whittaker, I—"

But she was already out the door.

***

Two hours later, close to five o'clock, Jesse was working the front desk when Clint breezed through the hotel door bundled in furs against the dropping temperatures.

"Brr. Cold out there for September." Clint shook himself. "Cold enough to snow."

"Find anything?"

"Not since the torn piece of dress. Went all over the area, me and a couple fellas from Rich Bar. It's like she disappeared into thin air."

"I know."

"I don't think the miners are going to keep this up much longer," said Clint, "especially south of here. After we told the search parties about the dress, there's no interest in searching anywhere except along the north fork. And every day fewer men show up. The cold doesn't help. The three of us didn't see anyone else out there looking today."

"I tried to explain this to Miss Madeline this afternoon."

"How'd she take it?

"Not well," said Jesse.

"Were you surprised?"

"No. She got upset and bolted out of my office."

"Speaking of Miss Madeline," said Clint as he began pulling off his buffalo coat and hat, "when I was over at the Malachi's stable, he told me she had come in today wanting to borrow a horse.

121

Malachi gave her one, but she was supposed to return it an hour ago and hasn't showed up. What would she want a horse for? It's damn cold for pleasure riding."

"She's not riding for pleasure." Jesse was on the other side of the front desk before the words were out of his mouth. "Take over here. I gotta go. And watch your mouth."

"Where you going?"

"To find Miss Madeline before she freezes to death."

CHAPTER SEVENTEEN

Malachi's "stable" was a three-sided booth constructed of poles for walls and pine boughs for a roof. It was primitive like most Hangtown structures, but it kept the horses he boarded out of the wind and rain and snow unless they blew sideways. Jesse hurried to it to ready his own horse for a frigid ride. Extra blankets and ammunition, a lantern. Another hour and the sunlight would be gone, making passage impossible. Worse, the sky had been dark and heavy all day, threatening snow. Only a desperate person would ride in such conditions.

He didn't even have to think about which direction Madeline had taken this afternoon. There was no question she had set out for the north fork, following the riverbank to look for Caroline. Except the bank wasn't easy to follow. In places the trees grew right up against the water line, and sometimes there was a steep drop-off into the river. Either scenario would send a rider deep into the woods, where she could get disoriented and lost as she tried to make her way back to the water's edge to follow the river northward.

The light from Jesse's oil lantern was swallowed by the night as the faint sun dropped deeper into the horizon. He could see about twenty feet in any direction. In a little while, even that halo would shrink. Had he been unwise to run into these woods in such perilous conditions? There could be two more Hangtown residents dead by morning.

After a monotonous hour of miserable cold and darkness, he thought he saw the telltale glint of an animal's eye reflecting off the lantern light. He halted his horse to listen and watch. The eyeball watched him too, followed by a noisy neighing. His own ride neighed and sniggered in solidarity. He urged it forward, and when he reached the other horse, he quickly dismounted and tied both steeds to a tree while looking over the stranded animal. He saw nothing amiss. This had to be Madeline's horse.

"Where is she, boy, where is she?" He smoothed the animal's mane to calm it. Then he chuckled to himself, fatigue overtaking him. "I'm interrogating a horse. This cold is making me crazy. I gotta get us all out of here."

He lifted his lantern higher as he searched the shadowy trees, wishing for a break in the clouds to expose even a slice of moonlight, but none came. And then, about ten feet away, he saw a body.

Madeline lay on her back, a pool of blood to one side of her head, another pool of blood by her waist. The blood had started to freeze, but not entirely, so he figured she had lain there less than an hour.

"Miss Whittaker. Miss Whittaker." He shook her shoulder but there was no response. Just then, he saw the first snowflakes fall by the dim light of the lantern. He groaned. Gingerly he turned her over to see the extent of her injuries. She had a bad gash on the back of her head, but it seemed the bleeding had stemmed. Worse was the actively oozing wound around her waist, also at her back.

He had to think fast. "I'm sorry, Miss Whittaker. You're going to hate me for this." He removed her shawls and coat. Then he pulled out his knife and slit the back of her shirtwaist, exposing her corset. Finding it impossible to remove—he knew nothing of ladies ' undergarments—he slit the back of that as well, cutting right through her chemise. By lantern light he examined her bare back. Something had punctured it violently, no doubt when she was thrown from her horse. A ragged gash, roughly four inches long, silently oozed blood.

He took his one clean handkerchief and pressed it into the wound. Then he cut the back of her chemise into strips, knotted them, and used the length like a bandage to firmly hold the handkerchief in place, moving her limp body side to side to apply the bandage. Throughout these invasions to her person, she never moved, not even an eye flutter.

Jesse was so focused on stanching the blood that he worked for several minutes before he noticed the bruise in the center of her back. She had been slammed with a rifle butt. From the yellow and purple hues, he surmised it had happened about a week earlier.

Snow was falling hard now. Visibility, even with the lamp, was nonexistent. There would be no return to Hangtown tonight. Jesse pulled two blankets off his horse, draped them over her, then went about setting a fire.

It snowed harder. His fingers were stiff.

Finally precious yellow flames leapt from the fallen branches he had gathered. He took a moment to thaw his hands, glancing as he did so at Madeline. She was still unconscious. Once his hands had warmed, he lifted the blankets he had laid over her and pressed one hand to her bare back. She was still unnervingly cold. If he could get the horses to lay down, he and Miss Whittaker could sleep between them and derive some warmth. But the horses, for reasons unknown, weren't ready to sleep.

He used his hatchet to set in a night's supply of wood, fed the fire, and extinguished the lantern. There was nothing to do now but turn in for the night. He gazed at the sleeping beauty.

You're going to hate me for this too.

He set his rifle on the ground where he could grab it quickly, then crawled under the blankets with Madeline. She was asleep or still unconscious, clearly oblivious to his presence. He gently put his arms around her, cradling her entire body against his as close as possible to share his heat with her, praying he wouldn't go to Hell for the pleasure the moment gave him.

CHAPTER EIGHTEEN

Madeline's first conscious thought was PAIN. Her head, back, hips—every part was on fire. And darkness. Something was smothering her face. Hard ground was beneath her, yet Caroline's warm back pressed against her. Where was she? She clawed at the blankets to look around and was instantly blasted by frigid air. She saw a silhouette of trees against dusky orange. Dawn. Snow on the ground.

I spent the night in the woods?

Before she could process what it meant, Caroline stirred and turned over. But it wasn't Caroline sharing the blanket with her. Madeline was face to face with Jesse Garry. Her mouth fell open as their eyes met, but before either could say a word, they heard the sound of a horse's hooves on fallen twigs and the metallic clink of a bridle.

"No room at the inn?" said Clint, halting his horse.

Jesse gave his brother the Glare of Death.

Madeline pulled the blankets over her head. *I must be dreaming.* But the pain in her body assured her she was very much awake.

And in Hell.

"What happened here?" asked Clint.

"I found Mad … Miss Whittaker unconscious and nearly frozen last night," said Jesse, madly shoving blankets off him and jumping to his feet. "She took a tumble from her horse. She's injured too. It was snowing and too dark to ride back to town."

"I see."

"I'm going to build this fire up. You water the horses," said Jesse. "And bring a flask of water for Miss Whittaker. She's probably thirsty."

Clint didn't move. Jesse looked up from his work. "Go. She needs privacy."

Clint nodded toward the blankets. "Privacy?"

"I got under the blankets with her because she was near death with cold."

Clint nodded. The smirk was still there.

"Go." said Jesse.

"You're not going to thank me for rescuing you?"

"Rescuing me?"

Brothers are the same everywhere, Madeline mused under the blankets. So Jesse Garry had found her unconscious, and Clint Garry had found her in bed with his brother, and all before breakfast. If she could, she'd have hidden under those blankets for the rest of her miserable life. But nature was calling. She pulled the blankets down to expose her head.

"Gentlemen, when you are done arguing, I'd like some help getting up, please. The pain is awful."

Jesse waved Clint away, then gingerly helped Madeline onto her feet. She groaned with each move. Then he helped her with her coat and wraps, which Jesse had laid under her like a mattress. Afterward she did what she had to do and returned to the campsite. Clint built up the fire and pulled some cold, hard biscuits from a satchel. Jesse and Madeline gratefully washed them down with water. They all moved quickly because of the cold.

"Clint, you take Miss Whittaker's horse. She'll ride with me."

"It would be easier on the horse if she rode with me. I'm lighter than you."

"I don't have time for games," said Jesse as he tightened the girth. "Now help me with Miss Whittaker."

Working together the brothers hoisted Madeline into the saddle. Mounting was awkward because of her wounds and bulky clothing. She yelped in pain when Jesse mounted up behind her and grabbed the reins.

"I'm sorry. We will get you back to the hotel as soon as we can."

"You mean Mr. Moore's Mercantile," she said.

Jesse did not respond as he guided his horse to the clearest path. Even with multiple layers of clothing between them, her warmth and nearness excited him. The snow had stopped but the cold would not let up. The morning was crisp, the sun brilliant, but the snow wasn't melting. They proceeded slowly because of Madeline's injuries.

"Considering I'm a part of your story now, I deserve to know what happened. You went looking for your sister, didn't you?" said Jesse.

Silence.

"It was foolish to search in such dangerous conditions. If I hadn't found you, you'd be dead right now."

Silence.

"You don't trust me, do you?"

Long pause. "I put a lot of faith in Mr. Turpin."

Jesse let out a breathy sigh. "Your faith was well situated. Harlin was a good man and the best friend I ever had. Trustworthy to the end."

"Yes."

"I take it you don't feel the same way about me."

Madeline squirmed. She found it difficult to articulate how she felt because she wasn't sure herself. Right now his body was, once again, pressed up against her, warming her back. He was tall, pleasant looking, and it certainly was brave of him to search for her in this deadly weather. And Mr. Turpin had vouched for his integrity. But the man had enticed Caroline to his hotel and she had not returned. And now this: Madeline had awakened under the blankets with him. He had touched her while she was helpless. Aside from the pain, were her injuries serious enough to require immediate attention? He had done all these things. *Had he done anything else?*

"I can't thank you enough for searching for me. I planned to ride until sunset. I never thought I'd spend a night in the wilds."

"How did you fall from your horse?"

"I was walking him. But suddenly there was a loud crack nearby. Not like a gunshot. More like a tree splitting and crashing to the forest floor. I couldn't get control of him. I remember flying off. I don't remember anything after that. Then I woke up and you were ... next to me."

"I'm sure you were shocked."

She shouldn't care what he saw when he removed her clothes. She was alive, and that was enough. But still. She burned with embarrassment.

"That's an understatement."

"I won't be telling anyone. You can count on that. And if Clint opens his mouth, I'll kill him."

"You needn't go to such extreme. But thank you."

"Who slammed the rifle butt into your back?"

Madeline's heart started to pound. "What do you mean?"

"I saw the outline and the bruising. I've seen rifle butt injuries before."

She took a deep breath. "It was a misunderstanding."

"Doesn't look like a misunderstanding to me. Looks like a rifle butt."

"You needn't concern yourself with it. I'm fine."

***

The three frozen riders garnered attention as they entered Hangtown, though foot traffic on Main Street was predictably lighter than usual because of the cold and snow. Jesse paused the trio in front of the Garry Hotel.

"I'm taking Miss Whittaker straight to her room," said Jesse to Clint as he dismounted.

"I'm supposed to begin service today at Moore's Mercantile," said Madeline.

"Not today," said Jesse.

"But—"

"You're in no condition to be waiting on anyone. Were you thinking of having Mr. Moore's mother tend to your injuries? Except for the harlots and you and your sister, she's the only other woman in town."

The image of Mr. Moore's crazy mother in her tattered nightgown and purple ostrich feathers rose in Madeline's mind. "You have a point. Then please help me over to the Casbah. My room might still be vacant."

"You're staying at the Garry." Jesses extended his hand to help her dismount.

"What?"

"I will explain your circumstances to Mr. Moore. Right now you need to rest. I think I have someone who can stitch up your back too. Your head will heal on its own. Now give me your hand."

"But—"

"It's alright, Miss Whittaker," said Clint as he dismounted his horse. "We'll make you comfortable at the Garry."

"I don't think this is a good idea," she said. "I need to get back to the Casbah." Residing at the Casbah meant frequently running into the wily Gull Dupont, which made her wince, but her old room was familiar, and sleeping in it made her feel closer to Caroline. It was the last place Madeline saw her sister's face or heard her voice.

"You can cooperate with me and my brother and let us help you off this horse," said Jesse, his hand still extended, "or I can pull you off right now and carry you upstairs to your room. You choose."

Clint's eyes got wide.

Madeline shuddered. She had drawn enough attention from Hangtown men to last a lifetime. She wanted off this horse and to hide away in her bedroom with some laudanum. Defeated, she extended her hand to Jesse while Clint stepped closer to assist. Once her feet were on the ground, Jesse began barking orders at Clint.

"Go to Moore's," said Jesse. "Tell him you need supplies to stitch up a wound. He'll know what you need. Put it on the hotel's account."

After Clint took off, Jesse helped Madeline into the lobby. Tien was behind the front desk. Half a dozen men at the bar stopped their conversations to stare. Jesse obtained a key from Tien then assisted Madeline up the staircase. She groaned with every step. Once they had reached the door to her room, Jesse departed to leave her some privacy. He returned to the lobby.

"Tien, I'm taking over here," said Jesse as he stepped behind the desk. "I'm putting you in charge of guarding Miss Whittaker. Don't let anyone into her room, and don't let her leave it. Do you understand?"

The old man nodded, his expression impassive.

"And Tien, I'll need your help later today."

Tien climbed the stairs and Jesse turned to his chores at the desk. Every few minutes he looked out the lobby window, searching for Clint. After about a half hour he saw Alonzo Moore walk through the door of the Garry. Jesse went on alert.

"Good morning, Alonzo. What can I do for you?"

The scent of Rowland's Kalydor lotion filled Jesse's nose as Alonzo approached the front desk. Wherever this fop went the fragrance enveloped him like the cloud following the Israelites. Jesse couldn't understand why a man wanted to smell sweeter than a woman.

"'Morning. I'm here to see Miss Whittaker."

"She's laid up right now, not accepting visitors," said Jesse.

"She'll see me. We have an agreement."

"The young lady is too badly injured to meet with you, but I'll tell her you came by."

"Injured? Is she alright? What happened?"

"That's her story to tell. When she's up and around."

"She is supposed to be boarding at the mercantile," said Alonzo. "I'm taking her back with me right now. She can rest up there. Call her. She will speak with me."

A vein began to throb in Jesse's jaw. "She's boarding here until I'm convinced she's well enough to leave."

Alonzo scoffed and looked down at his emerald cufflinks, mindlessly turning them around and around. "I hear you spent the night with Miss Whitaker out in the woods."

Jesse's heart skipped a beat. *Clint.* He forced his face to hide his shock and consternation. "Where'd you hear that nonsense?"

"Malachi."

Now it s all over town. "Malachi is a foozler and a windbag. You know better than to believe his gossip."

"Make sure she knows I stopped by to speak with her," said Alonzo, leaning into Jesse for emphasis.

Jesse set his face like a sphinx. He didn't even blink.

He watched Alonzo exit the Garry. Gull and Alonzo. Alonzo and Gull. Both showed inordinate interest in Madeline Whittaker. Why? He was still pondering the mystery an hour later when Clint returned with a parcel.

"What took so long?" said Jesse, unwrapping the brown paper.

"I had to go to the apothecary. Alonzo didn't have laudanum."

"Alonzo came by. He's unusually miffed that his employee is put up here instead of at his store. You told him, didn't you?"

"He already knew," said Clint.

Jesse grimaced. "News travels around this town faster than the devil can fly. Look, I told Tien and now I'm telling you. No one visits Miss Whittaker, and she doesn't leave the room."

"Why?"

"Someone smacked her in the back with a rifle butt. I saw the outline and the bruises when I was bandaging her up."

Clint slapped the desk. "Who did such a thing?"

"I don't know." Jesse started refolding the parcel paper to secure the bandages. "She won't say. But based on the color, it was recent, maybe a week old. Sometime around when she arrived in town. I have my ideas as to who did it."

"Who?"

"I can't say right now."

"Why?

"Because the whole town would know my suspicion as soon as you left the hotel."

"You have a bigger problem anyway," said Clint. He leaned over the front desk and lowered his voice. "Uncle's in town. I ran into him after I left Moore's. Someone's filled his head with wild stories of you and Miss Madeline. He told me he's coming over here to talk to you about holding her against her will."

CHAPTER NINETEEN

Gull leaned back in his oversize wooden chair and pulled slowly on a cigar. Its pungent blue smoke curled upward, filling his narrow office but doing nothing to help him unravel the mystery of the burglary of the Whittaker sisters' room.

It had to be a Casbah employee. He contemplated the various faces he saw every day in his hotel. None were bright or sinister. Every man in town with muscle and health was panning for gold, and, as for capable women, they were selling their bodies in saloons or doing high kicks in Hangtown's many fandango halls. The Casbah, like the Garry across the street, was staffed with the elderly, the misfits, the slow. Gull had heard from guests that it was as bad in the big city of San Francisco, where entire able-bodied crews had abandoned ship and headed for the gold fields as soon as anchor struck water. Sailors didn't even stick around long enough to unload cargo. Heck, even the Garry had a snaggle tooth coolie cleaning rooms and tossing slops. Only the desperate would employ a Chinaman for inside work, and a feeble one at that. Gull was smarter than his staff. He would figure this out.

He heard a knock at the door. "Come in."

Alonzo stepped into Gull's office and shut the door behind him.

"Have a seat," said Gull.

Alonzo sat down but did not make himself comfortable. He sat rigid in his chair, his mouth drawn tight.

"What's bothering you?" said Gull, tapping his cigar onto an engraved silver ashtray. "You don't make it a habit of visiting the Casbah."

"Have you heard the news?"

"About Madeline Whittaker?" said Gull.

"Yes," said Alonzo. "She spent the night with Jesse Garry out in the woods. They came back together this morning. Clint rode out early and found them."

"It's all over town. What's that to me?"

"You said she would start working for me today. But Jesse refuses to let her move into the mercantile. He stashed her in one of the rooms at the Garry."

"What?"

"I just left the Garry. Jesse claims she's injured. Says he'll decide when she's well enough to work for me."

"Well, well," said Gull. "You got yourself some stiff competition. He's going to have Miss Whittaker working behind that lobby counter and smiling at guests as soon as she's on her feet. You wait."

"We have a deal."

Gull sat upright, crushed his cigar into an ash tray, and leaned over the desk. "I've kept my part of the deal. Madeline Whittaker is your problem. If you can't keep track of your one employee, don't expect me to get involved. I have plenty of employee problems here at the Casbah to take up my time."

"You got the younger one like we agreed. I never got Madeline. You were supposed to deliver her safely to my store." Alonzo blew through his nostrils as noisily as a charging bull. "And you let Caroline Whittaker slip away, too."

Gull clenched his fists. "For every hundred bodies in this camp, three are women. That's ninety-seven men for Caroline to run off with. It's not my fault she took a shine to some yokel who hit pay dirt. It was bound to happen eventually. Sadie ran off the same way."

"I've kept quiet up till now about the wagonload you swindled from those girls. I've done my part. I took the goods off your hands and paid you fairly. Now you do what you promised. Get Madeline Whittaker into my store."

Gull stared at Alonzo. "What do you expect me to do? Throw a rope on her and drag her over to the mercantile?"

"Deal with Jesse Garry. He's the problem, not Madeline Whittaker."

Gull scoffed. "She can work wherever she chooses. I already told you, she's your problem, not mine."

Alonzo began to play with his emerald cufflinks, avoiding Gull's eyes. "Why is it pretty young things who work for you go missing? Could it be there's something else going on around here?"

"Shut your trap before I shut it for you."

Alonzo slapped his thigh with his hat. "Hold up your part of the deal like you promised." He stood to leave. "I won't be quiet until Madeline Whittaker is working at the mercantile."

CHAPTER TWENTY

Justus Garry barged into the lobby. Jesse saw the fiery darts in his eyes and knew he was in trouble.

"Uncle," said Jesse, looking up from the front desk at the sound of the hotel door. "We didn't know you were coming." He stopped examining receipts and gave his uncle a guarded smile. The ire he read in Uncle's face made Jesse's whole being go on alert. His smile disappeared in a flash.

He and Clint shared a look. They'd seen Uncle angry before.

"Both of you," said Uncle, jerking his head toward the hotel office, "in the office."

"Let me call someone to watch the desk," said Jesse.

He turned around and yanked the call bell, and in a minute Tien padded into the lobby. Uncle took one look at the man's shabby clothes and the long gray braid down his back and his nostrils flared.

Jesse and Clint had seen that flare before too.

"Who's this?" said Uncle, pointing at Tien, who kept his head down.

"Tien helps us with chores around the hotel," said Clint.

"You can't find anyone better?"

"Let's talk in my office," said Jesse.

"Look at his clothes," barked Uncle. "Like a shroud on a cadaver. And what's this ghastly tumefaction on his face?"

Tien shrunk down, only looking up once or twice at Jesse.

"Please, Uncle. My office."

Uncle huffed a righteous huff but started toward Jesse's office.

Jesse turned to Tien and gave him an apologetic shrug. "Keep an eye on things." Then he grabbed a chair from the lobby and the brothers followed Uncle into Jesse's office.

"Uncle," started Clint, "it's good to see—"

"What in hell is going on around here?" Uncle yanked off his hat and ran a hand through his mostly white hair. Justus Garry was about fifty, tall like his nephews, and quite dashing, with a gleaming pocket watch gracing his stylish wool suit and full, silvery beard.

"What do you mean?" asked Jesse. But he knew.

"I hear you enticed an innocent young woman into a relationship of a carnal nature and are holding her against her will in my hotel." Uncle glared at Jesse. If steam could blow out of angry

142

people's ears, it would be billowing like a geyser right now out of Uncle's.

"Where did you hear this?" said Jesse.

"What does it matter where I heard it? Explain yourself."

"Jesse was forced to sleep with her," said Clint, "to keep her warm."

Jesse covered his face with his hands.

"You hold your mouth," said Uncle.

Clint clammed up at once and studied the floor.

"Whatever gossip you've heard is exaggerated," said Jesse, recovering his composure. "The young woman you speak of is Miss Madeline Whittaker. Her younger sister, Caroline, is missing. Miss Madeline rode into the woods to search for her. I found her unconscious and near death in a blizzard, so I did my best to protect her through the storm. There was nothing carnal about it."

The memory of Miss Whittaker's partially exposed breasts suddenly surfaced in Jesse's mind. What Uncle didn't know wouldn't hurt him.

Uncle stroked his beard, his eyes boring into Jesse. "Hmph," he snorted. "And how did Miss Caroline go missing?"

Jesse squirmed. He was prepared for the first question but not this second one. Clint watched his brother intently. The tension in the room was as thick as apple butter.

"She disappeared after leaving the Casbah one morning," said Jesse. "Though no one is certain if she ever left."

"Where was she headed?" asked Uncle.

So he knew. Uncle already knew about the note Jesse had written to Miss Caroline. Jesse took a deep breath, bracing for what was coming. "She was on her way to the Garry for an interview. I sent her a note and asked her to meet me here."

"And then she up and disappeared," said Uncle, revealing an undertone of sarcasm. "Anyone see her arrive here?"

"No," said Jesse.

"Anyone see her leave the Casbah?"

"No."

"She sent a note to her sister saying she was eloping with a miner," added Clint.

"Then why would her older sister risk her life to go looking for her?"

"She believed her younger sister wrote the note under duress," said Jesse. "And Miss Caroline took none of her possessions with her, not even her clothes."

Uncle's foot tapped madly under the desk. "Two years ago I nearly lost this hotel to fire because of your negligence," he said, bellowing at Jesse. "Now two scandals at once, both involving young women. I should fire you both and put that Chinaman in charge."

"That's not fair," said Clint. "Jesse sent the note because he was trying to get the younger sister to work here at the hotel to draw in more guests. And Madeline would have died if Jesse hadn't gone after her."

Jesse looked at his brother, grateful for once for his ever-running mouth.

Uncle eyed them both. Unspoken words hung in the air. Would this be the last day he would earn a wage? What would he do for a living in this one-industry mining camp if he didn't work in Uncle's hotel? He supposed he could establish another store. Merchants in this mining camp seemed to do well—better than miners.

"Where's the elder Miss Whittaker now?" said Uncle.

"Upstairs," said Jesse. "She was injured when she fell from her horse. I gave her a room and I'm arranging for her to have some stitches put in today."

"How bad is she injured?"

"She has a big gash on her back that needs attention, but her head wound should heal by itself."

"I want to talk to her," said Uncle.

Jesse gasped. "Uncle, she's laid up."

"She will talk to me."

Clint and Jesse exchanged looks of shock.

"What?" said Uncle. "You don't want me to talk to the young lady?"

"It's fine," said Jesse. "If you're done, I'll go upstairs and prepare her for a visitor."

Uncle rose from his chair. "We are done."

***

The elder Mr. Garry wants to talk to me? Jesse Garry had kindly sent up a metal tub and arranged for the Chinaman to fill it with warm water. He had also ordered her clothing and few belongings be brought to her hotel room. But her cuts oozed, and she ached all over.

She moved slowly. With effort she applied fresh bandages then pulled a gray wool dress with handmade lace at the neck and cuffs over her hoops, plaited her long hair and piled it neatly at the back of her head. She splashed some rose water onto her neck. Looking so fresh and smelling nice after lying abed for hours made the pain recede somewhat.

She left the room and walked painstakingly down the stairs, grasping the handrail with each step. As she approached the lobby every set of eyes fastened on her, but her attention was drawn to a finely dressed older gentleman who gazed at her with a broad smile on his face. She surmised it was Justus Garry. He stood as she alighted onto the first floor.

"Miss Madeline Whittaker?" said Uncle, extending his hand.

She took his hand, then he clasped his other hand over hers.

Jesse and Clint watched this introduction intently from their hiding place behind the dining room door.

"Let us move to my nephew's office," said Uncle. "It's private."

***

Jesse looked at Clint then back to Uncle and Madeline. In a moment the office door closed. The brothers abandoned their hiding place and moved to the lobby.

"What do you suppose he'll say to her?" asked Clint.

"Probably trying to confirm my story. After Gull tried to destroy the hotel, Uncle never trusts what I say or do."

"There you go blaming everything on Gull," said Clint.

"Pipe down."

"Did you see how he looked at her?" said Clint. "Practically gobbled her up with his eyes."

"I saw."

"All your chances of winning over Miss Madeline just went down the creek."

"Oh, shut up."

"Uncle's got money, hotels, a fancy new carriage. And for an old guy he's not bad looking. Women like those things."

"Would you stop flapping that noisy clapper of yours?"

Jesse stepped behind the front desk where Tien was sweeping. "Thanks for helping out," he said.

Tien nodded.

"And ignore my uncle. He's … he's … my uncle. You can go now."

Tien nodded again and walked out of the lobby.

Jesse turned to Clint. "Go into the kitchen and make yourself useful. Biscuit needs help. Lunch will be served in an hour."

Clint didn't move.

"What are you waiting for? Go."

"I'm not moving until you promise to tell me what Uncle says to Miss Madeline."

"Alright, alright. I'll tell you what he says to Miss Madeline. Now go."

As he worked Jesse listened intently for any snippet of conversation that might penetrate the thin walls of the hotel, but the lobby was noisy with the comings and goings and chatter of guests. He heard nothing. After about forty-five minutes his office door opened and Uncle and Madeline walked into the lobby, both smiling. Jesse watched as Uncle shook Madeline's hand—again with that intimate hand on top of hers—then she climbed the stairs to her room. Uncle watched her until she was out of sight. He turned to his nephew.

"Miss Whittaker assured me you made no advances on her. I was too harsh on you."

Jesse looked up from the ledger he was writing in. "Thank you."

"I'll need your help, though."

"Anything you need."

"Get someone to nurse Miss Whittaker's injuries immediately," said Uncle. "Then move her things downstairs and into my carriage when I tell you. She is going to accompany me back to San Francisco as soon as she is well enough to travel."

CHAPTER TWENTY-ONE

Jesse was unnerved at this news but had the presence of mind to hide his reaction. "She agreed to this?"

"Yes. She seems excited. I offered her a job."

"But I've been trying to get her to work right here."

"Visitors to this mining camp have only two places of accommodation to choose from," said Uncle. "That should keep you full. You don't have a vacancy problem, do you?"

Jesse shook his head.

"Competition is stiffer in the city. She will be an asset. And besides," said Uncle as he pulled a fresh cigar from his breast pocket, "it appears pretty young women distract you from your work."

"That's not true."

"Don't think I'm looking out for *you*," said Uncle, his tone turning stern. "There is her reputation, which you have unforgivably tarnished. We owe it to her to make things easier. A fresh start in a nice position in San Francisco is exactly what she needs. It's ideal."

Ideal for who? Jesse remembered well the excited look in Uncle's eyes as he watched Miss Whittaker descend the hotel staircase, her skirts swaying ever so feminine like. Was something other than her welfare guiding his generous offer? He hated thinking such thoughts about Uncle Justus. He had set up Jesse and his brother well at the hotel, and though Uncle had a temper and was often hard to please, deep down he had judged him to be a man of integrity.

But that look—Uncle was a man, after all.

Then again, who was Jesse Garry to get in Miss Whittaker's way? It was a fact: She would prosper and be more comfortable in a glittering city like San Francisco than here in this dirty mining town where its two hotels offered accommodations barely resembling civilized living. And what of her future here? If she fell for some smooth-talking miner, she could end up living in a tent and washing clothes in a creek like the Indians. But now she was leaving, and Jesse hadn't had a chance to woo her …

"Why did you ride alone into a blizzard to find her? Taking others with you would be the quickest way to avoid scandal."

My first thought was her safety. "I acted, that's all."

Uncle shook his head. "Foolish."

"Uncle, she's injured."

"She's young. She will heal quickly."

"What about her sister? I would think she'd be hesitant to leave town until her sister is found."

"I took care of that," said Uncle. "Don't worry about it."

***

"You wanted to speak with me?" said Madeline as she slid the note she had received from Jesse minutes ago across his desk. He gestured to her to take a seat and she did so.

"My uncle informs me you'll be leaving us soon to work for him at the Bridlington—his hotel in San Francisco," said Jesse.

"Yes."

"How do you feel about this?" He watched her intently. "I mean, I thought you'd stay in town until your sister is found."

She looked down at her hands. Truth was, she felt guilty about being so happy when she still didn't know Caroline's whereabouts or condition. But she was leaving this awful mining town. She was going to San Francisco. Her heart hadn't been so light in weeks. Yet, how peculiar it felt to rejoice and grieve simultaneously.

"Your uncle assured me he would enlist some miners to continue the search," she said. "I was reluctant to accept his offer. But he wisely pointed out that whether I work in Hangtown or San Francisco doesn't affect the search."

"I suppose that's true."

"And when Caroline is found, he will arrange for her to join me in the city."

She squirmed a little under Jesse's gaze. She could see the wheels turning behind his eyes. *What was he thinking?*

"I see. And Mr. Moore? You're supposed to start working in his store as soon as you mend," said Jesse.

"Your uncle said he'd take care of that too."

He nodded. "It looks like Uncle has thought of everything."

"Your uncle has been ever so solicitous. He's even giving me accommodations in his hotel without charge until I return to Independence."

Jesse sat upright as if ordered to attention. "He did?"

She nodded.

"We must discuss treatment for the gash on your back."

Madeline flushed with embarrassment. That again. She hated being reminded of how this handsome gentleman had seen her at her most vulnerable. Unconscious. Half naked. But the wound oozed continually—she was constantly changing bandages. And it hurt like crazy. She was taking tinctures of bitter laudanum multiple times daily. It suppressed the pain, but the wound would not heal without stitches. Her time assisting Uncle Finney had taught her that.

"Hangtown has no doctor and there are no women in town to assist you," he continued. "A few miners 'wives live up the mountain, but I know little about them or their skills. Only one person I know is skilled at stitching wounds—and is sober. He's available immediately."

"Yes?"

"The hotel employs a Chinaman. His name is Tien. He speaks little English, but he has experience stitching wounds."

Madeline's eyes got wide. "That little old man I've seen working around the hotel with the swelling on his face?"

"It's alright. I've seen Tien's work. His stitches are as good as any doctor's. I'd let him stitch me up if I ever had a need."

A Chinaman? What would Pa say?

"Well," she said, clasping her hands together, "I used to assist my Uncle Finney in Independence with surgeries and lesser procedures. He's a doctor, and I helped him in his clinic for years. I learned a lot from him. I even helped him treat a few Indians who were at death's door. I suppose being stitched up by a Chinaman isn't so outrageous."

"All blood is red," said Jesse. "And I've already purchased everything Tien will need from Moore's."

How thoughtful of him." I've been using the laudanum you sent up. It helps with the pain. But ... how long has Tien had that growth on his face?"

"Hmm," Jesse chewed his lip. "For as long as I've known him. He's been with the Garry a little over a year. It comes and goes. I suspect he drains it then it comes back."

"If he can drain it, then it's not a tumor. It's probably nothing more than an ordinary cyst," she said. "Sometimes they can swell to be quite large. Draining it makes the sufferer feel and look better, but it fills up again if the doctor doesn't remove the sac. Perhaps he'll let me remove it. It's not a procedure he can do himself. Not even a seasoned surgeon would perform such a delicate procedure on himself."

"I see you were an attentive medical student."

"The practice of medicine is a form of service. The more I know, the more I can serve. In fact, I know how to stitch the wound on my back. If I could reach it, I'd do it myself.

"And you are an unusual employer to hire an elderly Chinaman with a swelling on his face," she added. "I don't know of another business in town that would take him in, even without the cyst."

"Tien showed up in the lobby one day asking for work. He came from China with his gold-digging son, but the son died soon after he reached Hangtown. Tien was left alone. As you can see, he's old and frail."

"Is he going back to China?"

"I'm not sure. He saves every penny. Maybe he's saving to return home. Anyway, it seemed a small kindness to let him work for the hotel. It's turned out well for both of us, though he doesn't talk much, and when he does we often don't understand each other. And certain people around here give me grief about it."

"Kindness is also service."

Jesse smiled. "Shall I speak to Tien about tending to you then?"

"Please do."

They sat awkwardly in silence a few seconds. What she had to say was difficult, but it needed to be said. She took a deep breath. "Once I leave for San Francisco I don't expect to return to Hangtown ever again. Likely this is our last meeting. Please accept my apology for raising my rifle at you when I first arrived. I realize now you meant no harm."

Jesse nodded. "And I apologize for the flippant comment about your legs. It was uncalled for."

Madeline looked away, blushing to her ears. "You were understandably angry." She smiled. "And thank you for braving the blizzard to search for me. You saved my life."

"I would do it again without hesitation. If there's anything more I can do for you before you depart, please let me know. If anything changes in regard to your sister, I'll send word to you."

Madeline stood and Jesse did, too. She started for the door but stopped.

"There is some unfinished business I have in Hangtown. Perhaps you can assist."

"In what way?"

"Mr. Dupont is holding our money—funds I need to pay for our journey back to Independence. When we first came to town, he sold our wagon and mining supplies to Mr. Moore—"

"He *what*?"

She nodded slowly. "After Mr. Dupont came upon us burying our pa in the woods."

"You buried your pa?"

"In the woods, yes. He died the morning we approached town. Mr. Dupont told me he was holding our money as bail to keep us from fleeing."

"Wait, *bail*? He was holding your money as bail?"

"Yes. He said he would work with Mr. Turpin to clear us as murder suspects. How were we to know that burying our pa like we did would tie us to the murders? Can you help me get our money back?"

"I'll do what I can. Where's your pa buried?"

She explained as best she could where and how they had left the body. "I asked Mr. Dupont to help us get Pa's remains back to town but he never committed himself."

CHAPTER TWENTY-TWO

Jesse pushed open the rough weathered door of Harlin's humble sleeping quarters. It could scarcely be called a cabin. It was tiny like a shed, windowless with a dirt floor, a stone fireplace its sole source of comfort. The scent of raw tobacco and bear grease clung to the walls.

His eyes went first to the sleeping platform where he had discovered his friend's lifeless body, as if he expected to see Harlin slumbering there. He had trouble grasping the reality of what had happened here—it seemed like a bad dream. Then he saw the stain on the earth where Harlin had bled out, and a cold wave of grief rolled over him. Someone had attacked Harlin a few feet from where Jesse was standing. The evil presence he had sensed weeks ago when he and Harlin had found the torched body on the way to Diamond Spring was still out there.

Except now it was here. But why Harlin? The man hadn't been even close to discovering who had killed the two miners buried under rocks on the creek bank. And like Jesse, Harlin had no idea where Caroline Whittaker was or even if she'd been taken against her will. Jesse could be wasting a lot of time searching for the younger Miss Whittaker. She could be happily starting a family in a cabin in the mountains round about unaware of the mad search her departure had instigated. It was anybody's guess. Their two big investigations had gone cold.

But Harlin knew Gull had the Whittaker sister's money. That made Harlin Gull's target. If Gull found out what Harlin knew ... and most bothersome to Jesse: If Harlin knew about Gull's trade with Alonzo, why hadn't he shared this information with Jesse?

Jesse spent little time in Harlin's cabin. There were few possessions to examine, the room was dark, the atmosphere depressing, and he saw nothing out of place—no clues whatsoever as to who had killed his friend. He didn't have much time to search anyway. As Harlin's partner, he had offered the cabin to the first man who had stepped forward to help bury the body. By tonight another miner would be sleeping here.

***

"They run after the rich ones," said Biscuit, delivering his judgment with characteristic assurance. "First Sadie Shaw. Then Caroline Whittaker. And now her sister. There's no hope for us ordinary wage men." He dropped another peeled potato into the bucket of water at his feet with a careless splash.

"Your bank account has nothing to do with it. There's no hope for you, period." Clint stopped wiping dishes to poke a finger into the old man's belly. "A woman wants a man she can get her arms around."

Biscuit reached into the bucket for a handful of water and threw it at Clint, who jumped backwards and fell onto Jesse, who was washing breakfast dishes. Deep in thought, Jesse pushed aside his brother and kept scrubbing. Tien sorted beans, tossing aside bad ones, as he sat silently in the corner on a stool.

"Who's watching the lobby?" asked Biscuit.

"Uncle," said Clint. "He's out there reminiscing about old times and chatting with guests before he and Miss Whittaker leave for Frisco tomorrow." He stopped working to look through the window. "No snow to stop them, but it's awful cold out there."

"Uncle will keep her warm," said Biscuit without looking up from his work.

Jesse and Clint turned and stared at the outspoken cook. "Why would you say such a thing?" said Jesse.

Biscuit scoffed. "Any man with a working cock is interested in that young woman. Uncle's no different."

"He's more than twice her age," said Jesse.

"So? He's well off and unattached. She's attractive, alone, needs a man, and because she's so young, she can be easily tamed. Marrying your uncle is the smartest thing she will ever do. And marry him she will. And if not him, there'll be dozens of well-dressed suitors in the city with more money than either of you. They'll be standing in line. She's not coming back to this dirty mining camp, missing sister or not."

Clint looked at his brother. "You think he's right?"

Jesse shrugged, turned back to his stack of pots, and grabbed the next on the stack.

"Of course I'm right. I see the way he looks at her," said Biscuit. "You think he's shanghaiing her to Frisco to *work*?"

Clint laughed. "She's going willingly enough. It's not like he's plied her with opium or banged her over the head and stuffed her into a sack."

"What did he offer her?" said Biscuit. "It must have been a real sweet treat. She's leaving town even before her sister has been found."

"A wage and free room and board," said Jesse. His tone was unusually somber even to his own ears. He had offered her the same arrangement but she declined it.

Is she interested in Uncle?

"That's no different than what you and Alonzo offered. So why not stay here?" asked Biscuit.

Good question. In Hangtown Madeline had her pick of two jobs with room and board. Why leave Hangtown for San Francisco—more than one hundred and forty miles away—when her sister was still missing? Jesse had never considered Uncle a man whom women desired. He dressed well but wasn't blessed with a handsome face or striking wit, and he was often crotchety and demanding. Was the pretty Miss Madeline's head turned by an older man's wealth? Was she that trifling? She was way too young for Uncle. The thought of Uncle touching Miss Madeline disturbed him. It wasn't right.

"She's from Independence," said Jesse. "She misses city life. And she's lost her entire family. Probably wants to get away from Hangtown's bad memories and live a normal life. Like she used to."

He hoped.

"That's what you believe?" Biscuit sneered. "You're more naive than she is. I would have thought after your woodland tryst you'd be chasing after her instead of offering her to your uncle."

Jesse threw down the dish rag, his face reddening, poison darts firing from his eyes at Biscuit. "There. Was. No. Tryst. I am not chasing her. And I am not leaving her to Uncle."

"Well, why aren't you chasing her?" said Clint, his eyes gleaming with mirth.

Jesse turned to his brother. "Push the stew off the fire. It's boiling too hard."

Clint grabbed a towel and pulled the enormous pot to a cooler area of the wood stove.

"She's gullible," explained Jesse. "Lived a sheltered life, always under the thumb of her hawkish pa. She even believed a cockamamie story Gull fed her about bail."

Biscuit stopped peeling. "What you mean?"

"The way she tells it, her pa died of fever the morning the sisters arrived in Hangtown. Gull came upon the girls burying the body in the woods that same night. They couldn't dig the grave deep enough, so they planned to get his body underground then pile it with rocks. Gull accused them of murder and took their wagonload and oxen as bail, hauled them back to town, and threatened to have them strung up if they tried to leave. Then Gull sold everything to Alonzo. Miss Madeline believes Gull was working with Harlin to absolve her and her sister."

"That's preposterous," said Clint.

"I know," said Jesse. "But there's more." Clint and Biscuit stopped working entirely. "Someone smacked Miss Whittaker with a rifle butt, hard, square in the center of her back. I saw the bruising when I bandaged her wound."

"You touched her back?" said Clint, practically hyperventilating.

Jesse glared at him.

"Who did it?" asked Biscuit.

"She won't say," said Jesse. "But I put my money on Gull."

CHAPTER TWENTY-THREE

Except for being mistaken for the elder Mr. Garry's daughter at two of the many roadhouses they visited on the journey to San Francisco, the trip had been uneventful and predictably long. Uncle Justus' carriage was modern and comfortable, with thick cushions on the seats, gleaming wood trim, and a stack of blankets to protect against the cold. Uncle was cordial and chatty, if not downright nosy about her life in Independence, but Madeline didn't mind answering his many questions.

Why should she mind? She was being treated like a princess and would soon be earning the money she needed to pay for the expensive return trip to Independence for herself and Caroline. By next summer she'd be doing what she loved most: helping Uncle Finney with his medical clinic. And, Uncle Justus had promised to continue to fund the search for Caroline.

Luckily Mr. Moore's Mercantile carried a few embroidery supplies, so needlework kept her hands occupied when the carriage wasn't bumping madly over trail ruts. She caught Uncle Justus staring at her several times, but then, it was the two of them in the carriage and the windows were covered by heavy drapes against the cold. With no scenery to distract and only books for entertainment, she figured he was bored.

Once they arrived at the stately Bridlington, Uncle Justus offered his arm and escorted her through the oversize doors. One step inside and she was in awe. The lobby was enormous, two stories high, graced with Italianate columns and two-dimensional relief on the ceiling embellished with fleur-de-lis and scrolls. The plush flowered carpet under her feet was finer and far cleaner than the carpet at the Garry, and the dazzling chandeliers caused her to stare.

When she and Caroline and Pa had passed through the city months ago, they had seen none of its glittering interior because Pa was in a hurry to arrive at the gold fields before fall. He had, however, acquiesced to the girls 'pleas and put them up at another forgettable roadhouse outside the city, mainly for a bath, but even that was for only one night because of the expense.

Madeline glanced at her faded dress and scuffed shoes. She looked like a field hand compared to these stylish women in their silks and elaborately coifed hair. She felt out of place.

"After we get you settled in," Justus Garry said, "I will call for a dressmaker to measure you for some new gowns."

Her mouth dropped opened. "But I haven't the money—"

"Don't have a care, Miss Whittaker. The hotel will cover the cost. Think of it as a uniform. I demand all my employees' attire is as refined as the Bridlington," he said as he swept his arm around the room.

"But you paid my traveling expenses from Hangtown."

"It's the cost of doing business."

She suspected Uncle Justus had not covered the traveling expenses of the dozens of other employees required to run his hotel, but she was dependent on his largesse and tired from travel, so she kept that thought to herself.

After he had helped her check in at the registration desk, she was relieved to bid him good night and follow the bellboy and a young lady in a crisp white-and-black uniform to her small room with a window overlooking the dark street.

Once she was alone, she fell onto the bed fully clothed and was soon sound asleep.

She awakened to the sound of someone knocking. Light filtered through the window. She smoothed her hair and skirt and opened the door. A maid stood in the hall, note in hand. Madeline dismissed the maid then tore open the envelope. Uncle Justus, the note said, was waiting for her in the dining room.

"I slept through our breakfast appointment!"

***

After hurriedly cleaning up and changing into her staid gray wool, Madeline entered the dining room, trying to look composed. The host escorted her to Uncle Justus' table, where he was chatting with a woman with striking snow-white hair—Madeline guessed she was in her eighties. From the dirty dishes and empty cups scattered across the table, she knew they had finished their meal. The host pulled out a chair and she sat down, apologizing profusely for sleeping through breakfast. Uncle Justus introduced the two women.

"I knew you'd like your feather bed, but I didn't know you'd like it that much," quipped Uncle to Madeline.

She blushed. Then a waiter brought coffee and she poured a little cream into her cup. She glanced at the woman long enough to admire her dignified brown silk bodice with bell lace extensions at the cuffs. So this was Uncle Justus' widowed great aunt, Mrs. Elizabeth Miller, who lived in the hotel. He had spoken of her during the carriage ride. She had outlived all her children and was dependent on her nephew.

Uncle stood up. "I must get about my responsibilities. I'll leave you two ladies to get to know each other. And," he said, turning to Madeline, "Mrs. Sarah Wilson will arrive after lunch to take your measurements and dress order."

"Dress order?" asked Mrs. Miller after he left.

Madeline was mortified at all this male attention. "Mr. Garry says I must dress the part of a hostess of a fine hotel. The wardrobe I carried from Independence is unsuitable for front desk duty."

Mrs. Miller chuckled. "My nephew likes things just so. Humor him, dear. I do."

Madeline liked Mrs. Miller at once. They exchanged stories over the next half an hour.

"What do you think of my nephew?" Mrs. Miller abruptly asked.

Madeline was taken aback. Think of him? Had she thought of Uncle Justus at all? "He's been very nice to me, and by extension, to my sister. I am grateful for all he's doing for us, giving me a job here in the hotel and forming a search party for Caroline."

"I mean," said Mrs. Miller, "What do you think of him as a man?"

Madeline screwed up her face. As a man? "He's a nice man."

Mrs. Miller scrutinized her, which made her squirm. Conversation after that was awkward. At the earliest possible moment, Madeline dismissed herself and returned to her room.

***

"Clint, what would you think about watching the hotel while I go out of town?"

Jesse leaned back in his office chair and eyed his brother across the desk. What he was about to do was awful risky, even reckless. Was he as crazy as Madeline when she went riding solo into a blizzard to search for her sister? Yes, he was. Uncle would surely fire him for leaving the hotel to the care of his impulsive younger brother. But his mind was set.

"Why? Where you going?" said Clint.

"Frisco."

"You're going after Madeline. I told you."

"Wrong. I'm going to deliver a message. It's nothing you send by letter on a pack mule."

"You're ending the search, aren't you?" said Clint.

Jesse slumped in his chair and let out a noisy breath. "It's cruel to give her false hope. Caroline's

gone. You know it, I know it. Madeline … she
deserves to know how it is with her sister. If she's
dead there's nothing we can do. If she up and got
married, she'll come back if she wants to. Uncle's
searchers haven't found anything either. I heard this
morning they're quitting and returning to their gold
pans."

"It's a long way to Frisco. You'll be gone for
weeks. You could get stranded in high snow. We
wouldn't find your body until spring. Maybe never
if a mountain lion gets it."

"I know about the weather. But once I enter
the valley areas the snow will be thin if there's any
at all."

"Well," said Clint, "I say go. You got
nothing to lose."

"Except my job here at the hotel—or my
life," said Jesse, flatly.

Clint scoffed. "Uncle won't fire you."

"What makes you so sure?"

"He grumbles like an ogre no matter what
we do, but he has no one else to run this place and
he'd rather burn in Hell than turn it over to me."

"That's a fact," said Jesse, chuckling.

"Quit worrying about Uncle all the time.
You gotta know for yourself what you want."

Jesse gave him a look. "What do you
mean?"

"If you think it's risky, then weigh the risk.
What do you want the most—your job or
Madeline?"

"I want to deliver the bad news in an easy
way. She's endured enough tragedies."

"Believe what you want. You fool only
yourself. It's quicker and safer to write a letter and
send it by pack mule." Clint stood and grabbed his

hat from the hat stand. "Only a man set on winning a woman's heart would be so darn careful about breaking it." Then he walked out. A moment later the door opened and he poked his head back in. "If you risk your life to brave snow and ice alone on a horse for a hundred and forty miles in the dead of winter and come back without her, then you're more stupid than I think you are." Clint banged his hat on his thigh for emphasis then walked out the door again.

Where did this bucking colt learn so much about men and women? Jesse marveled.

Madeline. Jesse closed his eyes in the quiet privacy of his office and called up his favorite memory: he and Miss Madeline cocooned under the blankets in the dark of a winter night, oblivious to the raging blizzard and its power to kill, all four-footed dangers forgotten as he held her warm, soft body next to his.

He wanted that again, to hold her, to be inside of her. He wanted it every night of his life. He wanted it more than his job at the Garry.

And then, like the gradual ascent of the morning sun on the horizon, awakening the world with its soft glow, realization dawned on him. For the first time, he acknowledged the truth: He wanted Madeline.

CHAPTER TWENTY-FOUR

The familiar aroma of cigar smoke and burning gas lamps filled Jesse with nostalgia as he stepped into the opulent lobby of the Bridlington. He had earned his first man-size wages in this place. Uncle had been patient, even kind, taking him on as a teenage greenhorn, ignorant of hotel business, as raw as they come. Nearly everything Jesse knew about running a hotel he had learned from Uncle in this grand enterprise. The old man was irritating and often unreasonable, but Jesse was indebted to him.

He glanced around the room, noting Uncle's lighting improvements and updated decor since Jesse had left for Hangtown. The hotelier spared no expense to make his establishment appear prosperous and sophisticated. No wonder the city's most elite moneyed visitors flocked to the

Bridlington to be pampered and conduct business in style.

He approached the desk. A young woman was standing behind it, her back to him. He took in her elaborately coiffed hair, a profusion of stylish brown ringlets cascading from a lush updo, yards of sage green silk draped over a wide crinoline, defining a small waist. He hadn't seen a woman dressed so ladylike in months.

This sure isn't Hangtown. "Excuse me, miss."

The woman turned around. Jesse was startled to see Madeline looking back at him. Her eyes widened and she smiled.

"I'm looking for Miss Madeline Whittaker," he said, teasing.

Madeline laughed. "I have changed, haven't I?"

"The clothes and hair are different, but the pretty face is the same."

Madeline blushed to her hairline. "What a surprise to see you at the Bridlington, Mr. Garry."

"Truthfully, I'm surprised too. I'm here on business."

"Oh?" her smile disappeared. "Is it about … Caroline?"

A vague answer would be cowardly. "Yes, Caroline, and another matter. When will you be free?"

Before she could answer, off to his side Jesse sensed a large form stepping toward him.

"Miss Whittaker," said Uncle, "go to my office and wait for me."

She looked at Jesse with pleading eyes then back at Uncle. "Yes, Mr. Garry." She reached under

171

the front desk for her bag, then quickly walked out of the lobby.

Uncle waited until she was out of the room. He turned back to Jesse. "Who's watching the hotel?"

Jesse knew this would be the first question out of Uncle's mouth. He was prepared. "Clint," he said, looking Uncle boldly in the eye.

"You'd better have a good reason for abandoning your responsibilities to a kid as unaccountable and unpredictable as your brother."

"I didn't abandon them. I temporarily reassigned them. Biscuit's there to help too," said Jesse. He started to say "Biscuit and Tien" but caught himself, remembering the ire the Chinaman provoked in Uncle. "And Clint is more grown-up than you think."

Uncle scoffed. "What are you doing here?"

"I have urgent business with Miss Whittaker."

"You should have sent a letter. Miss Whittaker is occupied with her duties," said Uncle. "She's not available."

"Then I'll speak with her at dinner."

"She's dining with me. If you have a message for her, give it to me and I'll see that it's delivered."

Jesse had been ready to defend putting Clint in charge of the Garry Hotel, but he was unprepared for Uncle's stonewalling when it came to Madeline. What was happening here? He remembered Biscuit's crazy ideas about Uncle courting her. Was Biscuit right? Did Uncle want Madeline for himself?

"I have to speak to her in person," he said.

"There will be time for that." Uncle waved his hand in the air dismissively. "Meanwhile, I need to speak to Miss Whittaker. Watch the desk until I send someone down here. Book yourself a room. How long will you be in town?"

"After I finish my business, I'll take a day to rest my horse and pick up some supplies. Then I'll head back unless I sense snow. Gotta ride while the sky is clear."

"Join us in the dining room at six," said Uncle. "We'll talk more then."

***

Jesse was seated with Uncle and Great Aunt Elizabeth when Madeline floated into the dining room wearing a shimmering copper gown festooned with yards of cascading white lace. Jesse didn't remember seeing her in it before. Another gift from Uncle? She was resplendent in the glow of the gas chandeliers—Jesse's heart fluttered at the sight. He rose quickly to greet her, but Uncle was quicker.

"Sit here, Miss Whittaker," said Uncle, pulling out the chair next to him and relegating Jesse to the seat farthest from Madeline.

Jesse watched Uncle's actions toward Madeline with consternation. But then she gave Jesse a warm hello and smiled, disarming him. Maybe he was imagining crotchety old Uncle Justus was smitten with a girl half his age—it was too outrageous to be true. He felt guilty to have swallowed Biscuit's gossip about a man who had done so much for him. And besides, she surely had no interest in Uncle.

Right?

Throughout the meal they shared small talk. While Uncle peppered Jesse with questions about business at the Garry Hotel, Aunt Elizabeth chatted with Madeline about life in Hangtown. The conversation turned to the town's lack of a doctor.

"We have a doctor right here at this table," said Jesse upon overhearing the ladies. Everyone stopped chatting and looked at him.

"What are you talking about?" asked Aunt Elizabeth.

"Miss Whittaker removed a large cyst on a fellow at the hotel before she left town." He turned to Madeline. "And you were right, if the sac is removed, the cyst won't come back. The man has been fine ever since. No cyst. He told me to tell you thank you."

"I'm so relieved," she said.

"You doctored one of those rough miners?" asked Uncle.

Jesse's eyes met Madeline's. "Not a miner," she said quietly. "Hotel employee. I assisted my physician uncle for years in Independence. I've removed many cysts."

"Which employee?" demanded Uncle.

Silence.

"Who?" said Uncle again.

"She took pity on our houseboy, Tien. You met him," said Jesse.

"You let her operate on a *Chinaman*?"

"Justus, please, we're in the dining room," said Aunt Elizabeth.

"That dirty mining camp is no place for a woman," said Uncle to Jesse. "How could you let a tender young lady like our Miss Madeline put her hands on a Chinaman?"

Madeline stared at her plate. Other diners were looking their way. Jesse's face was reddening.

"Nephew," said Aunt Elizabeth to Uncle, "let's discuss this later, shall we? Besides, you told me you have good news to share."

"Yes," Uncle said finally, "I have good news. I've promoted Miss Whittaker. Starting tomorrow morning she will be off the front desk and will serve as my personal secretary. I'm setting her up in a small office next to mine."

Alarm bells clanged in Jesse's head. *It s true. Uncle is courting her.* He looked at Madeline to study her response. She was still head down, face impassive, eyes fixed on her plate.

"That's wonderful, Justus," said Aunt Elizabeth. "Your workload has become burdensome lately. You rarely find time to accompany me to the shops." Her attempt at lightheartedness failed to lift the atmosphere at the table.

Suddenly Jesse stood and placed his napkin on the table. "If you will excuse us," he said, "Miss Whittaker and I have urgent business to discuss."

Madeline had no chance to respond. "Miss Whittaker is not available," said Uncle, also standing. "I'm going to show her the area of the hotel I've designated for her new office."

Jesse pulled out Madeline's chair as she rose. "You're coming with me," he said. "My uncle is forgetful. Even the slaves in Egypt went home at night," he said loudly enough for everyone at the table to hear. And taking her hand, he walked her out of the dining room.

***

"But this is your uncle's office," protested Madeline as she sat in an overstuffed chair near the wood stove where Jesse was building a fire. Behind Uncle's desk was a wall covered entirely in books. "My, he is quite the bibliophile."

"He made us read too, growing up," groused Jesse. "All kinds of boring literature. And isn't it like Uncle to conscript me like a foot soldier to work the lobby the minute I walk into his hotel?" He lit a match and set it under the tinder. A flash of blue, a tiny puff of smoke, and soon slender orange flames erupted from the shavings. "That makes me an employee. We can use his office to talk. Besides, there's no other private place in the hotel and it's too cold outside to walk."

"True."

People would talk if they saw them together. But her desire to hear news of Caroline overshadowed her qualm. She watched him blow on the fire until the flames got bigger. Lean and muscular, competent, and sure of himself—she found these aspects of him appealing. Finally, the fire took off. He left the stove door open a little then sat down across from her. She braced herself, her heart pounding.

He paused unnaturally long before speaking. "I have ended the search for your sister."

Madeline's face screwed up in pain.

"I know this is hard. I am very sorry."

He pulled a folded handkerchief from a pocket and pressed it into her hand. She dabbed her eyes.

"It's been three months. We have looked everywhere, miles of searching."

She nodded, her eyes cast down to the floor.

"Snow hasn't left the ground in weeks. If she were lost in the forest she could not possibly survive. She is either dead or truly ran off like that note said and is married now. If the latter is true, we both know we shouldn't worry."

"I've come to the same conclusion these last few weeks."

He leaned back in the chair, shoulders slack with relief. "My uncle's men have stopped searching as well."

Madeline nodded morosely. "It's probably wise. No use risking more lives—and our wagon and oxen? Did you learn anything?"

"I spoke to Gull. He denies everything."

Madeline's mouth fell open. "And Mr. Moore? He told you about the sale?"

"He told me about it. He said you agreed to it."

"What?"

"I can't string them up without proof."

She let out a huffy breath. "I can't believe what you're telling me. Mr. Dupont stole everything we had except our clothes. And I suspect Mr. Moore was party to the theft."

"I believe you. My investigation isn't over yet. But I need your cooperation to continue. That's partly why I'm here."

"Partly?"

"I found your father's grave."

Her head shot up. "You'll help me bring his body to town? I want him buried in the place he longed to see."

Jesse shifted in his chair then picked up his hat from the side table and fingered it. "His body wasn't in the grave."

Madeline looked away and squeezed her eyes shut. "Gone? Nothing left at all? An animal dug it up? Or a man?"

"I couldn't tell. The grave was greatly disturbed. There were drag marks. It could have been a large animal or a human. I saw no signs he had been … eaten."

Madeline buried her face in her hands.

"Miss Whittaker, without a body as evidence, your case against Gull and Alonzo isn't as strong as it could be. You need to return to Hangtown to testify. Tell your story to the miners. We have a justice system. It's crude but the miners are fair-minded. And Gull's reputation isn't exactly sterling. I think the miners would give you a favorable judgment."

"I will never go back to Hangtown," she said. She fairly spat the words. Go back to that hellhole where she lost Pa and Caroline? Go back to what?

She could save the entire sum needed for the journey East by working for Uncle Justus as his secretary, though it would take far longer to get home if she couldn't collect the money Mr. Dupont had swindled. Without the money from the sale of Pa's wagon and supplies, she would be stuck in San Francisco at least two years.

"Your testimony is the one thing I can use to go after Gull," he said. "And if you don't go back, he wins by default. You lose automatically if you don't show up to the fight."

She bristled. "I'm sorry, Mr. Garry. I am *never* going back to Hangtown. Please don't misunderstand my words. I appreciate everything you have done to find my sister and how you saved me from freezing to death in the wilderness. I am grateful. But Hangtown is the place that robbed me of what little I had left of my family: my Pa and my sister, not to mention all my money. I wish I had never heard of Hangtown! If there isn't sufficient evidence to indict Mr. Dupont and Mr. Moore, I won't waste precious funds on travel to Hangtown. I need that money to return to Independence."

"But—"

"You can't be certain of the miners' judgment. They might disagree with your assessment of Mr. Dupont's culpability. I will stay in San Francisco. At least here at the Bridlington I have a roof over my head and the means to earn money for my trip East." Her voice quavered. She stood to leave. "And your uncle is very good to me," she added. "Thank you for making the long trip to deliver your message. Good night."

Madeline left Justus Garry's office in time to see him step into the hallway from the dining room. Embarrassed to be seen coming out of his office, she merely nodded an acknowledgement then hurried to her room.

***

Madeline sat up in bed and looked out the window of her hotel room into the starry night, cold moonbeams streaming ghostly blue across her white nightgown. Her tears slipped silently onto the windowsill. "Where are you, Caroline? Where are you?" Night after night she had performed this elegy. The sky didn't care. No one cared. She fell back onto her pillow, defeated.

How had her life come to this? Pa, the boys, Caroline—gone. Pa's dreams of fields of gold gone with him. Here was his eldest daughter living in the big city of San Francisco of all places, working in a fancy hotel among strangers. What would Ma think? Her daughter had been swindled of all her earthly possessions and was now penniless, living on the generosity of a middle-aged man.

She grimaced.

The story of Madeline Whittaker was downright salacious. A dime store novel couldn't read more outrageously. Ma would be worried to death if she knew about her situation, but Pa would find some humor in it.

Then she remembered how Jesse had taken her hand at the dinner table. She hadn't had time to protest. It was nice, warm and comforting, his grip firm. She liked holding his hand. It was a … friendly feeling, protective. There wasn't anything debauched about it.

When she was young, Ma had warned her many times not to let a man touch her. Now that she was a grown woman, she understood Ma's concern.

But Jesse's hand was nothing to fear.

CHAPTER TWENTY-FIVE

"What did you say to Miss Whittaker to make her cry?"

Uncle Justus hadn't even sat down at his desk before he began spewing accusations. A cloud of pungent cigar smoke followed him through the door.

"She's mourning her sister."

"You sure that's all?"

Jesse started to rise.

"Sit down," said Uncle. "I want to talk to you."

Jesse obeyed. The tension in the room was as a tight as a drumhead stretched to its limit. Uncle was worked up more than usual. Jesse was wary.

"What business do you have with Miss Whittaker that caused you to risk your neck and your horse over one hundred and forty miles of snow and ice?" asked Uncle.

"Why are you so interested in my business with her? Or … is the real focus of your interest Miss Whittaker?"

Uncle tapped cigar ash into a crystal ashtray on his desk and glared at Jesse. "Answer my question."

"I came to speak to her about the search for her sister. It's been called off. It's been three months. She's either dead or married somewhere. The miners you hired have abandoned the search too. Everyone knows it's useless."

"Just as well," said Uncle. "She lives with false hope. It could distract from her work."

"I have to get back to my room," said Jesse, standing up.

"Sit down. I'm not done."

Jesse sat down.

"Is there anything you've failed to tell me? Specifically, is there any other reason you've pursued Miss Whittaker all the way to San Francisco?" asked Uncle.

Jesse focused mindlessly on the slightly open door of the wood stove. He didn't have to endure questions. The other reason he'd risked his life to speak to Madeline was none of Uncle's business.

After a period of terse silence, Uncle set his cigar down and leaned over his desk. "You might as well know, nephew: I plan to ask Miss Whittaker for her hand. I can offer her a much better life than most men, and we are well suited."

Well suited? Well suited? So Biscuit was right. "She's less than half your age."

"Age doesn't matter." Uncle took up his cigar again and inhaled deeply. "She's attractive,

182

alone, eligible, and I like her company. All I need is her consent."

"What makes you think a woman so young will give it?"

"She has no other options," said Uncle. "She's penniless and far from her aunt and uncle. I will take good care of her."

The thought of the lovely Madeline in bed with Uncle—as much as Jesse respected the man—made him sick. The old flapdoodle had lost his mind. "Ultimately," said Jesse, starting to leave, "Miss Whittaker will decide whom she wants to marry."

"Sit down! I'm not done!"

Once again Jesse sat down.

"I know why you pursued Miss Whittaker all the way to my hotel. You have designs on the young lady."

Jesse sensed Uncle was waiting for confirmation, but a team of wild horses wouldn't pull it out of him.

"Is it not true?" said Uncle.

A long, pregnant silence.

"You have nothing to offer her," said Uncle. "And it's immoral to drag her back to that mining camp. I won't allow it. A gentle lady like Miss Whittaker belongs in the city, living in a nice stone house and supervising a dozen servants with lots of little children underfoot." Uncle angrily stamped out his cigar butt. "Miss Whittaker belongs to me. You stay out of the way. Do you understand?"

Jesse glared at Uncle, his jaw set like stone.

"If you insist on running after her, that will be the end of your life at the Garry," huffed Uncle. "Same goes for Clint. You'll both be unemployed and uselessly digging in the dirt like all those other hapless miners. I'll cut you out of my will too."

Jesse stared in disbelief at his uncle. "Madeline Whittaker belongs to no one, he said."

And then he wordlessly walked out of the office.

***

Uncle wasn't done with Jesse yet. The old man pressed him into service at the front desk the during the midday dinner hour. Jesse was certain it was to prevent him from dining with Madeline. That's where Jesse was when he saw him—the big man who entered the Bridlington Lobby was commanding not just for his size but also by the air of assurance about him—a man used to getting what he wanted. Jesse looked him up and down. The stranger was dressed unlike the city folk that daily entered the hotel. This was a recent transplant, a countryman, not a cowboy or rancher, but perhaps a merchant or banker based on his eastern suit and smart shoes.

Something slimy about him caused Jesse to go on alert. The man approached the desk.

"Welcome to the Bridlington," said Jesse. "You have a reservation?"

"No," said the stranger. "I'm not here to book a room. I'm looking for a guest who's lodging here."

"Guest's name?" asked Jesse.

"Madeline Whittaker."

"Madeline Whittaker?" Jesse's muscles went rigid.

"You have that right."

"I can leave a note for her here at the desk," said Jesse. "May I ask who is calling?"

"William Blakely, her fiancé."

CHAPTER TWENTY-SIX

Jesse knew Madeline was nearby in the dining room enjoying lunch but shamelessly failed to volunteer this knowledge to Mr. Blakely. *Fiancé? Miss Madeline s fiancé?* The shoe did not fit.

"How can she reach you?" he asked.

Mr. Blakely gave him the name and address of a nearby hotel. Jesse recorded it on a slip of paper.

"I'll make sure she knows you came by," he said.

But before he could slide the note into a mail cubby, Madeline stepped up to the desk. "William," she cried. "I'm speechless."

Jesse watched as the two embraced like long separated friends. His sense of uneasiness wasn't lessened when Madeline formally introduced him, even though she referred to the dubious Mr. Blakely as a "friend from home"—not her fiancé.

"You're from Independence?" asked Jesse.

"New York. I manage a bank there. Bank of New York."

That explained the clothes. "What brings you West?" asked Jesse.

"I'm working with some investors to start a bank here," said William. "And I have other business to take care of." He said this as he smiled at Madeline, who returned the smile, eyes sparkling.

Jesse observed this annoying coziness with curiosity. He hadn't seen Madeline so animated since she first arrived in Hangtown. Mr. Blakely had undoubtedly been an intimate part of her past life. She had addressed him by his first name. But how intimate? If they were truly engaged, why had she never mentioned him? Why did she leave Independence without him? A man who planned to marry a girl this pretty would have put a ring on her finger before shipping her to a mining camp howling with woman-hungry wolves.

" Madeline, will you give me the pleasure of joining me for dinner?" asked Blakely. "The dining room of my hotel serves exceptional food." Without waiting for her answer, he turned to Jesse. "My man, please arrange for a carriage for hire for the evening so I can escort my lady in style."

Jesse blinked.

"William, Mr. Garry is not a desk clerk," said Madeline. "He manages a hotel north of here in Hangtown, an important mining camp. He's in the city on business and is filling in at the desk to help his uncle, who owns the Bridlington."

"I see," said William.

"I will speak to the concierge about hiring a carriage," said Jesse. "What time do you want it delivered to your hotel?"

187

***

"I've never had seafood before. This is delicious," said Madeline. "You were right about this place."

The dining room of the Winston Hotel, though smaller than the Bridlington, was lavishly appointed with imported wood furnishings and romantic, candlelit chandeliers. The food was equally sumptuous—large pink shrimp swimming in lemon butter and the most angel-like rolls she had ever eaten—all served on delicate porcelain dinnerware carried by uniformed waiters. William even ordered a bottle of wine, which he polished off alone. He repeatedly offered Madeline a glass, but she declined. Ma said a young lady ought never to drink when out with a man.

"I knew you'd like this place," said William. "And you're even prettier than when I last saw you."

Madeline smiled coyly and looked down at her plate.

"How did you end up in San Francisco?" he asked. "And where's your family? I remember your father and brothers were hellbent on reaching the gold fields. Is that where everyone is now?"

She set down her fork. "John, Charles, and Samuel died of cholera at Fort Atkinson. Pa died of fever the morning we arrived in Hangtown. We buried him in the woods outside town."

William stopped eating, his fork still in the air. "You and Caroline arrived in a mining camp alone?"

"Yes."

"Where's Caroline?"

Madeline told William the entire story of Caroline's disappearance, including Madeline's rescue at the hands of Jesse Garry and his continued search for Caroline.

"You have lost your entire family?" said William, shaking his head.

"Yes."

"How did you end up in San Francisco?"

"Jesse Garry's uncle—Mr. Justus Garry, the man who owns the Bridlington—also owns the Garry Hotel in Hangtown. On a visit to the mining camp he offered me a job at the front desk here in the city. I was offered positions in Hangtown, but I desperately wanted to leave that awful place. I needed money to return to Independence, so I accepted his offer."

"Why hurry to Independence? San Francisco overflows with opportunities. And besides, you have no family back home anymore other than your aunt and uncle, and they are getting up in years."

"My uncle promised to leave his medical practice to me."

William scoffed. "There you go talking doctoring again. You haven't changed."

Madeline sighed inwardly. Why did everyone think her silly for wanting to serve as a doctor? Even Pa—God rest his soul—hadn't taken her desire seriously, even after childless Uncle Finney had told him he would leave his clinic to her. Instead Pa had dragged her and her siblings across the country to pursue his own dream. And what had become of that?

"Have you written your aunt and uncle? Do they know what happened to your pa and the others?"

"I wrote them a while ago and told them everything but haven't heard from them. Now that

I'm in the city I hope mail goes through more reliably. I wrote them again just recently."

"They hadn't heard from you when I stopped in to see them," said William. "That was about two months ago."

"That explains the silence."

"What's your relationship to this uncle fellow?"

Madeline stiffened. "Relationship? He's my employer. Justus Garry has been very kind to me. He bought me this dress and a few others."

His eyes widened. "He buys you clothes?"

"Yes, so I can be appropriately attired to work in his hotel."

"He's exceptionally generous to one as young as yourself."

Madeline screwed up her face into a question mark. "What do you mean by that?"

"You met the younger Mr. Garry in Hangtown then?" asked William, ignoring her question.

"Yes," said Madeline. "Why do you ask?"

"I'm curious about your relationship with him. You cast him as a knight in shining armor."

Madeline laughed. "Jesse Garry is a very kind and responsible man. But he's no knight. He's … like one of my brothers. And how did you find me in San Francisco?"

"I passed through Independence on my passage West. I stopped in to see my folks, your aunt and uncle too. They told me your pa and everyone had left for Hangtown. When I heard that a mule train had arrived in the city this week from the camp, I inquired about you with the train captain. He told me you were staying at the Bridlington."

After the meal, William suggested they ride to the wharf to see the great sailing ships tied up in the harbor. Madeline noticed William had a little trouble hoisting himself into the carriage, but she dismissed her unease when they pulled up to the wharf, where she was utterly enthralled by the ships. They were enormous and oh so majestic in the moonlight. The only "big" boats she had ever seen were the boring, smelly cargo barges that plied the Missouri River. That same full moon provided the sole light along the dusky paths of the wharf, its rays shimmering on the water in undulating ribbons of gold.

It was a beautiful night, ideal for a stroll, though chilly. For the first time in months Madeline allowed her heart to be happy—fleeting thoughts of Caroline's disappearance could not dampen her light-hearted mood. It was joyous to be with someone from home, and she was so tired of grieving.

William stopped walking and faced her. "You know, Madeline, now that your pa has passed on, there is no one to object to our marriage."

His speech seemed a little slower than she remembered. *Is he drunk?*

"Are you happy to see me?" he said, pressing her hands to his lips.

"Of course I am happy to see you. I've sorely missed all my friends and family back home."

"Aren't I more than a friend?" he asked.

They had stopped on a wooden pier alongside a warehouse that faced the bay a few feet from the water. It was nearly midnight. The only sound was the undulating lapping of tidal waves against the bollards. Suddenly William grabbed both her arms, pinning her to the wall of the warehouse. He pressed his body hard against hers. She felt the firmness and heat of his loins pressed into her feminine area. Her heart was in her throat.

"Come up to my room tonight," he said, his words slurred but deliberate. "I will show you the difference between me and a brother." Then his mouth was on hers, voracious and violent and tasting of wine, while his hands ran up and down her hips.

"William, stop it!" she cried, turning her face to avoid his mouth as she pushed and clawed. "Stop it!"

Suddenly someone struck William on the side of the head with a wicked thwack. He went sprawling to the ground on his backside, looked around dazed for a moment, then slumped over unconscious. Madeline jumped back in shock, then looked at the stranger. It was Jesse Garry.

He put his hand on her shoulder. "Are you alright?"

"I'm fine," she said, her voice shaky. "But what did you do to William?"

"I stopped him from doing what men like him do."

She kneeled on the ground to get a close look at William. "You knocked him out."

"Don't worry. He's just going to bed earlier than planned. He'll be fine in the morning. A headache, that's all. Here." He extended his hand. "Let me help you up."

"I hope you didn't hurt him." She petted his cheek to awaken him. He didn't move.

" If I wanted to hurt him, I'd gone after him with my piece." He put his hand on his sidearm. "I wanted him to stop."

"I wanted him to stop too. It's the liquor."

"It's the man." Jesse looked at William and screwed up his face in disgust. He bent down and put his hand on hers. "I'm taking you back to the hotel."

She allowed him to help her up. "But what about William?"

"I will take care of William. Come with me."

Jesse tracked down the coachman, explained the situation, and together they walked back to the unconscious Blakely and dragged him up into the coach. He and Madeline watched as the coach rolled down the street until it disappeared.

"I hope he'll be alright," she said somewhat forlornly.

"He's fine. I paid the coachman extra to carry the tosspot right into his bed at the Winston. Don't waste a thought on him," said Jesse.

"Tosspot? Don't call William that."

"What should I call him? He's as liquored up as a bowl of Christmas nog."

Madeline shook her head in frustration but couldn't think of an argument. It was a fact: her date had imbibed too much. Nothing else could explain his scandalous behavior.

Jesse offered his arm. "The Bridlington is nearby. We'll be in the lobby in less than ten minutes. Stay close to me. Fog is rolling in. You could trip on these dark streets. And there are rats. Big ones, mean as grizzly bears."

"Rats?"

"Much more aggressive than eastern rats. Western rats will climb your petticoats."

She scooted close to Jesse at once.

"How do you know Mr. Blakely?" he asked.

"I used to handle deposits for my uncle's medical practice. William managed our small savings and loan before he moved to New York."

"You refer to each other by first names. It sounds like you were more than friends. He was your beau, am I right?"

Madeline sighed and pulled her wrap more tightly around her. "He was."

"More than a beau?"

"My, you have a lot of questions tonight."

"That's how investigators investigate."

Madeline laughed. "Yes, he was my beau."

"Why didn't you marry and accompany him to New York?"

"I wanted to. He asked me to marry him."

"And?"

Madeline looked down at her shoes. "Pa disapproved."

" How very unfortunate. So … will you marry him now that your pa is gone?"

"I have to think about it," said Madeline. "How did you happen to be on the wharf tonight?"

He hesitated. "I needed some air."

"When will you depart for Hangtown?"

"Tomorrow. Do you think we could take breakfast together in the morning? There's still something I'd like to discuss with you," said Jesse.

"I'd like that."

They agreed on a time, and before long Jesse pushed open the heavy doors of the Bridlington. The lobby was quiet—it was about one a.m.—and empty except for one person: Justus Garry. He sat stiff and mute in a wing back chair grinding a cigar in his teeth. He stood up when he saw them walk into the lobby.

"Miss Whittaker," he said, "go to your room. We will discuss your shameless behavior in the morning in my office."

"But Mr. Garry, I—"

"Go," he said.

Madeline looked pleadingly at Jesse then turned and walked toward the stairs.

"What are you doing with Miss Whittaker at this ungodly hour of the night? She has duty in the morning," said Uncle Justus.

"I walked her back to the hotel, that's all. Her dinner date drank too much and fell asleep."

Uncle Justus shook his head as if to clear it, then anger took over. "What did I tell you about staying out of my way? You should not be dallying with Miss Whittaker anywhere at any time for any reason."

"Should I have left her to the desires of her drunk escort?"

"What are you talking about? Who is this escort?"

"Ask her," replied Jesse. "Good night, Uncle." Jesse turned and headed for the staircase.

"Nephew!" exploded Uncle at Jesse's back, "Go back to Hangtown and keep an eye on my hotel!"

Jesse kept on walking.

CHAPTER TWENTY-SEVEN

The next morning Jesse packed his few belongings, all the while reflecting on Uncle Justus, who had generously put him up in this comfortable room at no charge. What an oxymoron the man was. Kind at times, grouchy often. Impatient but fair-minded, driven by profit. Loud and convivial one day, brooding and tight-fisted the next. Jesse struggled to stay on Uncle's good side, but the target was always shifting. Despite his mercurial temperament, Jesse respected the old man—after all, they were blood relatives. But why was a man who revered common sense and tolerated no fools pursuing a girl as young as Madeline Whittaker? It's all Jesse could think about as he gathered his possessions.

All except for that troublemaker: the slimy womanizer William Blakely. Remembering last night and the boldness of the wolfish fop set Jesse's teeth on edge. How dare he put his hands on Madeline.

Jesse left his pack in his room and descended the grand staircase to the lobby. He glanced about hoping to see Madeline, but she wasn't present, so he walked to the front desk to arrange for check-out. Before he could speak to the desk clerk, a delivery man walked through the lobby doors carrying an attention-grabbing, grandiose bouquet of white lilies and an enormous heart-shaped candy box, also white. Jesse watched as the delivery man set them on the desk. The heavy fragrance of the flowers permeated the front desk.

"Who are these for?" said the desk clerk.

The delivery man pulled a slip of paper from his breast pocket and read it. "Miss Madeline Whittaker." Then he turned and headed for the door.

In an instant Jesse swooped up the flowers and candy. "Don't bother calling a bellhop," he said to the desk clerk, "I'll deliver these to her." The desk clerk thanked Jesse and returned to his other business.

Jesse bypassed the grand staircase to the guest rooms and quickly walked down a long, little used hallway where he left the hotel through a side door. Once outside he angrily threw the flowers and candy onto the jumping orange flames of the hotel burn pile. "You won't buy her hand with your filthy money, Mr. Blakely," he said. "At least not while I'm breathing."

***

Madeline sat alone at a table in the dining room beneath a sunny window, silently sipping coffee in the nearly empty room while she waited for her early breakfast meeting with Jesse. But her mind was on Uncle Justus. She had done nothing wrong. Would she lose her position at the Bridlington? Madeline Whittaker—fired. Penniless. Selling matches to buy a crust of bread. Sleeping in a grungy alley fending off hordes of petticoat-climbing rats. Shameful. Hangtown may have been desperate for young female clerks—even those totally lacking in experience—to fill positions miners refused, but the city was populated with plenty of people, sophisticated young women with useful skills. What could she do to earn money other than low-paying domestic duties? And she had no references.

"Miss Whittaker," said Jesse, pulling out a chair opposite her. "Good morning."

She looked up. "Good morning."

"You don't look like you're having a good morning," he said. "You shouldn't let Uncle Justus intimidate you."

She chuckled and wiped her mouth with her napkin. "How did you know?"

"Uncle bellows like a bull, but underneath he's more beneficent than people know."

"He's been very generous to me."

Jesse took in her deep scarlet dress with matching glass buttons. "Yes, I know. He's generous to me too."

"You're dressed to ride this morning. What time will you depart?" she asked. He looked more handsome than usual with the morning sun's rays lighting up his face. She was surprised at how delighted she was to be dining with him. Suddenly she realized she would miss their visits. The city would be lonely without him. The thought saddened her.

"After breakfast," said Jesse. "Gotta get back while the hotel is still standing."

"You're worried about the hotel? Who'd you leave in charge?"

"Clint."

"Your brother will rise to the occasion. You'll see."

"Only after he's chased every pretty girl in town and spent every dollar of his wage on the next lucrative game of cards. What little energy he has left will go to the hotel."

"I've met Clint. You misjudge him. You should exercise charity toward your brother. At least you still have one."

Jesse became silent. After a space he said, "You must have wanted to go West a great deal to take such risks."

"My pa and brothers wanted to go West. Gold was all they talked about day and night."

"You didn't want to make the trip?"

She shook her head. "I grew up helping my Uncle Finney with his medical clinic. He and Auntie Hannah are childless and he's getting on in years, so he told Pa he wanted to leave the clinic to me. I wanted that clinic more than life itself—I still do—but Pa wouldn't hear of me staying behind, especially for something he deemed so unladylike. He was a good man but very old-fashioned. Of course—Pa would never let Caroline stay behind. She needs constant chaperoning."

They chuckled. A waiter took their order. After their meal was delivered, Madeline mindlessly pushed her food around the plate. "I will miss our conversations when you're gone," she said. "I hope when you return to San Francisco on

business again you'll look me up. Of course, I may
be unemployed by then."

Jesse set his fork down. "I will miss seeing
your face and speaking with you as well. But don't
worry, Uncle won't let you go."

"How can you be sure?"

"I'm sure. When you have a good thing,
something hard to replace, you don't let it go
easily."

She scoffed. "Destitute females willing to
work as a personal assistant in this elegant hotel—
especially with the luxurious wardrobe that comes
with the position, not to mention room and board—
are a dime a dozen. This country bumpkin is easily
replaced."

Suddenly Jesse reached across the table and
clasped her hand. "No, you're not, Miss Whittaker.
No replacement exists anywhere for you."

He was holding her hand. *What does it
mean?* She did not pull back. The touch of Jesse
Garry, she had learned, was very pleasurable. And
besides, they were mostly alone in the dining room.
No one would spread rumors.

"Miss Whittaker—Madeline—I want to
make you an offer. I want you to reconsider
returning to Hangtown with me to recover the
money Gull took from you."

She shook her head vehemently. But she
didn't let go of his hand.

"You're the one person who can bring that
scoundrel to justice. I need your testimony. Plus, the
miners need you. The camp has no doctor."

"I'm not a doctor."

"Maybe not officially, but you have skills
the miners need. Look what you did for Tien's face.
You can do that for others too. Miners suffer

sickness and injury all the time. Alonzo Moore can get you anything you need for doctoring."

"But I'm *not* a doctor. And the men won't accept treatment from a woman."

"Maybe not for minor stuff. But if a man hurts bad enough, he will accept help from anyone, even a woman."

Madeline shook her head.

"I read in the Mountain *Messenger* a while back that Geneva Medical College in New York graduated a woman doctor a few years ago," said Jesse. "That could be you."

"Truly? They gave a medical degree to a woman?"

He nodded. "And there's more." They were both ignoring their meal now, and Jesse was still holding her hand. He gazed directly into her eyes. "Please consider returning to Hangtown as my wife."

Madeline's mouth fell open. She was so shocked she couldn't respond.

"It's not as sudden or crazy as it sounds." He emphasized the point by putting his other hand over hers. "We get along well. I need a wife and you've lost your family. And the miners need a doctor. If you return to Hangtown you may very well get your money back. If you do, you'll have the funds you need to return to Independence. But maybe you'll decide to stay—as my wife."

"And if I don't get my money back? What then?"

"You can stay on as Mrs. Garry and minister to sick and injured miners. You told me you like serving."

"That's true."

"But if you're sincerely unhappy in Hangtown, I'll arrange passage back to the city for you. I'm sure Uncle Justus will jump at the chance to hire you again. And if he doesn't, I know he'll help you find another situation. Like I said, deep down he's a beneficent man. He took me and Clint in when our parents died."

Madeline nodded.

Jesse waited expectantly for an answer that didn't come.

"I enjoyed our breakfast, but I must hurry to Uncle's office."

"You'll keep me waiting for an answer?"

"I'm sorry. I need more time." She stood. "I wish you Godspeed."

CHAPTER TWENTY-EIGHT

Madeline took a deep, steadying breath as she stood outside Justus Garry's office. What was he going to do? Beat her with a fire poker? Yell like he sometimes did at his nephews? She gathered her wits and knocked.

"Sit down, Miss Whittaker," said Uncle Justus, gesturing to the same chair she'd occupied when Jesse Garry had told her he'd called off the search for Caroline and found Pa's grave. Justus Garry walked around his desk and sat down opposite her. A fire crackled in the wood stove like the fire Jesse had made a few nights ago. But she didn't feel at ease as she had with Jesse. Her stomach felt tight and a little sick. Uncle Justus lit a cigar and leaned back in his chair.

"I imagine you're tired after gallivanting about town into the wee hours."

Madeline smiled weakly. "Yes, I am a little tired this morning."

"I hear you dined last night with a gentleman. Can you tell me about that?"

Madeline was taken aback at such a personal question. "A friend arrived from Independence. From home. He asked me to dinner."

He didn't say anything, waiting.

"We ate at the Winston," she continued hesitantly. "It was lovely. Then we drove down to the wharf to see the ships. Time got away from us. It won't happen again, Mr. Garry."

"I see. You know this gentleman well?"

"Fairly well, yes." *Why is he investigating William?*

"What's his line of work?"

"He manages a bank in New York City. He's come West to establish a new branch here."

Uncle ground his unfinished cigar into his crystal ashtray and leaned forward, resting his hands on his knees. "Has he asked you to marry him?"

Madeline squirmed. "I've received no proposal from Mr. Blakely since he arrived in San Francisco."

"And my nephew? What do you think of him?"

"Jesse?"

"Yes," said Uncle.

She blushed. "He's very responsible. He does a good job of managing your Hangtown hotel."

Uncle Justus halted his questions and eyed Madeline. She felt his intense gaze and began fiddling with a fold of her dress.

"Has he made an offer to you?" He drummed his fingers noisily on a side table.

Madeline was slow to respond. She fiddled with that dress fold and stared at her shoes.

"Well?"

"What do you mean by that?" she asked. But she knew.

"A marriage proposal."

Why is this man so interested in my love life? Something felt off. Then, from within that deep well of Whittaker gumption, Madeline drew up some courage. She didn't have to answer all these intrusive questions, employee or not.

"He thinks I should return to Hangtown to fight for the items I was swindled out of. He offered to help me get my money back."

"Good for Jesse," said Uncle. "That's his innate sense of justice coming to the fore. But I'm sure you told him how virulently opposed you are to returning to that filthy mining camp."

"I did."

"Good girl." Uncle Justus got up and walked to his desk. He opened a drawer and pulled out a tip cutter, trimmed the smashed end of his cigar, set aside the cutter and cigar, and returned to his chair across from Madeline. "Miss Whittaker … Madeline," he said as he took her hand in his. "I have a proposal of my own for you."

Her first inclination was to draw back her hand, but instead she froze. *Whatever is this about?*

Uncle Justus pulled a small, emerald-green, velvet box from his pocket and pressed it into her hand. "Open it," he said.

Madeline opened the box. Inside, nesting on cream satin, was the loveliest, most opulent ring she had ever laid eyes on—an oval ruby surrounded by three concentric rings of diamonds set on a gold band. For a moment she stopped breathing. She felt faint. This could not be happening. Did this mean what she thought it meant?

"Mr. Garry, I—"

"Please," he said, leaning forward, "let me speak my mind first before you answer. I am well aware that you are much younger than I. I may be older, but I am in good health, and I can offer you everything a younger man cannot. You will never work for wages again…"

He is proposing. He is actually proposing.

"…You'll live in a large, comfortable house in this fine city and have maids to do the worst of the household chores. You'll never lack for anything, Madeline. In fact, once you are my wife, you'll never give your losses in Hangtown another thought. Our children will receive the finest education, and you will have time to pursue personal interests too, like books and music. Most important, you will have a family again. I am fond of you, Madeline. I will be good to you."

She stared at the ring, not because it was exquisite, though it was, but because meeting his eyes was too painful. In a flash of latent insight, it struck her that all the generosity she'd enjoyed under his providence made sense. Uncle Justus didn't want a personal assistant. He wanted a wife. She closed the ring box and pressed it gently into his hand.

"Mr. Garry, your offer is precious to me," she said, "but I cannot accept it."

"Are you rejecting me personally or is it the age difference?"

"I can't imagine why any woman would reject you for you. You are a fine man, and it's a privilege to work for you. It's just—"

"My age. I understand." Uncle Justus abruptly slipped the ring box into his pocket. "Well, I'm disappointed. But I'm sure you're wondering if I'll let you go after this. You needn't worry. Your position is secure. You're welcome to stay here as my assistant as long as you like."

She let out a breath of relief. "Thank you."

"Did you receive the things I sent?" he said as he stood to return to his desk.

"Things?"

"They should be in your room by now."

"I'll check for them before I report to my duties this morning," she said, also standing to leave. She walked to the door and turned. "Thank you for everything."

He merely nodded without eye contact, then turned his attention to his papers.

***

"Oh, Pa, what should I do? I like Jesse Garry. I like him a lot and I want children. But give up the clinic and live in Hangtown? I am so conflicted."

Madeline flopped onto her back on her bed and stared at the ceiling. "Two proposals in one day. Caroline would love this." She laughed aloud at the absurdity of her predicament.

After resting a bit, she jumped up and smoothed her hair. Before she left the room, she remembered Uncle's talk about "things" he sent. She glanced around the room. Seeing nothing, she closed the door and descended the grand staircase.

Uncle Justus had the grace to act like nothing had transpired between them. To onlookers it was an ordinary day, but to Madeline everything seemed askew. She alerted him to his afternoon appointments as usual, then spent most of the morning answering his correspondence.

Midmorning a bellhop approached her desk with a note. It was from Jesse's Great Aunt Elizabeth Miller, inviting her to take lunch with her in the dining room today.

"Please let Mrs. Miller know I'd be delighted to join her," she said.

Lunch hour arrived. The dining room buzzed with scurrying waiters, chatting diners, and the clink of silverware on china. Madeline's mouth watered at the savory aroma of roast beef wafting from the kitchen. She stood at the entrance, eyeing the room, then she saw Elizabeth Miller giving her a little wave from a table not far away.

"Aunt Elizabeth," said Madeline as she sat down, "so good to see you. We haven't visited in a while."

"How have you been, dear?"

Madeline reflexively started to say "fine," but stopped. She wasn't fine. Her insides were all tied up in knots. "There's a lot happening in my life right now."

"Yes, I know."

"How do you know?"

Mrs. Miller smiled. "My nephew asked you to marry him."

Madeline looked down at her hands on her lap, embarrassed. Just then the waiter came and took their order. All the while Mrs. Miller's declaration hung over the table like a heavy black cloud. Madeline had to fight the urge to flee to her room. Finally the waiter returned to the kitchen and left them some privacy.

"And you rejected him."

Madeline felt like an anvil was sitting on her chest. "Yes, I did."

"I tried to tell him. But he had his heart set on this match."

Madeline's head shot up. "You knew a proposal was coming?"

"Of course I knew. I've known Justus all his life. It wasn't hard to figure out he was wooing you. You're the only person who didn't know."

"I'm terribly embarrassed."

"Don't be. You did nothing wrong. Is it his age you object to?"

"He is older than my father."

"Of course, dear. I understand. It's a compliment to you that you didn't accept him for his money. You are an upright young woman. I'm sure your parents are very proud."

"I like Uncle Justus. I do. He's been so kind to me." *Because he wanted to marry me.*

"Will you stay on at the Bridlington? Do you have any other offers, dear?"

"I can't possibly stay here. That's what's causing me agony. Uncle Justus is acting like nothing happened between us, but it's awkward. I don't feel it's right to be here anymore."

"He's acting nonchalant to hide his bruised ego."

"Oh." Of course. She had rejected him. He must be mortified, and she was the source of his pain. The weight of her big No must be weighing on him as heavily as it weighed on her.

"I have no other situations here in San Francisco. And I know only one other person in the city not connected with the Bridlington—but that's a complicated relationship."

Aunt Elizabeth's eyebrows shot up with a question mark. Madeline noticed but didn't care to speak of William.

"The only other open door is to return to Hangtown. Jesse has offered me a job at the hotel. He says I should fight the man who swindled Caroline and I of our possessions. But I hate the thought of returning to that awful mining camp."

"Of course, it holds painful memories."

"But I keep thinking about what Jesse said, and I feel like a coward."

"Why?"

"He said not showing up to fight was like letting Gull Dupont win by default. I know he's right, but I am distraught. I cannot marry Uncle Justus. You do understand? But I can't go back to Hangtown either."

"But you're a strong young woman. You can fight Gull Dupont, and win too."

"No, I can't. I *was* strong. When I arrived in Hangtown I believed I could do anything. I had no idea a person could suffer so much. I don't want to walk back into the fire. I've been burned enough."

"I understand." Aunt Elizabeth pushed aside her empty plate and clasped her hands together. "But a door meant to be opened—the one you should walk through—is not always easy to open. We tend to think the hard and rocky road, beset with dangers, is the wrong one. We think a smooth highway indicates the right path. It's human nature to seek the easy way. But it's not always the best way."

"You mean Hangtown is the hard way, don't you?"

"Yes. No one wants to fight. It's natural to avoid conflict. But at times it's necessary if we are to hold on to what's been given us. The world is full of bad apples—people who would like to take what we have. You have to learn to confront them."

"True."

The ladies sat a while sipping their coffee, enjoying the moment. Then Aunt Elizabeth set down her coffee and looked directly at Madeline. "You like Jesse?"

Madeline paused to form an answer. "He saved my life when I was injured and freezing to death in a blizzard. And he organized the search for Caroline. We are in his debt."

"I know he did those things. But do you like him?"

Even longer pause. "I don't know how I feel about him ... he's very nice looking."

They laughed.

"Yes, my great nephew catches the ladies ' eyes," said Aunt Elizabeth. "But Justus has kept him busy learning the hotel business day and night for years. He's had no time to court a woman. He's twenty-six, and very eligible, you know. Someday he will inherit the Hangtown hotel and be as wealthy as his uncle. Give him some thought."

"I have."

"And?"

"If I marry Jesse I'll get stuck in Hangtown the rest of my life and never inherit my uncle's medical clinic, which he promised to me."

"Medical clinic?"

"My uncle is a doctor, married, but never had children. He promised to leave me his clinic because I assisted him for years when we lived in Independence. I want to help sick and injured people find health again."

Mrs. Miller seemed thoughtful. "I see," was all she said.

Soon the elderly woman stopped talking about Jesse. Madeline was grateful.

***

"Did anything come for Miss Whittaker?" Uncle peered over the front desk looking for any recently delivered parcels.

"Two items. Flowers and a box. Looked like chocolates," said the clerk. "Your nephew took them. Said he'd deliver them. That was early this morning."

"Thank you," said Uncle Justus.

Uncle Justus was still in the lobby when Jesse walked through the door, his travel pack hoisted on his shoulder. He saw his uncle, nodded, and approached the desk.

"What are you doing back here? I thought you left."

"Can't. My horse has thrush," said Jesse. "Too many miles on wet ground. He needs treatment before he can ride."

"You going to find another horse or wait it out?"

Jesse dropped his heavy pack to the floor with a thud. "Haven't decided yet. I don't like pushing him so soon after an outbreak, but I don't want to spend money on another horse either. Have you seen Miss Whittaker?"

Uncle Justus turned to the desk clerk. "Get him a room."

"Yes, sir."

He turned back to Jesse. "Drop your pack in your room and come to my office. We need to talk."

***

Jesse saw Madeline's eyes get wide when he approached Uncle's office. Her desk was located right outside his office door.

"Jesse, you're back. So soon?"

"I'll tell you all about it at dinner," he said, tipping his hat. "If you're free?"

She nodded.

Once in Uncle's office, Jesse plopped himself down near the fire in the visitor's chair. He had been summoned to Uncle's office so many times since he was a kid. He was unfazed at today's indictment. Uncle liked to battle on his own turf, that's all.

"Your great aunt tells me Miss Whittaker is considering leaving my employ and returning to Hangtown," said Uncle. "She says you offered to help her win back the money the Casbah owner swindled from her. Is this true?"

"It is."

"Are you thinking of escorting Miss Whittaker to Hangtown yourself?"

"If she agrees to accompany me, yes."

"That does make things easier, for you, I suppose," said Uncle.

"What do you mean?"

Jesse watched as Uncle leisurely lit one of his ever-present cigars. Something was on Uncle's mind, for sure. Jesse shifted in his chair, growing impatient with the way Uncle was drawing this out. Finally Uncle's cigar was lit and he took a long drag.

"After all I've done for you, nephew, you could at least play fair when it comes to Miss Whittaker."

"What are you talking about?"

"The gifts I ordered for her never made it to her room. If they had been delivered, she would have mentioned them as soon as she reported this morning. Clerk tells me you walked off with them."

Uncle sent the flowers and chocolates? Jesse felt sick. He blew out a big, noisy breath. "I ... uh... thought they were from someone else, Uncle. I'm sorry."

"That drunk New York friend of hers?"

"New York jackass."

Uncle laughed. "Well, if Miss Whittaker agrees to accompany you back to the mining camp, make sure she goes in comfort. Take my carriage. I'll send your horse back with the pack train next time it heads up to camp. Your horse will need more time to mend, anyway. Thrush develops slowly and heals the same way. The ground will be damp another month. No use injuring him further."

"Thank you." Jesse felt the tension drain from his shoulders. This meeting with Uncle was going better than he expected.

"As for expenses, have the cashier front you Miss Whittaker's travel expenses. And ..." said Uncle, poking his cigar in Jesse's face, "... don't you dare pressure the young lady, you hear? If she wants to stay here and work for me, you leave her alone. I'm not happy she's thinking of leaving us, but I don't want to get in her way."

"Thank you."

"And Jesse—I'm docking your pay for the chocolates and flowers."

CHAPTER TWENTY-NINE

"I do believe you will be sick of me by the time we reach Hangtown," said Madeline as she gazed at the countryside through the tiny stagecoach window. "Even married people don't spend this much time together."

Jesse smiled. Over his dead body would he reveal his jubilation about spending one whole week traveling alone in this bumping, rocking, swaying carriage with the lovely Madeline. No rugged trail, no freezing mornings, no aching legs and buttocks, no dread of Indians nor fear of bandits could drag his soaring spirit back down to Earth. It was floating in Seventh Heaven, and there it would stay, untouched by mortal pains until she agreed to be his wife.

To fill the long hours on the trail, at least an hour a day they read books they'd brought with them. Madeline did a little needlework when the sun was on her side of the carriage, but mostly they chatted—often the ride was too bumpy to do anything else—about her life in the East and Jesse's childhood with his parents in the Yerba Buena trading post before its name changed to San Francisco. Before his parents' deaths and the death of hers.

Every few hours the coach stopped to change to fresh horses and exchange mail and/or freight. Every night they pulled into a different stagecoach stop to eat, sleep, and share conversation with other travelers. After a few days all the stagecoach stops looked alike.

"I wish I could have spoken to William before we left," volunteered Madeline late one afternoon.

"He didn't respond to the note you sent?" asked Jesse.

Madeline shook her head. "I've heard nothing. I was hoping to get some assurance he's recovered from … that night."

"If he were ailing, the Winston would have called a doctor to tend him. He's fine. Probably busy setting up his new bank. And I have a wish too."

"Oh?"

"I wish you'd tell me who slammed a rifle butt into your back."

Madeline made a face. "It's embarrassing."

"Because someone did it or because I saw the evidence?"

She squeezed her eyes tightly shut for a moment. "Both."

"Surely it wasn't Caroline?" said Jesse.

Her eyes flew open. "Of course not."

"Your pa?"

Madeline grimaced. Jesse saw it and reached across the carriage for her hand. "Your pa?" he repeated.

Madeline shook her head. "I was struck with my own rifle."

Jesse waited.

"Mr. Dupont hit me with my own rifle," she said.

I knew it. Gull was without scruples.

"It was the night we arrived in Hangtown when he came upon us burying Pa in the woods and accused us of murder. I was scared out of my wits. Caroline was too. I didn't know who he was or his intent, so I ran for my rifle, but he got to it first. Then he hit me."

Jesse scooted across the carriage to sit next to her. For a long while they sat together in silence as the sun dipped low in the West. Leafless winter trees appeared black against the fiery glow of an orange-red sky when the stagecoach pulled up to another stop for the night.

***

With the help of the stagecoach driver Madeline hoisted her skirts into the coach and sat down, smoothing her enormous crinoline around her. She had worn her scarlet dress several times already this trip, but thankfully there was no visible dirt.

Despite her tired clothes, she felt refreshed this morning. Jesse had paid the innkeeper extra to send a copper tub and hot water to her room before bed. A hot bath and shampoo last night coupled with biscuits and coffee this morning had renewed her as nothing else could have. They would arrive in Hangtown by dinnertime tonight. It was going to be a good day.

Jesse climbed into the coach a few minutes after she did. They had already exchanged morning greetings at breakfast, so he took his seat across from her without a word as he had every day for a week. They sat like this for a long time, which was odd, because the stagecoach driver ordinarily rushed his guests at scheduled stops.

"I wonder what's taking so long this morning," said Jesse.

"I've no idea."

There was a sound of movement outside the coach, then the door clicked open. William Blakely's face appeared in the doorway, blotting out the morning sun like a dust storm across the plain.

"William?" said Madeline.

"How fetching you look this morning," he said. In one fluid movement he was in the coach and seated next to her. "I thought I'd join you for the remainder of the trip." He turned to Jesse and tipped his hat. "Mr. Garry."

Jesse gave him a barely perceptible nod in return. His face was inscrutable.

"How nice to see you again," she said. "But Hangtown? What about your work in the city?"

"I've more important work here," he said. "I'll tell you about it once we arrive." He was all smiles as he voraciously took in Madeline's elegant city attire. "And besides, with so much gold being mined, Hangtown might need a solid bank in which to store it."

"Have you mended completely?" She cocked her head to assess the spot where Jesse had whacked him.

"Aw, it was just a scratch," said William, smoothing his hair. "It takes more than a little lamb punch to keep me down."

Madeline smiled at William. Jesse chewed his bottom lip.

"You owe Miss Whittaker an apology, sir," said Jesse.

William stopped fawning over Madeline. "And a good morning to you, too, sir. Perhaps you will explain to her why you followed our carriage to the wharf like a viper slithering after a mouse."

Jesse shifted forward menacingly on the carriage bench and locked eyes with William. "Why don't you move over and give the lady some room? Your hips are practically smooching hers."

"I'm quite alright, Jesse," said Madeline. "But truthfully, William, you were out of order that night. I know the liquor was to blame, but still ..."

"Then I apologize, sweet Madeline," said William. He lifted his hand to her lips and kissed it.

Jesse crossed his arms across his chest and clenched his jaw.

"And Jesse," she added, "you should apologize to William. You struck him without even trying to reason with words."

"Mr. Blakely and I will discuss the events of that night later," was Jesse's tart reply, "alone." Then he grabbed his travel pack, pulled out a book, and though it was too dim in the coach to see the words on the page, pretended to read.

Madeline was anxious as the stagecoach pulled into town that afternoon. Memories of this place and what happened here were still vivid. The truth was, after losing Pa and Caroline, the money she'd lost to Mr. Dupont didn't seem as it important as it once did, though she still needed it to travel back to Independence, and she could earn it anywhere. She pulled the curtain aside to look at Hangtown as they entered the main street. Then she closed her eyes and slumped against the side of the carriage. Maybe she should have stayed in San Francisco and searched for work at another hotel.

"Madeline, are you alright?" asked Jesse.

"You're tired, aren't you?" asked William. "I'll book us two rooms as soon as the stagecoach stops."

"I'm alright," she said. "Memories, that's all." She forced a smile. "A room sounds nice."

***

Jesse directed Madeline to the Garry, of course. When William followed them, Jesse stopped walking and pointed to the Casbah across the street.

"I will lodge at the same hotel as Madeline," said William.

"We're full," said Jesse.

William's expression grew hard. He opened his mouth as if to protest, closed it again, then turned to Madeline. He reached for her hand as before and put it to his lips. "I'll come by for you tomorrow, dear one. Say, at noon, after it warms up a little? We can bundle up and go for a drive. I'll find a hack somewhere, or we can ride horseback."

"That sounds lovely."

Thisbu man does not give up. What does she see in the philandering clodpoll?

After Jesse watched William cross the street to make sure he entered the Casbah, he picked up Madeline's bags and escorted her into the lobby of the Garry. He stood a moment and looked all around, expecting to witness some disaster unique to his brother's management involving raging fire or stinking barnyard animals, but the hotel looked the same as when he had left weeks ago.

Clint left the lobby desk when he saw Madeline and Jesse.

"Well," he said, "a thousand grubby miners out panning for gold, and we've got the diamond of the first water right here in our lobby."

Madeline blushed. "Good to see you again, Mr. Garry. I had no idea you were fond of Shakespeare."

"Not fond. Uncle forced us," said Clint.

Jesse gave his brother a hug. "Clint, get a room for Miss Whittaker. Send up a tub and hot water. It was a long trip and she's tired. You can fill me in about the happenings around town after dinner." He turned to Madeline. "Miss Whittaker, I need to speak to you about something of a business nature. Can you spare some time at breakfast?"

Madeline agreed to meet Jesse in the morning at seven-thirty. He carried her bags to her room and they parted. After dinner was over and darkness had descended—when the rare brave traveler showed up needing a room—Jesse joined Clint in the lobby. Tien, afflicted by fever, had retreated early to his tiny room for the night. Biscuit had gone home to his cabin a little way up the hill from the hotel hours ago. The lobby was empty when the brothers sat down.

"So," said Jesse, scanning the hotel again, "the place looks good. Still standing. Have any problems while I was away?"

"No," said Clint. "We were full up mostly every night. Had the usual saloon fights about town. No shootings, though. It was pretty quiet. We still need another set of hands around here."

"I'm working on it. What about Gull?"

"He struts around town like he owns the place. I'd like to be in the room when he hears Madeline Whittaker's come back. I'm sure he thinks he's got away with the crime of the century. He probably thought she was gone for good."

"Probably," said Jesse. "The bastard hit her in the back with a rifle."

"What?" Clint drew back.

Jesse told his brother the awful story.

"I'll kill him," said Clint.

"No, I will," said Jesse. "And the body of her father is missing. She told me where he was buried. I found the grave. Body wasn't there."

"Gull?"

"Probably. Don't know. With no body, her story about him coming upon them in the woods falls apart. And Caroline can't confirm anything Madeline says. But it could have been an animal." Jesse ran his hands through his hair as if to clear his head. "No body, no evidence. What about Moore?"

"All he cares about is making money. If he knows she's back, I don't think he's worried at all about her testimony."

"I agree. Anyone come forward with information about Harlin?"

"Nothing."

At Harlin's name the brothers grew quiet. They sat in silence a moment, mourning their friend. Jesse stared at his empty hands on his lap.

"Ah, I forgot," said Clint. "Tien has been asking about your return every day for days. He seems worked up. I asked him why he was bothering so much about you, but he couldn't or wouldn't say. You should look in on him."

"I'll do that."

"And Jesse," said Clint with a smile, "Congratulations."

"Huh?

"You brought her back."

Jesse blew out a noisy breath and shook his head. "She doesn't want to be here. Says Hangtown is the last place she'd choose to live because she lost her pa and sister here."

"Then why did she come back? Not because she's in love with you."

Jesse grimaced. "I promised to help her get her money back from Gull."

"Good luck."

"I know," said Jesse. "And even if the miners string up Gull, whether she gets her money back or not, she still might leave. She hates this place, and her doctor-uncle says he will leave his medical clinic to her. She wants to go home to practice medicine."

"Too bad. Someone should write a book on how to win a woman's heart when she's grieving and hellbent on leaving the area," said Clint.

"There's worse," said Jesse.

"What's worse than her hating this place?"

"Her fiancé from back home looked her up in San Francisco and followed her to Hangtown. Thinks he's going to have a good time with her before he returns to New York City." Jesse clenched his fist.

"That fancy easterner who's staying at the Casbah? Big tall guy with slicked hair and spectacles?"

Jesse nodded.

"He's got money," said Clint. "Why aren't they married?"

"Her pa didn't like him."

223

"But her pa is dead."

"Makes him bolder." Jesse shook his head. "She's smart but not like that. Five minutes with the guy and any man can figure out what he's like. Her pa did the right thing."

"What about Uncle? Biscuit insists he was after Miss Whittaker."

"He was."

" Did he propose? Did she reject him?" Clint was on the edge of his chair.

"I think so. When I saw him last, he wished me good luck."

Clint let out a whoop. "The stars and moon are aligning in your favor."

"I don't know about that."

"Try harder, brother. Try harder."

After Clint retired to the room the brothers shared at the back of the hotel, Jesse walked to the kitchen for a glass. He filled it with well water from the pump outside the kitchen door and carried the water and an oil lamp to Tien's room. He knocked but there was no answer, so he opened the door a few inches and looked in.

Tien was asleep, looking small and pathetic on his old rope bed. Jesse quietly entered the room, set the glass on the bedside table, then touched the old man's forehead. He was hot with fever. Jesse saw a small book nearby, so he laid it on top of the glass to keep out dust and crawling things. Then he dipped a clean handkerchief he pulled from his pocket into the last of the water he found in the pitcher on the washstand. He wrung out the excess, folded the handkerchief into a rectangle, and gingerly draped it over Tien's forehead. Having done all he knew to help, he picked up the oil lamp and tiptoed out of the room.

It was nearly midnight. He should have joined Clint in their room—it had been a long day for him too, but he was restless. He needed fresh air to clear his head. He walked through the lobby and out the door of the Garry, intending to sit and think a while on a bench in front of the hotel. However, no sooner than he had sat down, he saw William Blakely and a local harlot walk out of the Casbah. He watched them walk arm in arm down the street until they entered the fandango hall not far from the Garry.

CHAPTER THIRTY

Madeline stood in front of the tall wardrobe taking an unusually long time to decide what to wear. She had two engagements with young men today, a situation so rare it demanded exceptional attire, and for the first time in her life she had a desirable choice of frocks to impress. Not her new scarlet with the glass buttons. She had worn it too many times on the stagecoach ride with Jesse. Her old gray wool was warm but boring. She wondered what Jesse's favorite color was, then caught herself. *Why am I concerned about his tastes?*

Finally, she chose the copper silk she had worn to dinner with him and his uncle and great aunt. It was fancy for day wear, and lightweight silk wasn't ideal for late winter weather, but she had seen his eyes light up when she walked into the dining room, so he must have liked it. She would throw on extra wraps if the afternoon was not warm enough for a comfortable ride with William.

The dining room was full when Madeline arrived, but the waiter guided her at once to their table. They exchanged greetings and ordered breakfast.

"Room comfortable?" asked Jesse.

"Very. Especially the bath. Thank you. Speaking of which, I can't take advantage of your hospitality. Your uncle paid me everything I was owed when I left the Bridlington, so I have funds to pay for my room."

"There's no charge for you."

"No, no." She shook her head vigorously. "I've learned my lesson. Your uncle was generous toward me when I served at the Bridlington. I naively accepted gifts from him, and it caused a terrible misunderstanding." She winced at the memory of Uncle Justus' proposal. "I can't let it happen again, and besides, we don't know how long I'll be lodged here."

"If you feel obligated, you can always help here in the hotel. You know how to run a front desk now."

"True, but ..."

"It's not like I'm straining to make a job for you. And you needn't worry—I have no hidden motive. I've made my motive when it comes to you quite clear, have I not?"

"You have."

"I need help at the front desk. Daytime coverage is a problem. Frequently Clint and I have business outside the hotel. Biscuit is busy in the kitchen and Uncle doesn't like Tien working out front. Tien has plenty to do anyway with cleaning rooms and helping Biscuit."

"I see."

"Surely you won't go and work for Moore's Mercantile?"

"When pigs fly."

Jesse laughed.

"I wouldn't work for Mr. Moore or Mr. Dupont no matter how much they paid. A couple of blackmailers, they are."

"Then manage the desk. It will pay for your room and board plus two dollars a week in gold dust. Until the trial, of course. Then we will talk again about your plans. Can you start tomorrow?"

"Yes. And thank you. Was that the business you spoke of last night?"

"Mostly," said Jesse.

The waiter arrived with their food. They made small talk while they enjoyed the hot biscuits, red eye gravy, and coffee. After they finished, Jesse pushed aside his plate and leaned forward on the table. "What about Mr. Blakely?"

Madeline looked over the top of her coffee cup at Jesse. "William? What would you like to know?"

"Are you going to marry him?"

"I can't believe you asked me such a question. It's decidedly personal, and truthfully, none of your business."

"It is my business. You haven't given me an answer yet."

What is it about this man? So easy to talk to. So disarming. More like an old friend even than William—and they came from the same neighborhood. "He has not proposed."

"Not yet," said Jesse. "And when he does?"

"I have thought about it a lot, but it's confusing. I was once very in love with William, so

228

when he proposed I was thrilled. But Pa was hotly against the union. I never understood why Pa disliked him so much. My siblings and I never dared question Pa's judgment. William was charming and attentive, courteous to my folks. He dressed well, earned good wages—he even owned a house. When we left Independence I shut my heart to him, figuring I'd never see him again. His presence at the Bridlington has stirred up all kinds of feelings again. I'm entirely alone now. A marriage proposal from a man from home is tempting."

"So that's what Mr. Blakely is to you— home?"

"Yes, home. Family. Love. Memories of a happy life."

"Then what keeps you from accepting him?"

Madeline sighed. "I keep thinking about Pa. I should respect his memory."

"You know what to do," said Jesse. Then he lowered his voice an octave and said in his best fire-and-brimstone preacher voice, "Obeying your parents is the fifth commandment."

Madeline blanched.

"I'm sure you'll make the right decision," he added. He folded his napkin and set it on the table. "I have to get to work. One last thing: Can you look in on Tien? He was terrible feverish last night. With all your doctoring experience at your uncle's side, maybe you can help him. Biscuit and Clint make lousy nurses."

"Of course."

"His room is behind the kitchen."

***

Biscuit wasn't in the kitchen when Madeline arrived, so Clint showed her to Tien's room, where she quickly assessed she needed willow bark powder to bring down his fever. He was delirious, but other than a very warm forehead, she saw no serious symptoms, such as rash or lesions, though his lips were dry and cracked. She tried to get him to drink from the water glass by his bed, but he took little. She dunked the damp handkerchief she found near him in cold water and laid it on him again, then returned to the kitchen.

"Biscuit," said Madeline, "greetings from San Francisco. Do you have willow bark powder and some grease?"

Biscuit gave Madeline a distant look, as if his mind were in another room. "I heard you returned."

"Yes, I've returned, at least temporarily. Tien is feverish. Do you have willow bark powder?"

"I have bacon grease but no willow bark powder. Moore will have it."

Madeline took some bacon grease on a rag from him, thanked him, went to her room to retrieve her wraps and bonnet, then descended the grand staircase to leave the hotel for Moore's. Once outside, she was delighted to feel the midmorning sun's rays on her back. The sky was clear and blue. Another sparkling mountain morning. A horseback ride through the trees with William would be invigorating.

She was aware of the usual male stares as she walked the few hundred feet to Moore's, but she wasn't the same innocent girl who had arrived here six months ago. She was refined, even hardened, and no longer intimidated. She had as much right to walk this street unmolested as any other Hangtown citizen. Let them stare. Having lost everything in this place made her fearless. She had nothing left to lose.

However, she didn't relish encountering Mr. Dupont again, not even in the public square. And as for Mr. Moore, she refused to fear him.

I can do this, I can do this, I can do this. She steeled herself for an encounter with the wily merchant.

She entered the mercantile to the usual tinkle of the bell over the door. She glanced all around for Mr. Moore but didn't see him or any other person, so she approached the counter to wait. As she did, she heard the sound of someone on the stairwell near the rear of the store. She looked in that direction, saw lime green and purple ostrich feathers swaying over the top of a leather boots display, and groaned.

"Is Mr. Moore in?" she asked as Mrs. Moore stepped behind the counter. "I'm in need of medication."

Mrs. Moore scowled as she eyed Madeline up and down, up and down. Madeline noted the woman was dressed as garishly as before, her scraggily gray hair longer and dirtier. It hung in oily strings over the yoke of her soiled nightgown. And she was still barefoot.

"You foolish thing," spat the crazy old lady. "I warned you about selling your body to break into theater. Serves you right if you got the clap."

Madeline's hand flew to her mouth. "Ma'am, is Mr. Moore available?"

"Carry on like a sporting lady, and you'll end up under a pile of rocks like that other floozy."

"Mother! I told you to stay in your room" bellowed Alonzo Moore from the top of the stairwell. "Get back up here."

Madeline trembled. Floozy? Pile of rocks? What did the old crone mean? Madeline was paralyzed, her shoes stuck fast to the wood plank floor as she tried to make sense of the insensible. After some scuffling noises upstairs, a woman's shrieks, then the sound of a door banging shut, Alonzo came down the stairwell and stepped behind the counter. He smiled and greeted Madeline as if nothing unpleasant had transpired at all.

"Miss Whittaker, how nice to see you in my store again. Did you have a satisfactory stay in San Francisco?"

"Uh, yes. San Francisco is quite—"

"I'm sure it is," said Alonzo. "What can I get for you today?"

Madeline purchased willow bark powder and escaped Moore's as fast as she could. The clock in the store told her she had thirty minutes to make an elixir and give it to Tien and to freshen up before William called for her. She hurried back.

She prepared the elixir the way she had seen Uncle Finney do it dozens of times. But Tien labored to swallow, consuming about half before falling back down on his pillow in an exhausted heap. Half was better than nothing. She would try to get him to finish the rest before nightfall. She wiped his cracked lips with a thin layer of bacon grease then left for her room to rearrange her hair and check her outfit in the looking glass. Once she was satisfied with her reflection, she laid her coat, shawl, winter bonnet, and rabbit muff on the bed and picked up a book.

She would have preferred to wait in the lobby where there were people to watch, but Ma said a young lady should not look too eager when a man is calling.

Time passed. No one called from the desk. Her stomach rumbled. The biscuit and red eye gravy were a distant memory. *What is taking him so long?* Madeline didn't own a timepiece, but she still had Pa's. She opened the bottom drawer of the high dresser and fished around among her small array of underthings until she found it. Twelve forty-five. Lunch was being served in the dining room.

Perhaps he left a note at the front desk. Room service was spotty since Tien fell ill, so she didn't bother using the bell pull. Frustrated, she left her room and went down to the lobby. Clint was on duty.

"Has anyone left a note for me?"

"Aw, you look pretty today, Miss Whittaker."

"Thank you."

Clint turned to check her mailbox behind him. "No note."

Her shoulders sagged. "If anyone delivers a message, please send it up to me right away instead of leaving it in my box. I'll be in my room."

"Of course."

***

Jesse sat at his desk in his office struggling to keep his mind on his work. Recordkeeping was the most tedious of the many tasks involved in running a hotel—his mind wandered repeatedly from the business at hand.

How far out of town had that cad Blakely had driven Madeline? It wasn't too late in the season for a sudden snow squall to bury the trail back to Hangtown. The witless greenhorn would probably get them both lost and need to be rescued.

Was this trip into the lush countryside around Hangtown part of Blakely's proposal plan or a second attempt to molest Madeline? Either scenario made Jesse crazy. He slammed shut the ledger and walked out of his office.

"Clint," he said as he neared the lobby desk, "I'm going to lunch. Everything alright around here?"

"All quiet."

"Good. Look, I've asked Miss Whittaker to start on the desk tomorrow. This will give you more time for repairs around the hotel. Can you take a few hours in the morning to help her get accustomed to the routine?"

"Sure."

"She won't need much instruction. She performed well at the Bridlington," said Jesse.

"I can show her around right now if you want. She's upstairs in her room."

"No, she's out riding with a friend."

Clint shook his head. "I just saw her. She came down looking for a message in her box, but there was none so she went back upstairs. Told me to call her if anyone left a note. She's waiting to hear from that city guy, isn't she?"

They didn't go riding. Jesse yelped on the inside. "Probably."

"Then she'll wait all day. Two miners carried him into the Casbah before sunrise. Passed out drunk as a lord," said Clint.

"You sure it was him?"

"Saw him myself. He's the only fella in town who dresses like a banker."

"He's sleeping it off while she waits in vain upstairs. I'd like to rearrange his face." Jesse smacked a clenched fist into his hand.

"Since he didn't show, why don't you invite her to eat lunch with you in the dining room or send a plate up to her?" said Clint.

"I would, but I don't want to embarrass her." Jesse paused, his eyes lighting up. "Wait a minute." He abruptly left the desk and went back to his office. He emerged a moment later with his hat and coat. "I'm leaving the hotel for a while."

"I'll see she gets some lunch," said Clint. "Where you going?"

***

Jesse stepped into the Casbah lobby and marveled. Despite the ugly qualities of the owner, the Casbah was beautiful: clean, tastefully decorated, with thoughtful lighting, an ambience exuding elegance and calm. It had been a few months since he'd set foot in Gull's place. The man had spent some money on it.

"Can I help you?" asked the young man at the front desk. Hank, Jesse thought his name was.

"I'm looking for William Blakely."

Hank looked Jesse up and down. "Aren't you the owner of the Garry across the street?"

"Manager."

Hank rubbed his thumb up and down his jawline.

"I made acquaintance with Mr. Blakely on the stagecoach from San Francisco," Jesse explained. "I heard he drank a little too much last night. I'd like to check on his welfare."

"Ah. In that case, room twelve. Up the stairs and to the right."

Jesse thanked him and ascended the stairs. Soon he was standing at the door to William's room. He knocked. No response. He turned the knob. The door was unlocked.

He entered the room as silently as possible and locked the door behind him. Blakely lay on his back the length of the bed, still in his street clothes and shoes. Jesse could easily imagine two men carrying the unconscious sot into this room, one at each end, huffing and puffing, swinging him back and forth to hoist him high enough to throw him onto the bed. The do-gooders hadn't bothered to cover him with a blanket even though the late winter nights were still nippy. No matter. Though it was well past noon, William Blakely was dead to the world.

A pair of woman's stockings lay draped over the footboard.

Jesse walked to the washstand and grabbed the water pitcher. In a moment, its full icy cold contents drenched William's head and torso, doing what an intruder in his hotel room had failed to do—wake him up. He woke yelling in protest loud enough for lobby guests to stop what they were doing and look up to the second floor. He bounded out of bed like he'd found a viper in it.

"What are you doing?" yelled William.

"You're late for an appointment with a lady."

William shook his head, befuddled. "What's it to you?"

"You don't deserve an afternoon with Miss Whittaker," said Jesse. But he wasn't standing still as he said this. With both hands he grabbed William by his collar and lifted him off the ground.

"Put me down!" William choked out. "You'll kill me!"

Jesse held him in the air, his jaw bulging with anger. Their eyes were inches apart. "I don't like you," he said.

"I don't like you either," said William, still dangling. His face was red, his eyes bulged. "Put me down!"

"I will kill you," said Jesse, "and not quickly either, if you so much as touch Miss Whittaker or play with her heart. Do you understand?"

William looked at Jesse with naked hatred. "I understand."

Jesse let his drippy prey dangle a few seconds then released his grip. William dropped to the floor with a thud.

"I will go to the law about you," said William, righting himself and loosening his collar where it had chafed his neck.

Jesse headed for the door. "I *am* the law," he said.

***

Someone was knocking on her hotel room door. *A message from William?* Madeline opened it to see Clint holding a tray of food. "A note for me?"

"No," said Clint. "I thought maybe you'd like some lunch before the dining room closes."

Her heart sunk with a thud. "How thoughtful of you. Thank you."

Clint left and Madeline set the tray on the end of her bed. No note. Why hadn't he sent a note? Maybe he was sorry he'd traveled all the way to

Hangtown. Surely it wasn't nearly as grand as New York City. Maybe he had already arranged to return to San Francisco.

Was he hurt or sick? Had she angered him somehow?

She looked down at her fancy frock and felt silly being all dressed up only to sit around her room, so she changed into her boring gray wool to match her mood. She left the tray untouched.

Around five o'clock she decided to check on Tien before heading for the dining room for the evening meal. As she passed the kitchen on the way to his room, she saw Biscuit at the big black cookstove. She said hello and he responded similarly, though he returned to his dinner chore immediately without the usual chit chat he liked to indulge in with her. *He must be very busy.*

She knocked on Tien's door, but there was no answer so she turned the knob and went in. Tien lay unmoving as before. She felt his head. Still hot. "Poor old man." She grabbed the pitcher on the washstand and left the room to get water from the well pump. When she returned she made an elixir as before, then gently shook him to wake him. When he opened his eyes and realized who she was, he became animated, trying to speak.

"Mr. Tien, what is it? Do you have pain anywhere?"

Tien's hands flailed and shook as he tried to form words, but she could make no sense of whatever it was he was trying to say. He was obviously upset, frustrated because he couldn't communicate.

"I'm sorry, Mr. Tien. I don't understand," she said. "Are you hungry? Do you need something?"

Tien fell back onto the pillow, exhausted. Saddened because she could do so little for him, she freshened the handkerchief with cool water and laid it on his head. The elixir would reduce his fever for a few hours and make him feel better, but she knew it would not cure him. Only time would do that.

"Do you have pain in your body, Mr. Tien?" Again, no answer. She left the room and quietly closed the door. She was passing through the lobby on her way to the dining room when Clint called her.

"Miss Whittaker, a note for you," he said, holding out a white envelope. "It just arrived."

Madeline took the note and thanked Clint. Then she carried it to her room to read in private. It was from William. He was apologetic. They couldn't ride this afternoon because he had been detained by business. But could he call on her at six for dinner together in the Garry dining room?

At once her gray mood turned pink. The day was redeemed after all. She flew to her wardrobe and pulled out her copper silk, her now favorite frock. She tidied the loose tendrils of her hair, pinched her cheeks to redden them, and wished for cologne. She took a long, appraising look at herself in the glass.

Her face fell suddenly. *Will William drink too much again?* Her dark thoughts were interrupted by someone pounding madly on the door.

"Miss Whittaker!" shouted Clint. "Miss Whittaker!"

"Wake the dead, Clint," she said as she opened the door. "What is it?"

"Rockslide. There was a rockslide up the North Fork. Three miners were buried alive in their tents. Their injuries are bad."

Her hands flew to her face. "No!"

"The miners carried them all the way down the mountain. Can you come? We laid them out on the floor in the hallway near the kitchen."

"Of course," she said. "Let me change into something more appropriate." She started to shut the door then stopped. "No," she said, suddenly overcome with guilt for worrying about soiling her favorite dress when men were dying, "I'm coming right now."

CHAPTER THIRTY-ONE

Madeline took a deep, steadying breath as she descended the grand staircase to the lobby behind Clint. She knew the scene she was about to walk into would be traumatic, and if she did not get control of the rising panic, she would faint. She had seen plenty of blood and gore, had her hands in it many times as an assistant to Uncle Finney. Now she must carry herself like a real doctor, like Uncle Finney, and mentally prepare herself to serve those in need.

However, even in the worst trauma cases in which she had assisted, there was usually only one injured person, and he or she was nearly always fixable because treatment was spearheaded by her competent uncle, working in his well-stocked medical office, whose presence calmed her as he quietly and confidently explained to her what he was doing to minister aid to his patient and why.

241

Now there were three crushed and crying men, possibly mutilated beyond repair, steps away, and they were depending on her alone to heal them. The commotion as they neared the kitchen made her heart pound. Dusty miners milled about the victims, who lay on crude gurneys on the floor, dripping blood into the wood planks. The miners had done their best to support broken bones and stem the bleeding with whatever they could find. Two of the injured moaned and yelled intermittently. The third, the youngest, about the same age as her oldest brother, lay silent and still, his head wrapped with strips of wool blanket. She consciously fought despair when she saw blood seeping through the layers. His injury was serious, possibly fatal.

"Clint, run to Moore's. Get whatever he has for trauma. Bandages, ointments, sutures, needles, scissors, salves, anything at all. Laudanum or any pain relief he has on the shelf. By now he's surely heard about the rockslide. He'll know what to send."

"Yes, ma'am."

Clint took off and Madeline turned back to the crowd, half searching for Uncle Finney's face. Everyone seemed to be looking at her expectantly. Then she saw Jesse. He gave her a "I'm so glad you're here" look of relief.

"Jesse, I need your help," she said.

"Tell me what to do."

She gestured for him to step away so she could speak in private. "The young man's injuries are the most serious, I think. I am uncertain if he can be saved, but I'll try. The blood seeping from his head wound gives me hope he's still alive. The other two have broken bones for sure, which won't kill them, but internal injuries might. I'll start checking for those right away. Meanwhile, I want you to tend to the young man."

"Yes."

"First, unwrap the blanket strips from his head and look for debris. If you see rocks or twigs or anything foreign, gently pull it out. Second—and most important—stop the bleeding. We can't wait for supplies from Moore's. Can you get me some clean kitchen towels?"

Jesse ordered a nearby miner to run to the kitchen for towels. The man left at once.

"Press a towel into the wound. Press gently but firmly. If his skull is crushed and you push too hard, you could press bits of bone into his brain. If one towel becomes sopped, use another, but don't remove the first towel. Put the second towel on top of the first. Do this until the bleeding stops or at least fifteen minutes. After fifteen minutes you may see some oozing or trickle for up to forty-five minutes."

"I understand."

"I have to help those two other men now," she said. "Thank you."

"They will be alright, Madeline."

She nodded courteously to confirm his assessment, but inside she was quaking. She worked automatically, asking herself a few times what Uncle Finney would do when a situation presented beyond her knowledge. She checked for broken bones, punctured lungs, and internal bleeding. Soon Clint returned with his arms overflowing with brown paper packages. She untied them and began to work like a machine, shooing away anyone she deemed not helpful, requesting help from anyone who seemed capable and calm.

Occasionally she glanced at Jesse, who sat on the floor, cradling the young man's head while he patiently put pressure on the wound. Maybe it was because he seemed, in that moment, as kind as her compassionate Uncle Finney. Maybe it was because the young man reminded her of her dear brother John. She was uncertain of what she was feeling, but the scene caused her heart to move within her.

***

Several hours later, Jesse and Madeline were alone with the youngest injured miner. The other two miners had been carried upstairs, where they were stable and sleeping. Madeline sat on the floor, holding the young man's hand and checking for a pulse from time to time. He was still alive.

"I think your work is finished here," said Jesse. "I'll help you to your room."

Madeline—exhausted, dazed, and bloody— gave him a blank look. "I think I was supposed to have dinner with someone tonight."

There s never a picnic without at least one ant. Jesse sighed a big ole silent sigh. "You were expecting Mr. Blakely?"

"I think so. But I haven't seen him. Would you mind checking my box at the front desk?"

"I'll be right back." He walked to the lobby. Of course there was no note. Pen and paper require sobriety. He returned to the hall outside the kitchen. "No note."

Madeline signed audibly then looked glumly at her blood-stained dress, too exhausted to respond.

"When did you last eat?"

She thought a minute. "Breakfast, I think."

"Stay here, I'll get you something from the kitchen. I'm hungry too. And I'll bring us some wet towels to clean up with."

Jesse returned after a few minutes with bread, butter, plates, and towels. "Couldn't find much," he said.

"It looks delicious," she said, reaching for a towel. She began to wipe away the blood from her arms and hands as best as she could.

"Would you like to eat under the stars?" he asked. "The sky was as clear as crystal earlier tonight. We should see lots of stars. The bench out front makes a great viewing seat. I'll get you a blanket."

"Sure."

Jesse left and came back quickly with the blanket. He helped her off the floor, and they walked to the bench in front of the hotel and sat down. He was right. The sky was ablaze with stars. Jesse draped the blanket over Madeline, then he sat down next to her and they ate their bread and butter in silence, too spent to talk. They watched drunk miners sashay their way down the street through the middle of town.

"You did very well today. Saved those men's lives. But I'm sorry you ruined your dress," he said, nodding toward her skirt.

Madeline glanced down again at the wide swath of blood splatter across the front of her nearly new, once shimmery copper gown. "Service requires sacrifice. It was my choice, though I couldn't have done it without your help and the others. As for savings lives, I'm worried about the young man."

"He has youth on his side."

"True."

He looked at Madeline in the filtered light of the Casbah across the street. Her face was lined with pain. "Are you alright?"

"I hope he lives," she said, her voice cracking.

He pulled a corner of the blanket aside and took her hand in his. She did not pull away. "We are required to do only what we can do. What we cannot do we leave to God."

She nodded.

They sat together in silence, Jesse contemplating the softness of her hand and his incredible luck, when two dark figures emerged from the fandango hall, singing and laughing like braying mules. They reflexively looked toward the noise. He could not make out their faces, but the voices were obviously those of a very drunk man and woman.

As they drew closer, the bawdy lyrics became more discernible, embarrassing Jesse in front of Madeline. The wobbling duo stopped in front of the Casbah. They fumbled in their inebriated states, trying repeatedly to open the door, laughing hysterically when they failed. Once it was open, the lobby chandeliers created perfect silhouettes of Mr. William Blakely and a local harlot.

Jesse watched in disgust as Blakely lingered in the doorway to give the woman a long, dramatic kiss while fondling one of her nearly naked breasts. *Does Madeline recognize him?* He turned toward her Madeline to see her staring at the bald display of debauchery across the street, silent tears streaming down her cheeks. Then she looked at Jesse. When their eyes met, she covered her face with her free hand.

Jesse reached across her shoulders and wordlessly, gently, and tenderly cradled her head in his hand, guiding her to rest it on his shoulder. She did not protest.

CHAPTER THIRTY-TWO

"Mr. Tien, good morning. How are you feeling today?"

Madeline touched the old man's forehead. His fever had finally broken, leaving him clammy, his hair stuck to his face. His eyes fluttered open at the touch of her hand. He looked dumbly at her, his countenance one big question.

"You were very sick, Mr. Tien. I'm relieved your fever is gone. Are you thirsty?" She held up a glass of water. Tien leaned forward and took a sip, then fell back on the pillow, eyes fixated on her, blankets pulled up to his chin as if to protect himself from a ghost.

"I know you're wondering why I'm here," she said. She smiled, but he continued to stare. "I've been taking care of you. You've been quite ill and haven't eaten in three days. How about I go to the kitchen and fetch you some breakfast."

"Mr. Garry. Jesse," croaked Tien.

"Jesse? You want to see Jesse?"

Tien nodded, still clutching the blanket for dear life.

"You want Mr. Garry to bring you breakfast instead of me?" *Mr. Garry was right. They only accept doctoring from a woman when they are writhing in agony or bleeding to death.*

"Alright, I'll ask Mr. Garry to bring you breakfast."

Tien shook his head. "Talk to Mr. Garry."

"Oh, I see. I'll send him in."

She left Tien's room and walked to the lobby. Clint was on duty. "Have you seen your brother? Tien is asking for him."

"Tien doing better?"

"His fever is gone. He should be on his feet in a day or two."

"Good," said Clint. "I'm sick of doing women's work."

Madeline drew back and gave him a look.

"No disrespect, Miss Whittaker. But I'm supposed to be doing repairs and more important chores around the hotel."

"Where is Jesse?" she repeated, ignoring the slights.

"Upstairs with the injured miners. Room seven."

She headed for the grand staircase. She found the door to room seven ajar. "Jesse?" she said, poking her head through the open door.

"Come in."

"How are your patients doing this morning, Dr. Garry?" she asked.

Jesse smiled. "*Your* patients are stable, Dr. Whittaker. But the kid is still unconscious."

She moved to the side of the bed where the young man lay deathly still. She checked his pulse. "At least he's alive."

"Thanks to you."

She ignored the praise. "I wish Uncle Finney could see this. Never in my life did I imagine I would set so many bones in one day," she said as she surveyed the room. "Now this one," she said to Jesse, after cheerily greeting one of the older miners laid out on the floor, "see his bandaged foot? You need to keep it elevated to keep the pressure off the wound. This promotes healing. A pillow is perfect for this." Jesse pulled a spare one from the lone bed in the room and handed it to her. "Lift his leg, please," she said. Jesse complied while she arranged the pillow under the man's calf, which lifted his bandaged foot off the floor.

The man groaned in pain. "Send the feller away," he said to Madeline. "He's not gentle like you are. And you're prettier too." She turned her head and covered her mouth to stifle a laugh.

"See? You're good at this," said Jesse, smiling.

"No, my uncle is good at this." She continued to check on each man's bandages, poking and prodding, asking about pain, while Jesse observed. She promised to send up a meal to the two conscious patients, then she and Jesse exited the room.

"How long will you lodge the men here?" she asked.

"I've been wondering myself about that. Uncle keeps tabs on the hotel's receipts in my monthly report. I'll have some explaining to do if I let them stay too long. Plus I put all their medical supplies on hotel credit."

"I'm sure they'll pay you back," she said. "Why doesn't this town have a clinic? Hundreds of miners, maybe thousands live around Hangtown and the other mining camps. What with their inevitable injuries and fevers, there must be constant need for a doctor and beds for seriously sick or injured patients." *And a church with a minister to bury people.* The thought of Pa's unceremonious interment followed by his removal from his grave still stung.

"They're waiting for you to build one," said Jesse.

"Don't be cheeky. You didn't answer my question."

"If the men need a clinic, it's to cure them of gold fever," he said. "It's the main malady around here. Ordinary life like a clinic, church, or school isn't important when the big nugget is around the next creek bend. Gold is all they care about."

They started down the grand staircase. Then she remembered. "I looked in on Tien this morning. His fever is gone, and he asked to speak with you."

"Me? Why?"

"He didn't say. I'll relieve your brother of desk duty now. But promise me you won't force Tien back to work right away. He's very weak. Let him rest at least a day."

"Whatever the doctor orders," said Jesse.

***

Jesse opened the door to Tien's room and was instantly repulsed by the sick room smell. *How does she do it?* He approached the bed. Tien had fallen back asleep. Jesse shook him.

"Tien. Tien. How are you feeling? You want to talk to me?"

Tien, weak and disoriented, took a minute to fully awaken. Then he tried to sit up. Jesse saw him struggle and gently supported his arms until the old man was upright.

"You don't have to sit up if you want to talk," said Jesse, remembering Madeline's admonition about letting him recuperate.

Tien shook his head. "Tien have something," he said. Then he turned himself in the bed, picked up his pillow, and felt along the seams until he came upon a slit. He put his hand into the slit and fished around for several seconds until he found what he was looking for. He pulled out a red silk drawstring pouch embroidered in an Asian motif with birds and leaves. He opened the pouch and pulled out a clump of long blonde hairs. Jesse's eyes got wide. It was obviously human hair. Tien handed the pouch and hair to Jesse.

"Where did you get this?"

"Tien show you." He started to get up but fell back onto the bed, dizzy and weak.

"Drink some water," said Jesse, offering the glass.

Tien drank thirstily. "Good now," he said.

Jesse helped Tien to his feet, pausing a moment to let him catch his breath. When he pointed toward the kitchen, Jesse nodded and led the way. The kitchen was empty when they arrived. "Buttery," said Tien pointing to the cramped lean-to pantry where Biscuit stored the bulk of the hotel's foodstuffs. This time Jesse let Tien lead the way to the back of the room. He squatted on his haunches and pointed to a crack in the wooden leg of a very

252

old, very dry table piled high with sacks and crates. "Hair in here."

Jesse squatted to see for himself. The table leg had split with age, creating a sharp crevice about four inches high and deep enough into the leg to be visible from a few feet away. "How long ago did you find this?"

Tien counted on his fingers. "One, two, three weeks."

Right after I left for San Francisco. The wheels in Jesse's mind started turning rapidly. A hunk of human hair wouldn't catch on a table leg so near the floor unless a person was bending low or lying supine on the floor.

Cold fear washed over Jesse. It was all too easy to imagine someone on the floor, bound in rope or some other restraint, rolling back and forth in a panicked attempt to free herself, catching her loose hair in the crack in the table leg.

That someone was Caroline Whittaker. "Have you told anyone about this?"

Tien shook his head.

Jesse put his fingers to his lips. "Tell no one."

Tien nodded.

"Go rest now, Tien. I'll take care of this."

Tien left the kitchen, and Jesse stepped into the dark hallway where the three miners had received medical treatment the night before.

Every inch of him wanted to find Biscuit and beat him to a pulp, cut off his balls for good measure, then hang him, but acting without considering the consequences was the mark of a fool. Hangtown miners respected Jesse as the law, a mantle passed to him from the even more respected

Harlin Turpin. He must swallow his anger and act like a lawman.

Biscuit was the likely culprit, but without evidence there was no case. Jesse needed to investigate. He didn't yet know what happened to Caroline Whittaker, whether she was dead or alive, or even if someone had harmed her. She still could have run off and married a miner. But one thing he knew for sure: Caroline Whittaker had been in the hotel buttery at some point, because no one for a hundred miles had long gold hair like that girl.

Looked like she had indeed arrived at the hotel that fateful day months ago when he invited her to speak with him about working at the Garry. She hadn't turned up her nose at his offer and failed to show. Something had happened to her after she arrived at the hotel kitchen.

He strode into the lobby where he saw Madeline behind the desk. The red silk bag burned like a hot coal in his pocket. Guilt tugged at him for withholding what he knew, but until he was certain of Biscuit's involvement, he figured silence was best. He donned his most inscrutable poker face.

"You know where Clint is?"

"He said he'd be in the barn sharpening knives," said Madeline.

"And Biscuit? He's not in the kitchen."

"Doing the marketing," said Madeline.

Jesse thanked Madeline then walked around the back of the hotel to the barn. He found Clint as Madeline had said, operating a sandstone grinding wheel. Piercing metal screams filled the barn with each push on the foot pedal.

"Clint," Jesse yelled over the racket, "I need you to stop what you're doing and come with me."

"What's up?" said Clint. But he didn't stop. He kept pushing down on the foot pedal, filling the barn with the screeching of metal and flying sparks.

"Stop that," yelled Jesse.

Clint ignored his brother. "What now? I'm busy."

"I have important work for you."

Clint scoffed. "You never have important work for me. What is it this time? Some dirty chore Tien can't do cause he's sick? I've had enough of filling in for the Chinaman, thank you."

There was some truth in what his little brother said. Clint was two years younger than himself, but at twenty-four, he was a grown man. Yet Jesse rarely trusted him with serious responsibilities. And as Madeline had said, he also rarely "exercised charity" toward the only immediate family member he had left in this world.

"I have a lead on Caroline Whittaker."

Clint halted the grinding wheel. "Tell me."

Jesse pulled the silk bag from his pocket and showed Clint the hunk of blonde hair. He shared the story Tien had related and explained about the crack in the table leg.

Clint fingered the hair. "The roots are still there. Her hair got pulled out hard. Quick too."

"I saw that," said Jesse. "Listen, I want you to search Biscuit's cabin with me. He's in town getting supplies. Afterward he'll return to the hotel to prepare lunch. We have time."

"If I don't show up to help with the midday meal, he's going to wonder where I am, and Tien's no help. Madeline says he's too weak to be on his feet."

"Don't worry about Biscuit. He'll have no idea we're searching his cabin, and he can fix a meal by himself for a crowd if he has to. He's done it before."

"Hopefully he won't ask Madeline to help him in the kitchen," said Clint.

Jesse sobered. "Get the horses ready as fast as you can. And say nothing to Madeline."

"You gonna let her know we're leaving the hotel? We usually tell her our whereabouts."

"I'll think of something."

CHAPTER THIRTY-THREE

Madeline was wiping down the front desk when the expected note arrived from William. She fingered the envelope. Whatever he'd written was going to hurt. Not that it mattered. She was done with Mr. William Blakely, even if he was her last treasured connection to home. She opened the envelope and unfolded the plain white paper inside.

Dearest Madeline,

> *I extend my sincere apology for not keeping our dinner appointment. I received a message from San Francisco and had to take a stagecoach yesterday afternoon back to the city immediately. I promise to make this up to you when I return. And I have a plan to help*

you acquire your medical clinic!
Please reply by sending a letter to
the Winston.

Fondly,
William

Madeline stared at the words, more disappointed than shocked. Somehow she was expecting this. *So, who was pawing that harlot's breast last night, William—your ghost? This must be why Pa disliked you so. And I'll get a medical clinic on my own, thank you very much.*

She tore the note into tiny bits and stashed them in her bag to burn later. *The big liar is probably sleeping it off at the Casbah right now.*

Jesse entered the lobby and approached the desk. She greeted him with a smile as she always did.

"Clint and I have business. It will keep us away from the hotel for several hours. Can you manage alright without Tien?"

"Of course. I'll be fine. Biscuit is the one who needs help. We have a full house for lunch."

"Biscuit can manage the kitchen alone. And if he asks for your help, do not leave the desk."

"You don't want me to help Biscuit?"

"No matter how much he complains, stay on the desk."

What an odd thing to say. "I understand. Shall I assume it's alright to look in on the injured miners?"

"I hope you do."

Jesse left and she went back to work. Traffic was slow this morning, so she finished cleaning up the desk, tidied the lobby, watered a few plants, then decided to sweep the boardwalk in front of the hotel—Tien's job. She drew out the chore, enjoying the fresh morning air and greetings of passersby. Hangtown was a pretty little place in the daytime: bustling with productivity, blessed with crisp mountain air, and only a few drunks to sully the picture. It might be nice to live here, once the town became more civilized with churches, schools, more stores to choose from, and of course, women and children.

Someone called her name. She recognized the voice. She stopped what she was doing and braced herself to engage with Mr. Gull Dupont.

"Miss Whittaker," said Gull, tipping his hat, "I see you found a position here at the Garry. I thought your move to San Francisco was permanent."

Madeline took in the customary dark suit and dashing hat Gull wore. She was no longer intimidated by this man. Anger had overcome fear. He lived well and dressed well because of his profitable hotel, yet he had greedily enriched himself by stealing everything she and Caroline owned in this world, leaving them penniless. Who knew how many others he had stolen from. He had threatened to expose her to Harlin Turpin as a murderer, and now Mr. Turpin was dead by the hand of an unknown party—maybe even this man standing before her.

Mr. Dupont is nothing but a fraud. A loud, bullying fraud.

"I'm sure you would have preferred I had stayed permanently in San Francisco."

"What an uncharitable thing to say, Miss Whittaker."

"Seeing you makes my charity sprout wings and fly. I returned to Hangtown to participate in a trial."

"Now that's a smart girl. You want your security money back."

"Yes, I want my money back," she said.

"When will the trial be?"

"Soon. It's been nearly six months. You would hang onto my money forever, but the law will not allow it."

"The wheels of justice turn slowly, Miss Whittaker."

"Maybe so. But if you have your way, they will be halted altogether."

"What is the source of this unjust accusation?" asked Gull. He had the audacity to turn up his mouth in a little smile.

He thinks I'm funny. "You know the answer," she said, her voice rising. "The miners will hear our complaints in due time, and you will be punished."

"I think you misunderstand how things work in this town," said Gull.

"I understand *exactly* how things work in this town." With an angry flourish of her broom she whisked a pile of dirt over his shoes. "Good day, Mr. Dupont."

That man. She heard Mr. Dupont chuckling as he continued down the street, which made her angrier.

***

Jesse and Clint tethered their horses to a tree in the small clearing where Biscuit had constructed his modest, one-room cabin. Jesse's chest constricted with a creeping fear as he glanced toward the door.

Simultaneously he was flummoxed. What were he and Clint doing up here investigating an old man's cabin, looking for Caroline Whittaker in the least likely place to find her? *Biscuit?* Was he capable of harming anyone? The man had a dirty mind and a tongue to match, but he was in his fifties, in poor shape, his life marked by nothing but idle talk and a penchant for fried potatoes.

Clint got to the door first. He unlatched the multiple wood crosspieces and pin bolts designed to keep out bears, and in a minute he and Jesse were inside the dingy cabin. They left the door open for light, but the cabin was shadowy in places, especially the corners. The room was small and sparsely furnished: washstand, bed, table, wood stove, large bear rug, oil lamp, and a few personal items including Biscuit's pipe and tobacco. Like all miners' cabins Jesse had been in, including Harlin's, there was little to investigate.

"Too small to hide a person," said Clint.

Jesse nodded. "Nothing suspicious. Let's check outside. Look for a grave or any physical evidence that Caroline was here."

As they left the cabin, they set the crosspieces on the door as they had found them. The ground around the cabin was packed down and cleared as one would expect—no sign of a grave. Clint suggested they search the woods, so they did.

"We're looking for a needle in a haystack," said Clint, returning to the front of the cabin. "Woods for miles. If he buried her, her body could be anywhere in these mountains."

"I know. I was hoping he had slipped up, maybe left some evidence behind," said Jesse as he scanned the area.

"You think he knows we suspect him?" asked Clint.

"He knows nothing. Let's get back to the hotel." Jesse began to untie his horse.

"You going to talk to him? Show him the hair Tien found?"

"I have to," said Jesse. "I wouldn't be doing my job if I didn't interrogate him."

"It's pointless. He'll deny everything."

"I know it." Jesse mounted his horse. He sat a moment and swept his eyes in all directions, searching. "Do you feel it?"

"Feel what?"

"Evil," said Jesse.

***

The lunch crowd had dispersed by the time the brothers rode up to the hotel. Jesse put Clint in charge of the horses as usual, then he headed for the back door of the kitchen to speak to Biscuit. He desperately wished he didn't have to have this conversation with his longtime kitchen help. The thought made him sick. He did not want to entertain the notion that Biscuit was capable of harming Miss Caroline. The awesome responsibility for her life and his middle-aged employee weighed on him. If Biscuit was guilty, it was Jesse's job to get justice for Miss Caroline. Biscuit would hang.

He consciously reached back into his memory, trying to recall anything from his time with his father to strengthen him in the moment, but memories of his father grew dimmer each year. It was because of Uncle's hours of forced reading and memorization sessions that Jesse was able to bring up the words of statesman Patrick Henry.

Adversity toughens manhood, and the characteristic of the good or the great man is not that he has been exempt from the evils of life, but that he has surmounted them."

How will I surmount this? He opened the back door to the kitchen.

"Hey, Jesse," said Biscuit, looking up from the dishpan where he was cleaning lunch dishes. "Tien needs to get better faster. We had a full house for lunch today."

"So I heard." Jesse steeled himself. "Can you sit down a minute so we can talk?"

"I gotta get this kitchen cleaned up and start preparing dinner."

"This is more important."

Biscuit looked quizzically at Jesse then shook the water from his hands, dried them, and pulled up a chair. Jesse grabbed a chair also and seated himself directly across from Biscuit.

"What is this all about, Jesse? I got a lot of work to do, and I'm behind schedule now because I didn't have Tien or Clint to help with lunch."

"Patience."

Jesse pulled the red silk pouch from his pocket, carefully keeping his eyes on Biscuit to observe his reaction. He saw Biscuit's face fall when he pulled out the long hunk of blonde hair.

"Do you know what this is?" said Jesse.

Biscuit took a long while to answer. "Hair," he said. He began to fidget with his fingers, rubbing his index finger against his thumb repeatedly.

"Yes, hair. Do you know anything about it?"

"Why would I know anything about hair?" said Biscuit. "What is this all about, Jesse? I have work to do."

"I know you have work to do. I have work too. I found this hunk of hair in your buttery. Do you have any idea how it got there?"

"Of course not. Hair is hair. It could have come from anyone long ago. Why are you bothering me with this when I'm loaded down doing the work of three people?" Biscuit was growing more agitated, shifting in his chair, his finger and thumb rubbing madly like he was trying to start a fire.

"Any idea whose hair this is?" asked Jesse.

"No."

Clint was right—Biscuit would deny everything. But Jesse had to try. "Biscuit," he said, "are you absolutely sure you did not see Caroline Whittaker come to the kitchen to keep my appointment with her months ago on the day she went missing?"

Biscuit sat upright now, arms crossed over his chest, looking Jesse straight in the eye. "I am sure," he said. "And you're crazy to try and pin some crime on me." His voice was rising now. "That whore ran off with a miner. Everybody knows it. The pretty ones always throw themselves at the ones with money."

"I don't know if she ran off with anyone," said Jesse. "And neither do you. I know I found what looks like her hair in your buttery, stuck in a cracked table leg near the floor. Any idea why her hair would get caught at the bottom of a table leg? What was she doing on the floor of the buttery?"

"Why do you ask me these stupid questions? I don't know! I don't even know if this is her hair.

You don't know either." Biscuit stood up. "Are you done? I have work to do."

"I'm done," said Jesse. "You can get back to work. Thanks for giving me some of your time."

***

Jesse and Clint lay in their beds in their dark hotel room, the clock ticking towards midnight. For over an hour they had dissected Biscuit's possible involvement in Caroline's disappearance. Jesse, convinced by Biscuit's defensive demeanor and scant physical clues, concluded he was likely involved. After much discussion, Jesse fell asleep, but slumber eluded Clint.

"Jesse, wake up! Wake up!"

"What? Fire?"

"I figured it out."

Jesse hoisted his drowsy self onto his elbows. "Figured out what?"

"Biscuit has a cellar." Clint paced with barely controlled energy.

"How do you know?"

"He had no food in his cabin. Remember? Tobacco but no food."

Jesse fell back onto his pillow in a stupor.

"Think about it. We unlock the bear-safe crosspieces and enter the dark room. Scan the interior—in your head, I mean," said Clint.

"Yeah."

"Take an inventory of everything we saw. There was no food. Biscuit had tobacco in his cabin but no food. No sacks. No crates. His food must be stored somewhere else."

"A cellar. You're right," said Jesse. "There was no food in his cabin. How did I not notice that?"

"He probably stores all his foodstuffs down cellar to protect them from bears. We're always hearing stories around the camps of bear break-ins." Clint stopped pacing and stood over Jesse's bed. "How soon can we go back and search?"

"We'll wait until Biscuit is occupied with breakfast preparation," said Jesse. "Go back to sleep now."

Clint returned to his bed and Jesse pulled the covers up to his chin.

"Good job," he said.

They hardly slept. Around 5 a.m., when Biscuit ordinarily showed up at the hotel to start work, the brothers were up and dressed and waiting in the kitchen, drinking coffee. Five a.m. came then 5:15. Biscuit did not appear.

"You think he's sick?" asked Clint.

"No," said Jesse. He pulled his gun from his holster, looked at it as if to make sure it was still there, then reholstered it. "He's trying to figure out what to do. Or maybe he's gone."

"What do you mean?"

"I knew showing him the hair would alert him of our suspicions. He may not even be in his cabin anymore. He could have fled after dark."

"Old Biscuit? In the dark? It's too dangerous. There are grizzlies out there."

"Fleeing after dark is a risk alright, but it's a risk he's willing to take to avoid the noose. If he harmed Caroline Whittaker, a noose is not a risk. It's a certainty."

"What are we going to do?"

"We will wait until 5:30. Then I'll wake Tien and ask him to get breakfast ready for the guests. Then we will head back up the hillside."

"That's fifteen minutes from now."

266

"Go to Malachi's and get me a horse. Mine won't be here from Frisco until next week."

Clint nodded.

Jesse stood up. "Pack extra cartridges."

CHAPTER THIRTY-FOUR

A pink-and-yellow sun peeped over the eastern hills as Jesse and Clint started for Biscuit's cabin—a sun lovely to behold but shedding insufficient light for travel through dense woods.

Jesse, in the lead, guided his horse slowly, partly because of poor visibility and partly because he dreaded what he might see and what he might have to do at Biscuit's cabin. Biscuit had been angry at his questioning a day earlier. How was he feeling this morning after brooding all night over their testy conversation? And almost as bad: If Biscuit was innocent of harming Caroline Whittaker, how would the three of them recover from this deadly accusation? The fact was, Jesse needed Biscuit's cooking skills. Replacing him would be difficult.

But right now, when it came to Caroline Whittaker, all Jesse could see was Biscuit's guilt.

When they arrived at the cabin, they tethered their horses, grabbed their rifles, and walked in silence to the door. Clint knocked. No answer. He knocked again.

"Biscuit, you there?" yelled Jesse.

"Think he's dead?"

Jesse shook his head. "Door is bolted from the outside. He's taken off somewhere. Let's go in."

Clint unbolted the door as before. The brothers clutched their long arms, ready to shoot, and entered the cabin, surveying the little room in every direction, half expecting Biscuit to jump out, but there was no sign of the old cook.

"Rug," said Jesse.

Clint bent down and pulled back the bear rug. As Clint had deduced, a cellar door was hidden beneath it.

"I'll go down," said Clint.

"You don't know what you'll see."

"Neither do you. I can handle whatever's down there." He jerked his head toward the corner of the room. "I'll need that oil lamp."

Jesse picked up the lamp, lit it, and handed it to Clint. "Go ahead. Be a hero," he said with a wry smile.

Clint set the lamp aside then pulled up the rope attached to the heavy plank door. The brothers peered into the inky darkness. "Here goes," he said as he grabbed the lamp and stepped onto the ladder that disappeared into the black hole.

Jesse's heart pounded as he watched his little brother descend the ladder. At least he knew—based on the exterior cross pieces on the door—Biscuit was outside the cabin somewhere and not lying in wait, armed, inside the cellar. He would have liked to join Clint on the ladder, but he needed to keep an eye on the cabin door. They couldn't risk being trapped inside on the off chance Biscuit returned and bolted the door from the outside.

Jesse strained to hear any sound coming from below. "See anything?" he yelled from above.

"Not much. Food. Root vegetables. Barrels. Boxes," was Clint's muffled reply. "The usual cellar items. It's dark in here." He paused. "There's a pile of blankets in the corner."

A few seconds later the screaming started. A woman's piercing screams filled the cramped cabin with her terror.

"Clint, what's happening?" yelled Jesse. "Clint!"

All Jesse could make out in the dim light of the oil lamp were indistinguishable shadows. The screams continued for several minutes. He checked the door for any sign of Biscuit, then ran to the cellar opening.

Finally, blessedly, the screams reduced to whimpering. "Send down a clean blanket," yelled Clint, who was halfway up the ladder now.

Jesse fetched a blanket off Biscuit's bed. "Is it Caroline Whittaker?" he said, handing over the blanket.

Clint nodded. "I think she's lost her mind. I'm trying to calm her down."

Jesse exhaled a giant breath. They had found her.

"Talk quietly. If you're calm, she'll be calm."

"I'm trying," said Clint. Then he disappeared again into the cellar.

Jesse looked through the doorway of the cabin for the umpteenth time, listening and watching for any sign of Biscuit, then returned to the cellar entrance. Their lives could be in danger if

Biscuit realized he was cornered. Jesse kept up this back-and-forth exercise for several minutes.

Finally, after what seemed like an eternity, he heard Clint call from below, "We're coming up. She can't walk. I'm going to carry her."

"Need help?"

"Grab the lamp from me as soon as you can reach it."

In a moment the top of Clint's head emerged on the ladder and he handed the lamp to Jesse. Over his shoulder was Caroline Whittaker wrapped cocoon style in Biscuit's blanket. Her long blonde hair, dirty and tangled, hung down in a rat's nest. She was thin, barefoot, and filthy. Clint set her down gingerly on Biscuit's bed. Mute and frightened, she looked wide eyed at Jesse.

"You're alright now, Miss Whittaker. Biscuit's gone. We're taking you home to Madeline," said Clint.

Caroline did not respond. She clutched the blanket high, covering her nose, her eyes two big saucers, taking in her surroundings like it was the first time.

"We gotta get out of here," said Jesse. "We don't know if Biscuit's gone for good or fetching water at the creek. I don't want to run into him while Miss Whittaker is with us."

"She rides with me," said Clint. He turned to Caroline. "Miss Whittaker, we're taking you home. Is that alright?" Caroline did not speak. "I'm going to pick you up and put you on my horse. It's a short ride back to town."

Jesse watched as Caroline calmly allowed Clint to pick her up and set her on his horse, then Clint mounted the saddle and sat behind her. Once they were situated, Jesse set the cross piece and pins on the cabin door and started for his horse.

The first shot rang out as he grabbed the reins. Clint's horse reared up then fell back to earth with a thunderous crash. Two more shots rang out, causing the horse to thrash crazily under Clint's reins.

"Go!" shouted Jesse. "Go!"

Caroline became hysterical, screaming and crying uncontrollably.

Jesse couldn't tell which direction the shots came from, though he saw the explosions of dirt they spewed into the air when the bullets slammed into the ground. He yanked his horse's reins and ran into the nearest clump of hardwoods.

From his hiding place he watched Clint until he was out of sight. Caroline's screams continued down the hillside. He dismounted and squatted down, listening for movement. The only thing he knew was Biscuit was armed and somewhere near the front wall of the cabin. The only thing he heard was the blood rushing past his ears, the breathy snorts of his horse, and an occasional twittering bird. It was dangerous to leave the tree camouflage. He and his horse were easy targets.

"Clint will have fifty men or more here in less than an hour. Give up now, Biscuit."

No response. The man owned no horse. His bad knees made horseback riding impossible. He couldn't possibly outrun Jesse on his old fat legs.

"You'll be dead before dinner if a mob of miners gets a hold of you," yelled Jesse. "Give up, Biscuit. They'll tear you apart like a pack of wolves. Give up now and I'll keep you away from them."

Jesse pondered the wisdom of his hasty promise. Even he couldn't stop an angry mob of armed miners. But he had no idea what to say to motivate Biscuit to put down his weapon. Biscuit was going to hang—there was no question. The only enticement Jesse could think of was to offer him a quicker, less painful end than being thrown to angry miners.

"I have information," yelled Biscuit. "Promise me you won't turn me over to the miners."

"What do you have?"

"About Gull."

Gull? Jesse was all ears, but he was also suspicious. Was Biscuit lying to save himself from being skinned alive by bloodthirsty miners? He didn't know the old man well. All of their encounters had been at the hotel, and all of their business had concerned the hotel and its operations.

"Promise," repeated Biscuit.

Jesse deliberated. He wasn't one to break a promise—he wouldn't turn Biscuit over to the miners. But he knew he couldn't save him. He would hang from a tree whether the miners got to him or not.

"Alright. I won't turn you over to the miners. But if you're lying, I'll tie you to a tree myself and set a pack of wolves on you," yelled Jesse.

"I'm coming out."

From his hiding place Jesse watched as Biscuit emerged from a thicket not far from the cabin, holding his rifle high above his head. As he approached the cabin door, he lowered the rifle to the ground and waited. Once he was convinced Biscuit was no longer a threat, Jesse emerged from the tree stand with his rifle aimed at Biscuit's head. On his belt was a rope he'd removed from his saddle.

"Face in the dirt," ordered Jesse.

"Aw, Jesse, my knees," whined Biscuit. "Down!"

Biscuit labored to lower himself. Once his nose was pointing toward Hades, Jesse created a hitch knot with an adjustable loop and placed it around his neck. "You move wrong, and I'll pull this rope and squeeze the breath out of you," he said. "Now get up. We're going back to town."

Biscuit struggled to right himself. Jesse could have helped him, but his mood had turned black, and there was always the chance Biscuit could strike him with a fist if he got too close.

Once Biscuit was standing, Jesse tied the other end of the rope to his saddle. He used a shorter length of rope to tie the cook's hands behind his back. He mounted his horse and urged the animal forward. He yanked Biscuit's leash.

"Start talking."

***

"One moment." Madeline was already dressed when she heard the knock on her door, but she took a second to check her reflection in the looking glass. She smoothed her hair and opened the door. Her eyes met Clint's, then moved downward to his bundle. She gasped.

"It's Miss Caroline," said Clint. "May I lay her down on your bed?"

" Of course." Clint entered and gently set Caroline down on the bed. She was awake but still not speaking. "Oh God, oh God. Where did you find her?"

"In a cellar."

"A cellar?"

"I gotta go, Miss Whittaker. Jesse's up the hill behind the hotel taking care of ... I'll tell you everything later," said Clint. "Miss Caroline has been through a lot."

Madeline locked the door behind Clint and approached the bed. She clasped one of Caroline's hands in hers. "Caroline?"

Caroline stared as before, her eyes big and round.

"Caroline, it's me, Madeline." She waited for Caroline's response, but none came. "Are you hungry, sugar bun? I'm going to get you something from the kitchen. I'll be right back."

Madeline locked the hotel room door behind her and flew down the grand staircase to the kitchen. "Tien," she said. "I need food. Caroline has been found." She glanced around the kitchen. "Where's Biscuit?"

Tien nodded and pointed to a plate he had already prepared, covered by a kitchen towel. He poured a cup of coffee and added some cream. "For Miss Caroline," he said as he handed the items to Madeline. "Happy day," he added.

"Thank you. And Biscuit?"

"Not work today," said Tien.

Once back in her room, Madeline helped Caroline sit up in the bed to eat. Caroline moved slowly, slothlike, as if every movement required painful physical effort.

"Are you hurt anywhere?" asked Madeline.

Caroline did not answer. She did, however, eat all the eggs and toast Tien sent up and drank the entire cup of coffee. When she was finished, she slumped down on the bed and closed her eyes. Soon she was sound asleep.

"What happened to you, dearest sister?" said Madeline in a low voice. "Where have you been?" She gazed at her little sister a few minutes. "I have to go downstairs to my duties," she finally said. "There's no one to cover for me in the lobby right now. I'll check on you every hour, sugar bun."

Slowly she left the room, watching for movement from the bed, but Caroline didn't stir. She locked the door and headed for the front desk.

Madeline was cleaning the lobby when she saw a few men on horseback in front of the Garry. She watched with interest as their number grew to six then twelve, then doubled in a few minutes, then doubled again until their combined shadows noticeably reduced the light coming through the window.

Curious why the miners would leave their gold pans on a sunny day, she stepped out onto the boardwalk to inquire.

A dozen pairs of eyes turned to Madeline. The men stopped talking among themselves and courteously removed their hats. She saw a strange discomfort in their faces. Her heart began to pound. Surely this assembly had something to do with Caroline's disappearance, or rather, her appearance.

"Good morning, sirs. Could you please tell me why you're all congregating like this?"

A few men exchanged words among themselves in low tones. Others looked down at their horses.

What is going on? "Is this about my sister?"

An older miner close to Madeline spoke up. "Yes, ma'am. We are forming a posse to go after the man who took her."

Took her? Caroline was kidnapped? She grabbed onto a hitching post to keep from falling over.

"Ma'am," the miner continued, "you ought to stay in the hotel until nightfall. There's going to be a hanging."

"Thank you," was all she could get out.

She turned and walked back into the hotel. She felt lightheaded. The lobby was spinning. She grabbed the doorpost, staggered a few feet, then fell into the first chair she came upon.

After a few seconds the dizziness passed. She climbed the grand staircase to check on Caroline, or rather, to assure herself the figure sleeping in the bed upstairs was her beloved little sister and not a dream.

***

"His real name is Guillaume Dupont," said Biscuit as he and Jesse made their way down the hillside toward the hotel. "Guillaume is the French form of William."

Jesse sat on his horse behind the old man to keep an eye on him—and to yank the rope around his neck if he tried anything funny. "He was born in Quebec to a French trapper and Abenaki squaw. He uses Gull because it's easier for Americans to pronounce. Could be hiding from the law in Canada. I don't believe everything he says."

"What happened to the Whittaker sisters' wagonload?" asked Jesse.

"He sold it to Moore."

"And the money?"

"Gull never parts with cash."

"Moore in on it?" asked Jesse.

"Of course. You know what Alonzo's like, grasping and squeezing at every penny. They're twins, those two."

Jesse was gratified Biscuit was talking, but what he'd gleaned so far was not news. He'd heard most of it from Madeline.

"Why'd you take Caroline Whittaker?"

Biscuit went silent.

"I said why'd you take her?" Jesse, furious, jerked hard on the rope around Biscuit's neck.

"Hey!"

"Answer me!"

Biscuit clawed in vain at the rope to loosen it from his neck. "I can't talk without air!"

Jesse was unmoved. "I can pull harder."

"Okay!" yelled Biscuit, still tugging at the rope. "I was trying to get her to tell me where the other box of gold coins was."

"What gold coins?"

"I found two compartments under the girls' wagon when I unloaded it for Gull. One had a box of gold coins in it. The other was empty. I figured the girls had the other box."

Biscuit was working for Gull? My cook was working for my competitor? Jesse couldn't have been more stunned.

Or so he thought.

"Did you find it?"

"No. I searched their room at the Casbah, too. Found nothing."

"Is that the only reason you took Caroline Whittaker and shoved her in your cellar?"

The old cook clammed up again. Jesse waited a few seconds then yanked hard on the rope.

"Ah! You're killing me!"

Jesse glared at his cook's fat, reddening face as he pulled madly at the rope around his neck, groaning and crying, trying to loosen it. Jesse was beginning not to care.

"There's more," yelled Biscuit. "If you kill me you won't know ..." He began to stagger.

Jesse halted his horse, dismounted—quicker than usual—and loosened the rope around his prisoner's neck. "Now you know I mean business," he said. "I'll keep my end of the deal if you keep yours."

Biscuit inhaled deeply, gasping for air. Jesse let him catch his breath a minute, then he mounted his horse again and they continued the slow trek to Hangtown.

"I will repeat the question," said Jesse. "For what other reason did you kidnap Caroline Whittaker?"

Biscuit looked at the ground. "Because she's pretty," he said.

Jesse swore under his breath. The old fool!

"It ... happened. I didn't mean to take her, Jesse, before God I didn't. It's not like I planned it. I don't know what came over me. It must have been the devil."

Jesse stared at his fat old cook in disbelief.

"And once I took her it's not like I could return her to the Casbah. So I held onto her. I didn't know how to fix the mess I made."

"You forced her to write that phony message about eloping, didn't you?"

Biscuit hung his head. "Yes."

"If I find out you touched her, I'll make sure they cut off your balls while you are still alive and hang you naked," said Jesse. "Idiot."

"I didn't do anything to her, Jesse, really I didn't. I know I did wrong in taking her, but the least I can do to redeem myself is tell what I know about Gull."

"I was taught in Sunday School that no one is beyond redemption, but *you* are the one exception, you moron. There's more?"

"That first body they found up by Diamond Spring? Along the creek bank? Sadie Shaw."

Jesse cocked his head and lifted one eyebrow. "Sadie Shaw?"

"Gull was after her husband's claim. He was the young miner from Ohio who struck it big. He and Sadie never set out for San Francisco. Gull lied to hide his plan. He kidnapped both of them and kept them in a cabin somewhere up by Diamond Spring. When he couldn't squeeze the exact location of the big gold strike out of Sadie's husband, he killed her, thinking the husband would give up and talk. But the man wouldn't budge, so Gull killed him a week later."

"The first body had a man's button on it stamped in French," said Jesse.

"Oh that. Gull had a pair of old pants too threadbare to wear anymore. He put them on Sadie so that whoever found her body would think another miner had fallen victim to a claim dispute or some common disagreement between miners."

Jesse removed his hat and ran his fingers through his hair. He was reeling. How long had he waited to have hard evidence on Gull Dupont? So much information. It was hard to take it all in.

"And Harlin?"

"Gull killed him too. A Casbah waiter overheard Miss Madeline tell Harlin about how Gull had dragged them back to town to try them for murder. The waiter told Gull. Harlin was the biggest threat to Gull's plans to hold onto the Whittaker sisters' money."

"How do I know you're not the one who's done all this killing?" asked Jesse. "It's easy to blame it all on Gull."

"If I was a killer, Caroline Whittaker would be dead and buried somewhere in these hills where no one would ever find her. I'm a gold-grubbing stinker alright, but I don't kill."

They walked a while in silence. Jesse wasn't sure who he was angrier at, Gull for stealing everything the Whittaker sisters owned—not to mention the loss of three innocent lives by his bloody hands—or Biscuit for causing so much heartache to Madeline and Caroline.

Poor Miss Caroline. What had she been through all these months? Her suffering was unimaginable.

"And what about the buttery fire? It nearly destroyed the Garry last year. My uncle wanted to kill me. What do you know about Gull's involvement?"

"I'm sorry, Jesse. That was an accident. My fault. I hinted it might be sabotage by Gull to cover my own ass. Gull had nothing to do with it."

After a while the upper story of the Garry Hotel came into view above the trees. As they passed the tree line that marked the clearing to the hotel, Jesse saw the mob of horseback riders heading toward them. He signaled to Biscuit to halt.

Jesse was about to dismount, thinking he could reason with the mob long enough to get Biscuit to repeat his confession before the inevitable happened, when an irate and impatient miner decided justice couldn't wait. He raised his rifle and aimed at Biscuit.

But he missed.

Jesse fell to the ground, splattered with blood and gasping for air, a bullet lodged in his neck.

CHAPTER THIRTY-FIVE

Madeline was working at the front desk when she heard the distinctive sound of a gunshot report from behind the hotel. Everyone in the lobby, including Madeline, stopped what they were doing and looked toward the rear of the hotel. A minute later a crowd of men spilled into the kitchen through the rear door, shouting orders and talking all at once. She heard several voices but recognized only Clint's.

Never a dull moment in this barbaric outpost.

Her first instinct was to run to the rear of the hotel to help, but if the miners wanted the kidnapper dead, this wasn't the time to play doctor, though she was keenly curious as to the identity of the man they had executed. Suddenly Clint ran into the lobby, looking crazed.

"Miss Whittaker, come quick! Jesse's been shot!"

Was she dreaming?

In a moment her legs were moving without any instruction. She ran around the desk and through the lobby to the kitchen after Clint.

There was Jesse Garry, carried from the yard on his own horse blanket and laid out like a corpse on the hotel kitchen worktable. The miners parted to let her through. The sight of Jesse, prone and helpless, gasping for air, blood splattered over his head and torso ...

Oh, Uncle Finney, how I wish you were here to show me what to do.

But these men believed she knew exactly what to do, and they were all watching her. She must not fall apart. She braced herself and began to work, drawing from within the training she'd had by Uncle Finney's side. She began to assess the injury.

"Jesse," she said, peering into his face, "I'm going to take good care of you. You're going to be alright."

She saw cold fear in his eyes, the same fear squeezing her heart.

"Towels! I need towels!" she yelled. Tien ran to a cupboard and returned with a stack. She pressed one into the wound to stop the bleeding. "Where's Clint?"

"I'm right here," he said, stepping forward.

"Bring me all the supplies remaining from the surgical work we did on the three miners a few days ago. Quick. Make sure you get plenty of laudanum. I need to do some cutting to find out where the bullet lodged. I don't see an exit hole." She turned to the men crowded around her. "Is anyone carrying a freshly sharpened skinning knife?"

A miner offered his knife. She thanked him and turned back to her patient. Jesse's skin was ashen, cool, and clammy. She lifted his hand to examine his fingernails. They were bluish. He was going into shock. She pushed down her rising panic. He had lost a dreadful amount of blood.

When Clint returned, she asked everyone to leave except him, Tien, and two miners in case they needed strong arms to reposition the patient.

"I can't stay, Miss Whittaker," said Clint. "I have to get back to the men outside."

"At least tell me how he got shot. Did the kidnapper do this?"

"No. An impatient miner aimed at the kidnapper and missed. Hit Jesse instead."

"Who's the kidnapper?"

Clint paused. "Biscuit."

"Biscuit?"

"I gotta get outside right now and stop the miners before they hang him. I got questions for him." Clint grabbed his hat and ran out the kitchen door.

Biscuit? Not possible. She could not believe it. But there wasn't time to ponder this news. She had managed to get enough laudanum down Jesse's bleeding throat to sedate him. She picked up the skinning knife.

"I'm sorry, Jesse. I so wish we had ether here in Hangtown like they do in the East." And then she began to cut into his neck to search for and remove the bullet.

When she had found it and had stitched up the wound, she arranged for the two miners to carry him to his room, and she asked Tien to send up meals for herself and Caroline. Then she headed for the grand staircase. The climb had never seemed so

285

strenuous. She was exhausted and covered in blood. She changed her clothes and washed herself before approaching the bed.

"Caroline?" Madeline pulled the covers down enough to see her sister's face. "I'm back."

Caroline opened her eyes, made eye contact with Madeline, but said nothing.

"Tien is bringing you a lunch tray, sugar bun. I thought maybe tonight I'd order a bath for both of us. Would you like a nice hot bath? I'll go to Moore's Mercantile and get you a bath bomb too. You like bath bombs. Doesn't that sound lovely?"

Madeline waited. Caroline no longer had an opinion on bath bombs. Madeline noted her sister's eyes following her movements around the room. What was going on in her mind?

She sat down on the edge of the bed. "I've been nursing three miners," she said brightly. "They were injured in a rockslide. One is young and very nice looking. About your age. When he gets better, I'll introduce you."

Nothing.

"I'm taking care of Jesse Garry, too. He was shot by accident. He took a bullet to his neck. I removed it. Uncle Finney would be proud. I believe Jesse—Mr. Garry—is going to be fine. The bullet lodged in his sternocleidomastoid. That's a muscle in the front of the neck, here." She touched a spot on her neck. "He was very lucky. The bullet missed an artery and his windpipe."

Nothing.

Madeline wanted to tell Caroline the good news of Biscuit's arrest, but she feared traumatizing her even more.

"Caroline," she said, "when you're feeling better, we will go to Moore's Mercantile and buy fabric to make you a new dress. You can choose the color. How's that sound?" Caroline loved pretty clothing. Madeline felt certain this bait would raise a response in her little sister, but as before, Caroline had nothing to say.

Someone knocked at the door. Madeline opened it to see Clint carrying an enormous tray of food.

"Tien sent this for you." He set the tray on the bed then signaled he wanted to speak to her alone. They left the room, carefully shutting the door behind them so Caroline couldn't hear.

"I was too late," said Clint. "Biscuit is hanging from a tree at the entrance to town. I didn't get to speak a word with him."

Madeline nodded, too numb with shock to respond. Biscuit's involvement in Caroline's disappearance didn't seem real. His death seemed even less real.

"And Miss Whittaker, I hate to tell you this, but the young man injured in the rockslide? He died about an hour ago."

Clint left and Madeline shut the door behind him. In an instant her legs buckled, and she crumpled to the floor in a heap of bloody skirts.

Caroline was lost to madness and might never return. Jesse Garry—her one real friend in Hangtown—was grievously injured, unconscious, a hole the size of a quail egg in his neck, crudely sewn up by a two-bit impostor posing as a doctor. The friendly but pitiful Biscuit was dead. The hotel would not be the same without him. And an innocent young man she had operated on had been robbed of his life.

What unforgivable sin had she committed to invoke the wrath of Heaven?

***

One week later Jesse stood in front of the looking glass in his hotel room wrapping a thick scarf around and around his bandaged neck. Madeline had said the support would reduce the pull on his stitches, and she was right. With the scarf he could sit and walk normally, but the bouncing involved in a horseback ride was still intolerable.

"How long you gotta go around dressed like a mummy?" asked Clint.

"Until the stitches heal."

"Isn't it hard to turn your head with that thing on?"

"A little," said Jesse. "But at least I still have a head to turn."

"Miss Madeline saved your life."

"I know. You've reminded me every day since I was shot."

Clint squeezed in next to Jesse in front of the mirror and began combing his hair. "You can't put off a hearing in front of the miners forever," he said. "Biscuit gave you the witness you need to arrest Gull. Miss Madeline will be gone as soon as she gets her money back. Got a plan to keep her here?"

"Yes."

"What?"

"Marry her."

Clint laughed. "I'm not putting any money on it."

Jesse scowled, absentmindedly turning toward his brother. He winced with pain. "She hasn't said no."

"You mean she hasn't said yes. That reminds me, I asked Miss Caroline to go riding up to the waterfall with me this afternoon. We are leaving in an hour."

"How did you get her to agree to this? She still isn't speaking."

"Masculine magic. I have it, you don't," said Clint with a smirk as he walked out the door.

Jesse walked to his first-floor office and sat down at his desk, neglecting a stack of invoices and his ledger. Clint was right. He couldn't delay a hearing in front of the miners any longer. A week of recuperation from his neck wound had given him a solid excuse, but his excuse had expired, and he still had not shared with Madeline the information Biscuit had spilled before his execution.

She would inevitably win her case against Gull, and he had assets aplenty to make her whole. But then what? Would she run back to Independence? He wasn't sure he wanted to know.

And what was that nonsense about him not having any masculine magic?

"Hmph. Clint doesn't know what he's talking about."

He got up from his desk and walked to the lobby to speak with Madeline. He knew how to show a lady a good time as well as his smart-aleck little brother.

***

"I know where there's a flower meadow south of here," said Jesse. "It's not as spectacular as the falls but I think you'll like it." He put his hat on his head, Madeline took his arm, and they walked out of the hotel. They garnered a lot of attention as they strolled through town. Jesse was glad. *Let them think she s mine.* After about twenty minutes they were far enough into the countryside to enjoy privacy and quiet.

"Sit here?" asked Jesse, pointing to a fallen log. He first checked the rear of the log for snakes, found none, and urged Madeline to sit down. He sat down beside her. They made small talk while taking in the balmy air, admiring the ring of old hardwoods around the freshly greened meadow, and gazing at the wildflowers. Delicate yellow Monkeyflower, lavender Douglas Iris with striped white-and-yellow center, starlike Baby Blue Eyes, and brilliant orange poppies dotted the meadow like confetti.

"It's like a painting," she said. "Thank you for bringing me here. Though I suspect you have more on your mind than flowers."

Jesse smiled. He reached across his lap and put her hand in his. "Biscuit did a lot of talking before he died. I gleaned details related to your case against Gull—evidence to arrest him—Moore too. I will assemble a hearing with the miners this week. But I must warn you, it will be difficult to bear. Gull will do his best to discount your words, maybe even smear your reputation, though I suspect he will direct his ire at me more than you."

"I understand."

"Biscuit…" Jesse shook his head and looked away. "He was a weak man. Not as evil as Gull, but he did evil things for no justifiable reason. He asked me to tell you how sorry he was for the harm he did to you and your sister."

Madeline squeezed his hand. He proceeded to tell her everything he'd heard from Biscuit on the long walk down the hill from his cabin.

"Gold coins? Biscuit found gold coins on the underside of our wagon? I'm astonished. I had no idea."

"So, you didn't take half of them from the wagon? He said there were two compartments."

"No. Did you find gold coins in Biscuit's cabin?"

"We haven't searched it yet," said Jesse. "Our priority was bringing Caroline back. I'll search the cabin tomorrow. You will win your case against Gull and Alonzo."

"I hope so."

The sun was sinking lower in the western sky, filling the heavens with splashes of resplendent pink and red like delicate watercolors. "It's getting late. We should get back," she said.

"A few more minutes." Jesse lifted her hand to his lips and kissed it. "You still haven't answered my question."

Madeline pulled her hand back to her lap. "I owe you an apology. I've made you wait a long time for my answer. I am sorry."

Jesse's heart sunk when she let go of his hand. *She is going to say no.* "Why can't it be yes?"

"You recently told me you've made your intentions toward me plain. But I have made my intentions plain too. I want to go home to Independence and inherit my uncle's medical clinic. I want to treat the sick."

Jesse groaned.

"But lately I've wondered if I would truly leave Hangtown once the miners force Mr. Dupont to return what he stole. I'm lonely for home, but the trip to Independence will eat up every penny I get back."

291

"So this is merely an economic decision for you."

"How crass that sounds."

"You're the one who framed it that way."

"Do people make a hard decision motivated by one thing? Making a decision is a complex exercise to determine what matters to you most."

"It certainly is for you," said Jesse. "Do you even like me? Is marrying me a 'hard 'decision?"

"Yes, I like you. I like you a lot. I was heartbroken when I learned it was you who got shot behind the hotel a week ago. You're the only friend I have in this town, and you have been so good to me and my sister. Marrying you would be easy, to tell the truth."

"That's good to know."

"The hard part is living in Hangtown. There's nothing here but hard-drinking, womanizing, gambling men. We don't have a school or clinic or even a church. And if we had a clinic, I don't believe the men would accept me. Everyone knows me in my part of Independence. They trust me because of my years of association with Uncle Finney."

"You just got here. Give them time."

"My heart is torn in two. Ever since we got swindled, my heart has been set on getting our money back as a means to go home to civilized society. Then Caroline went missing. All these months I've been kept going by these two things, getting our money back and finding Caroline. Now that she's found and I'm close to getting my money, I keep wondering if I really want to leave. My heart says Jesse is here …"—she reached for his hand—"and there are many nice features to the West— outside of Hangtown. I'm confused."

He abruptly pulled his hand away from hers. "Obviously."

"You're angry."

Jesse did not respond, just stared straight ahead.

"I don't blame you for being angry. You've been waiting a long time for an answer. But Jesse, there is another person I have to think about. Have you considered my sister's welfare? I am responsible for her now. Likely she will never marry and will depend on me for support the rest of her life. I keep wondering if she might come back to herself when she's in the familiar surroundings of home, in Independence."

"My brother sure seems to like her." He put his hand over hers, softening his stance. "I see your point about your sister. But what's so wonderful about Independence? Your folks and brothers aren't there anymore."

Madeline smiled. "It's a nice place, city living with shops and churches and all. But mostly, while I was tending the sick with my uncle, I began to have this crazy dream of taking over his practice. Nothing is more rewarding than seeing people get well by my hands."

"You seem to come to it naturally."

"When I was stitching up the miners I felt so strongly … like … like I was born to do this. Like this is my calling. To make people well."

Jesse stood up. "You have some big ideas. Sun's going down. We should get back."

CHAPTER THIRTY-SIX

Jesse and Clint surveyed the ocean of blue flannel shirts and black felt hats, hundreds of miners who had left their claims for a few hours to observe the trial. It was morning, and the chill of early spring added to the energy, causing miners to move briskly, patronizing saloons and shops while they waited for the big spectacle. Jesse stood above the crowd on the bed of an uncovered wagon hitched up to two horses, a wooden box a little bigger than a man's foot resting near his boot. Beside him were four vacant chairs pulled from the Garry Hotel dining room.

"Why all this?" said Clint as he pointed toward the wagon and chairs.

"You'll see soon enough. It's time to start. Tell them to bring out Gull and Alonzo."

Clint returned a few minutes later with the accused. They were accompanied by four armed miners but walked freely, unrestrained. Behind them walked Madeline and Caroline, wrapped up well against the cold. Clint climbed onto the wagon to assist Caroline while Jesse assisted Madeline. When their eyes met she saw loving concern, but no one was smiling this morning.

The ladies sat in the two chairs closest to Jesse. Then one of the armed miners climbed onto the wagon, positioning himself between the ladies and the two vacant chairs. Upon Clint's command, Alonzo and Gull climbed into the wagon and sat down. The other three miners stood guard around the wagon, their firearms at the ready. The crowd grew quiet once the miners saw the defendants and accusers in their positions.

"Men of Hangtown," began Jesse, "I've called you away from your claims today to hear accusations against Gull Dupont and Alonzo Moore." He gestured toward the two men. "They are accused of theft, fraud, violence against innocent women, false imprisonment, and murder. The accusers are sisters Madeline and Caroline Whittaker." He gestured toward the women. "After they speak, anyone who has information to support their claims as a witness is invited to speak. Afterward the defendants and their witnesses will speak."

Madeline trembled. She was seated a few feet away from Gull, and hundreds of pairs of eyes were on her and Caroline. Would she be able to choke out even a word? She had waited so long to be vindicated, but now that her moment had arrived, her stomach felt like a tight belt around her middle. Terrified of Gull Dupont, terrified to speak up, terrified to see two men hang because of her testimony, terrified of having to make the hard decision to stay or to go once she was made whole.

She wanted to run back into the hotel and hide in her room.

She also wanted to be held in the warm, strong arms of Jesse Garry the way he had embraced her under the blanket when they were stranded in the freezing darkness months ago. She wanted him to take all her problems off her shoulders, to feel safe again like she had on that blizzard-driven night. She was tired of carrying her troubles alone.

She looked over at her sister, hoping for a comforting smile, but Caroline's face was inscrutable. However, Madeline knew, after a week of being reunited, Caroline's mind was active and processing everything going on around her.

Madeline heard Jesse calling her name. She stood and clasped the back of her chair to steady herself. *I can do this. I can do this.* She looked at Jesse, who nodded and mouthed a silent, "You can do it."

She pulled a sheaf of paper from her shawl and began to read. "On the night my sister and I arrived in Hangtown, we couldn't afford a hotel room and we needed to bury our pa, who had died that morning of fever. We were in the middle of digging his grave late that night when Mr. Dupont came upon us in the forest …"

Madeline spoke of being accused of murder, forced back to town, their belongings sold without their permission, and their money held as bail. She looked straight ahead as she spoke, not wanting to lock eyes with Gull or Alonzo. She also feared if she looked at all the miners staring at her she would become tongue-tied.

The miners listened in silence. When she had said her piece, she thanked them for making a fair judgment and sat down.

Jesse spoke next. "I regret my hotel cook, Mr. Bartholomew Pyle—you folks knew him as Biscuit—is not here to testify, because he shared some information with me before he died relevant to this trial."

Gull, who had been studying the ground until this minute, suddenly looked up at Jesse. Jesse ignored him. Alonzo woke up also at the sound of Biscuit's name and began to watch Jesse more intently.

"Unbeknownst to me, Biscuit was working for Gull Dupont while he was employed at the Garry Hotel. It was Biscuit who found this." Jesse picked up the wooden box at his feet. "This box was hidden on the underside of Miss Whittaker's wagon by her father. When Gull hired Biscuit to unload the supplies from the sisters 'wagon to sell them to Alonzo Moore, he found this box of gold coins."

Jesse opened the sliding lid box to reveal a cache of small gold coins. He lifted the box high in the air for the crowd to see. A murmur of awe went through the crowd.

"After we are done with these testimonies, you are all welcome to investigate the underside of the wagon I'm standing on. I borrowed it from Malachi, our stable owner, who purchased it innocently from Alonzo Moore. You will see this box was made to fit perfectly into a secure holder. Both are constructed of eastern oak by the Whittaker sisters' father." Jesse turned to Madeline. "Further, Gull Dupont, in an effort to coerce the Whittaker sisters into returning to Hangtown so he could sell their wagon, oxen, and goods for his own gain, struck Miss Whittaker on her back with the butt of her own rifle. Is this not true, Miss Whittaker?"

Madeline lowered her head. "It is true."

Gull stared across the tops of the heads in the crowd, fastening on none of them, arms crossed, his mouth a straight, grim line.

Jesse proceeded to testify against Gull and Alonzo after that inflammatory accusation, revealing every salacious detail Biscuit had shared with him. The crowd booed when Sadie Shaw's name was mentioned, but they became positively frenzied upon hearing of the murder of Harlin Turpin. Angry, shouting men started to close in on the wagon.

"Gentlemen! Gentlemen! Calm yourselves. We will hear both sides of this story before anyone takes action," shouted Jesse.

But the crowd grew noisier. Madeline, though shaking herself, threw her arms around Caroline to keep her calm. After several seconds of chaos, Clint climbed onto the wagon and shot his sidearm into the air.

The men halted their approach to the wagon, though many still complained loudly about Harlin's murder.

"I haven't had a chance to speak," shouted Clint. He picked up the coin box and held it high in the air. "I didn't hear Biscuit's confession because he was strung up before I could question him, but I was with Jesse when he found this box of coins hidden in Biscuit's cellar."

Jesse jerked his head to signal Clint to get off the wagon, which he did. Jesse continued. "Biscuit found two compartments under the wagon for coin boxes. One was empty. He assumed, wrongly, the sisters had removed a second box of gold coins from the wagon, so he tore apart their room at the Casbah to find it. Biscuit told me himself. That's why he kidnapped Miss Caroline Whittaker."

Gull drooped a little and stared glumly at the wagon floor, his bravado fading away like a slow leak in an old balloon. Alonzo looked straight ahead, dazed. Then Jesse announced it was Gull's turn to defend himself. Though the smirk was gone, Gull stood up, looking as polished as any career politician.

"Gentlemen, Jesse Garry and Miss Madeline Whittaker have lobbed serious accusations against me. But they have nothing but the alleged word of a dead man to support their claims, which is not valid testimony in any court of law. It is true I came across the Whittaker sisters outside town one night last fall, but as you may remember, Hangtown was suffering then from unsolved murders. I found Miss Whittaker here—" he gestured toward Madeline "—digging a hole and preparing to cover a corpse with rocks. I must remind you this is the same method an unknown party used to dispose of two miners."

"You don't know if they were miners," said Jesse.

"And you don't know if they were Sadie Shaw and her husband," retorted Gull. "And it's my turn to testify." He turned back to the crowd. "As for the Whittaker sisters' possessions, I converted them to cash by selling them to Mr. Moore strictly to use as bail to prevent their flight from Hangtown until they could be tried. Their money is safe, set aside for them should they be cleared of all charges."

Jesse's face grew red. He tapped his foot uncontrollably. A murmur rose from the crowd once again. Jesse motioned with his arms for the crowd to quiet down. "Let him finish," he shouted.

"I shared my concerns about the sisters ' actions with Harlin before he died," said Gull. "Had someone not taken his life, the ladies would have been tried already. I have never hidden my actions in regard to the Whittaker sisters from anyone. It is outrageous for Biscuit or Mr. Garry here to try and pin Harlin's murder on me, when Jesse Garry was the person who stood to benefit from his death. With Harlin dead, Mr. Garry became the law in this town. It's what he wanted all along."

Jesse jumped up from his chair, grabbed his hat and banged it against his thigh. Gull looked toward the noise then back to the crowd.

"And as for striking a woman with a rifle to coerce her to return to Hangtown," Gull turned back to Jesse, "that's a lie from the pit of Hell. I have never and would never strike a woman."

Madeline covered her face in her hands. How could his man tell one lie after another? Had he no fear? Who would the miners believe? Destitute, powerless newcomers to Hangtown like herself and her sister? Or this imposing, wealthy man who wielded so much influence over the doings of this little mountain town?

"I saw the butt mark on her back myself," said Jesse. "She had to have her back stitched up when she got thrown from her horse last fall. It was clearly a rifle butt mark."

"Did it have a name on it?" barked Gull. "All you have is the word of this fanciful young woman. That's no evidence at all. And what were you doing looking at her naked back?"

Madeline sank lower in her chair, her face still covered by her hands. Would she ever escape from the humiliation of that awful injury when she was thrown from her horse? Now the entire town was reminded of her exposure. This was not how she expected the trial to unfold.

Suddenly from off to the side she heard a fracas. She removed her hands from her face in time to see Clint Garry sprint onto the wagon. He lunged at Gull, decking him with one swift blow to the head.

"Gull DuPont stole their father's body from the grave!" yelled Clint. "He tried to hide evidence!"

With lightning speed Jesse grabbed his younger brother, who was still pounding on Gull, by the back of his shirt and flung him toward the rear of the wagon.

"Get down!" yelled Jesse.

Clint grabbed his hat from the wagon floor where it had fallen, flashed furious eyes at his brother, then jumped off the wagon. Gull pulled himself into an upright position and dusted himself off.

"My brother will cause no more problems," said Jesse to Gull. "Do you have anything else to say in your defense?"

"I'm guilty of nothing and you have no proof," said Gull, a crack appearing in his well-practiced cool facade. He returned to his seat, rubbing his head where Clint had popped him. Then he angrily placed his hat back on his head, clenched his jaw, and refused to make eye contact with the crowd.

It was time for Alonzo Moore to defend himself. As Madeline knew he would, the man claimed to know nothing except Gull had wanted to sell him a wagonload of mining supplies. Alonzo said he had no reason to think the goods were stolen since they were brought to him by an honest citizen, Mr. Dupont. His testimony was short and unadorned.

"Are there any more witnesses to support the testimony of the Whittaker sisters or Mr. Dupont or Mr. Moore?" asked Jesse.

The crowd grew quiet and waited.

Caroline slowly raised herself from her seat on the wagon. She scanned the crowd as though she thought they would eat her, then turned to Jesse.

Madeline stood up and put an arm around her sister. "Caroline," she whispered, "Do you want to say something?" Caroline's eyes brimmed with unshed tears. "It's alright, Caroline. Whatever you have to say is alright." Caroline looked at Madeline, then she looked at Jesse. Hesitantly she looked at Gull. His eyes were full of hatred—she buried her face in Madeline's shoulders. Madeline embraced her and whispered something into her ear a second time. After several seconds Caroline put her head up again, more composed this time, and faced the miners. She clutched her sister's hand tightly.

"I saw Mr. Dupont hit my sister with Pa's gun," she said. Then she collapsed back onto her chair in a heap of sobs. Madeline sat down next to her and embraced her.

"If there are more witnesses, please step forward now," said Jesse. He waited, scanning the heads of the miners looking for a hand. "I see no hands. Now, as to my brother's remark about the body—I have personally searched the area where the Whittaker sisters' father was buried. It's about twenty minutes outside town, exactly where

Madeline Whittaker told me it would be. I took my brother to examine it as well. The body is gone. Whether it was removed by a human or an animal is unclear. As a result, the disposition of the body is not material to this hearing. Therefore, I declare the period of testimony to be over."

Jesse looked over the crowd. "All those who find Gull Dupont guilty as charged say aye." With one voice the miners roared a guilty verdict. "Are there any nays?" No one responded. It was the same with the charges against Alonzo. "I pronounce the defendants guilty as charged."

Madeline sat with her arms around her sister. She couldn't rid herself of the tightness in her chest despite what she had just heard. Caroline whimpered quietly.

Jesse and Clint helped the ladies descend from the wagon. Once on the ground, Jesse put his arms around Madeline to support her. She couldn't stop shaking, though she managed to turn around and take one last look at Gull and Alonzo. A huge crowd had begun to surround the wagon, noisy but not as raucous as before, likely because of the four armed miners guarding the accused. Madeline watched in wonder as a man climbed into the wagon seat and grabbed the reins. The two men who had caused her and Caroline so much pain were going to die. It seemed unbelievable.

The crowd dispersed in front of the horses, and in a minute the wagon carrying the doomed was slowly making its way to the hanging tree at the entrance to Hangtown..

CHAPTER THIRTY-SEVEN

Madeline was finishing her work at the lobby desk around five o'clock when she saw Jesse walk through the front door of the hotel accompanied by a dozen men dressed in the usual blue-and-black panning garb. Miners rarely spent their precious gold dust on a pricey room at the Garry or the Casbah—though they spent freely at the bars inside both hotels. They preferred to sleep on the floors of other miners 'cabins or to pitch a cheap, crude tent of oil cloth near their claims.

She looked at Jesse, wondering, but his expression was inscrutable.

"Welcome to the Garry Hotel," she said. "Something tells me you are not here to book a room."

All the men removed their hats as if on cue.

"The citizens of Hangtown have something to say to you, Miss Whittaker." Jesse said, and he winked. "Please come and take a seat."

Madeline closed the guest book she had been working in and walked around the desk, bewildered, giving Jesse a What's-this-all-about? look as she passed him. He smiled. She seated herself in the first upholstered chair she came to in the lobby and looked up at Jesse again. *He sure seems to be enjoying himself.* The other men, all older miners above forty years of age, favored her with a smile when she happened to meet their eyes. The oldest looking miner, notable for his long white beard, stepped forward.

"Miss Whittaker," he said, "there's been a meeting of the leading miners of Hangtown about the disposition of Gull Dupont's estate."

Madeline looked up at Jesse. His expression gave away nothing. She turned back to the bearded one. "Yes?"

The old man continued. "He died with no known family or dependents. We spent the day speaking with everyone who was acquainted with the deceased, and we are certain from our investigation he arrived in Hangtown alone and has no family in this country."

"But what does this have to do with me?"

"It came out in yesterday's testimony that you and your sister were grievously wronged by the late Mr. Dupont, swindled of all your worldly possessions and taken by false pretenses back to Hangtown. You were also physically assaulted."

Madeline nodded. She glanced at Jesse again. He was about to burst with some secret—she could see it in his eyes. *What is going on?*

"I have always hoped to get the value of the oxen, wagon, and its contents returned to me and my sister," volunteered Madeline. "Can you do this for us?"

"Yes, we can do that," said the old man, "if that's what you want. But we met with dozens of miners today. And after much discussion, we have something in mind you might like even better."

"I am listening, sir."

"The miners of Hangtown would be pleased if you and your sister would accept the Casbah Hotel as payment for the loss of your goods and the distress caused to you by the unforgivable treatment you received at the hands of Mr. Dupont."

Madeline was incredulous.

Jesse nodded rapidly. "Miss Whittaker, they are *giving* you and Miss Caroline the Casbah Hotel," he said.

Madeline shook her head as if to wake herself.

"The Casbah is yours to do with as you wish," said Jesse. "You can keep it and operate it as a hotel or another business or you can sell it. But the miners asked us to tell you they are hoping you use it to start a clinic. We are all grateful for the lives you've saved since you arrived. Hangtown needs a doctor."

A volley of "yesses" and "amens" arose from the men.

"You're all we have, Miss Whittaker," Jesse continued. "I know you don't think of yourself as a real doctor, but to those you have helped with your medical skills, including myself, you are an angel from Heaven. Hangtown will have a medically trained doctor in good time. More miners arrive every day, eventually a doctor will set up shop here.

Perhaps you can be tutored by him and help us even more."

"I don't know what to say," said Madeline, twisting her hands in her lap. "What about Mr. Moore's mother? What will happen to her now since he's gone?"

"The store will pass to his sister," said the old miner spokesman. "She used to work for him. Now she's living in Sacramento with her new husband. We expect she will take in her mother as well. We're working on getting them together as soon as possible."

"That's good news," said Madeline, unable to think of anything intelligent to say.

"Well?" said Jesse.

"I should think on it overnight," said Madeline, rising from her chair. "Thank you, everyone, for your concern for myself and my sister."

***

"Do you believe in fate, Caroline?"

Madeline sat on the bed in her nightgown, her knees to her chest, gazing through the window into the starlit sky. Caroline was already under the covers, her long hair billowing across the pillow in golden waves like sunshine, watching her older sister's every move. "Or Providence? Or how about destiny? Do you believe one door closes so another can open? Or is this wishful thinking?"

Madeline had learned not to expect a reply from her sister. But after her one-line testimony at the trial, there was always a slim thread of hope. She leaned into Caroline's face.

"I've been waiting all day to tell you the most amazing news, Caroline. Wanna hear?"

Silence.

"Well, I'm going to tell you anyway. The miners have decided to give us the Casbah, as compensation for our losses and suffering. Can you believe it? And all these months I was hoping to get only the value of our belongings back in cash. They've granted us the entire hotel! Do you think we should accept it? I can't think of a reason why we shouldn't. The man has no heirs so it's not like we're robbing his children."

She was disappointed at her sister's silence, but she forged ahead anyway.

"They told me they are hoping I start a clinic to serve sick and injured miners. Think, Caroline—we'd have a roof over our heads and a way to earn our keep. What would Auntie Hannah and Uncle Finney think if I ran a clinic in a gold mining camp? It's too fantastic to even think about. What do you think of all this, sugar bun? Would you like your sister to be a businesswoman? I could teach you the basics of tending the sick, too. Of course, this means we won't be returning to Independence. You once told me you'd like to stay in Hangtown. Do you still want to stay?"

Caroline's eyes were half-closed.

"There's one more thing, Caroline. I've saved the best for last. You're never going to believe this one. Jesse Garry has asked to marry me. I've become very fond of him, Caroline. I think I … I love him. He's sweet and of solid character, and so thoughtful towards me. Pa would like him, don't you think? He's been a friend since our first day in Hangtown when he stopped to offer us help. I'm going to say yes unless you give me a good reason to say no."

Eyes fully closed now, Caroline groped blindly for Madeline's hand, found it, and gave it a squeeze. "Say yes," she said with a big smile.

CHAPTER THIRTY-EIGHT

Clint and Jesse entered the lobby of the Garry Hotel together and walked directly to the desk where Madeline was setting up for the day.

"Good morning, gentlemen. I see you're coming from the kitchen. How's Caroline doing?"

"She's a godsend to Tien," said Clint. "He likes working with her because she's quiet, and her biscuits and gravy are the best."

"Our mother's recipe," said Madeline. "Now what I can do for you this morning?"

"Come with me," said Jesse, "we have business to discuss. Clint will take your place on the desk for a while."

Clint was already walking around the front desk to where Madeline was. She excused herself to return to her room for her shawl then joined Jesse in the lobby.

"Let's ride this morning," said Jesse as he opened the hotel door and they stepped out onto the street. He took her arm.

"You sure you're up to it?"

"I'm always up to riding with you, though I think a wagon would be easier on my stitches than horseback. I borrowed one from Malachi."

They walked to Malachi's stable, where he had the wagon hitched and waiting. Malachi removed his hat and looked up at Madeline after helping her onto the wagon board. He chewed his lip like someone worried about something.

"I'm returning it to you, Miss Whittaker. I didn't know it was swindled from you when I bought it."

Madeline straightened her skirts around her feet on the wagon board. "You keep it," she said. "You did nothing wrong and paid honest money for it. I won't be needing it anymore."

Jesse's heart leaped in his chest. *She won t be needing the wagon! Could this possibly mean—"*

"You sure, ma'am?" asked Malachi.

"I'm sure."

Jesse and Madeline rolled leisurely through the parklike spring foliage, enjoying the moment as Jesse kept an eye out for deep ruts caused by runoff. The deciduous trees sprinkled among the evergreens were all dressed in soft green leaves, the first new growth of the season. The air was pure and sweet, the morning sun warm and comforting.

"I thought we'd go back to the flower meadow you liked so much," said Jesse.

Madeline nodded. "Let's do."

This time Jesse had brought a blanket to place on the fallen log because of the damp. He checked it for snakes then spread the blanket and they both sat down.

"Have you made your decision about the Casbah?" he said.

"I have. I'm going to take it."

Jesse closed his eyes briefly. *She s staying.*

"Owning a clinic is a dream come true. Running a clinic will also make a way for me to support my sister. I thought about it all night, and I can't think of a reason to say no."

"Caroline will marry. She won't always be dependent on you," said Jesse.

"What makes you so sure?"

"She's pretty and doesn't talk much. She's every man's perfect wife."

They laughed.

"And my little brother is at the head of the line." Jesse took her hand in his. "It makes me so happy to hear you're staying in Hangtown. Only one thing can make me happier." He pulled an emerald green, velvet box from his jacket pocket.

Madeline's eyes grew wide. She drew back a little.

"You've seen this before, haven't you?" he said.

"I saw a box like that in San Francisco."

"I thought so," said Jesse. He grimaced. His hunch had been right. Uncle Justus had proposed to Madeline. *Well, Uncle is unlucky despite his wealth.*

He opened the box and pulled the ruby ring with three concentric rings of diamonds from its satin holder and slipped it onto her finger. "Will you marry me, Madeline Whittaker?"

"I don't know." She shook her head in mock consternation. "They'll say you married me only to acquire Hangtown's first medical clinic."

He scoffed. "They'll say you married *me* to inherit the Garry Hotel."

She rolled her eyes.

"And for my handsome face," he added. He slipped the ring onto her finger. "It looks pretty on you." Then he sighed, put his head down, and stared at his lap. "I have a confession."

"Oh?"

"I might have made you think Tien was a doctor in China. He wasn't."

She gave him a quizzical look. "You said he knew how to stitch wounds."

"That was the truth. But he didn't stitch up people."

"My back healed fine."

"I knew it would."

"Jesse, what are you getting at?"

"Oink, oink."

"Huh?"

"He was a pig farmer. He learned to stitch wounds by working on his pigs."

She laughed. "Well, that will be one more crazy story to share with our grandchildren." She lifted her hand and gazed at her engagement ring. "Why do you have the ring your uncle offered me?"

"It's a family heirloom. It first belonged to Aunt Elizabeth's grandmother. Her husband was a sea merchant a century ago, so they were fairly prosperous. You'll be the fifth bride to wear it. If you choose to wear it."

"I choose," she said.

Suddenly his arms were around her and he was kissing her for the first time, sweetly yet passionately. "I love you, Madeline." Every muscle in his body was on alert with desire. He could think of nothing but how much he wanted her.

"I love you." She laid her head on his shoulder. "Aunt Elizabeth gave it to you then?"

"Right before I left San Francisco. She likes you," he said. "And she's an excellent judge of character."

"I like her too. She's a wise lady. She taught me a lesson to remember."

"What's that?" said Jesse.

"I need to stop running from difficulties. Stop panicking when obstacles look impossible to overcome. Because sometimes the hard way is the right way."

"True."

"I've cried more tears in the last six months than I had my entire life before I left Independence. But sometimes the way to find the pot of gold at the end of the rainbow is to take the most difficult path."

"Are you saying choosing me was the difficult path?"

"No, Jesse, you're the pot of gold."

The End

About the Author

Virginia Hull Welch was raised in Santa Clara, California. After graduating from Santa Clara University with a Bachelor of English, she married and moved to northern California where she earned a Master of Communications at Chico State University. She spent decades working as a freelance editor and writer before retiring and moving to Virginia with her husband. She has four grown children and many grandchildren. *Hangtown Hearts* is her second western romance and fifth book.

www.virginiahullwelch.com